MELINDA A DI LORENZO

Snapshots by Laura

Teresa:
I hope the
book makes
you smile!
Melinda Di Lorenzo

DEDICATION

Thank you to my husband, for being my sounding board and my number one fan.
Thank you to my parents, for always believing in me and for supporting me.
You all give my life and work meaning.

PROLOGUE

NOW

She opened the letter on the afternoon before the funeral.

She had been staring morosely at the pile of mail, thinking of how to proceed. The pile had been building for nearly a year, and was justifiably large. She knew that the envelopes contained words of sympathy, well-intended, but almost meaningless in the wake of her desolation. The long white ones with their plastic windows were easily identifiable as bills—probably gone long unpaid—accumulating since God knows when. There were a few anomalous ones—pink ones, blue ones, a large manila one—that could not be classified immediately by their appearance. All of them implied a future. A sense of carrying on that she was trying to contend with. A future that seemed dauntingly close, but much too far away to be the here and now.

She did know that immediate closure would not come in the form of friends and family, nor from paying off a cable bill ten months overdue. But sorting the envelopes was a starting point. And her life had been so full of endings lately.

So she gazed at the stack of mail, still deciding how to sort it. By size? By the categories she could identify? Or by those she might open now, those she might open later, and those she might never open at all?

She sighed and decided to sort by colour. Making that small decision lightened her spirits marginally, and she reached for the first stack. White and off-white together. Pastels together, cream in a stack of their own. It was a slow process, and midway through, she admitted that she was actually exhausted. This one small task had drained her—and finally, when only a single stack remained, she resolved that she would finish organizing and go straight to bed. As she reached for the last pile of unsorted envelopes, a small, stark black card slid out and onto the floor.

She stared at it, confused by its difference from the others. There was no comfort in its blackness, no hint at its intention at all. She picked it up, almost reverent in her handling of the envelope.

It was four inches by four inches in size, and it was sealed with an iridescent black sticker. The writing on the front also shimmered, faintly silver in colour. It was necessary, she absently surmised, to use a special pen when addressing this card. A traditional black or blue ball point pen would have been virtually invisible against the dark paper. She turned the envelope left and right, bending it a little to admire the fluid lettering that addressed it. She forgot, momentarily, why she had to sort this mail in the first place. She looked blankly at the stacks in front of her, and shook her head to clear it.

She set the black envelope apart from the others, feeling oddly energized by its presence. She buzzed with a strange sense of life that she hadn't felt in nearly a year.

Her eyes burned ravenously as she stared at the envelope, and all thoughts of rest evaporated from her mind. She turned her face away from it, slightly embarrassed by her intense reaction. But the glossy lettering drew her eyes back.

She would open each and every card, each and every bill. Now. And then, lastly, she would open the black envelope.

Her brain tingled with anticipatory glee, her fingers itched to open it first.

But the last year had taught her nothing if not will power.

And she knew, somehow, that this envelope and its contents were dessert-like in nature—sweetest when left until the end of the meal to enjoy.

Chapter 1
THEN

My experience of *The Cafe* had never been a good one. Everyone I knew, from my parents, to my peers, to my friends, had been singing the praises of the trendy, tucked away restaurant for as long as I could remember. Their biscotti was the crunchiest. Their coffee was the richest. Their atmosphere was untainted by the ever-growing commercial coffee shop package. Or so they claimed.

But as I stood in line for my thirteenth or fourteenth minute, I couldn't help but sigh dramatically. I heard someone behind me muffle a mocking laugh.

And that was definitely at the top of my reasons *not* to spend a significant amount of time or money in this overrated coffee shop. I had made my own mental checklist, starting with its pretentious customers and their mocking laughs. Followed by the fact that their wait times were the worst, their staff was a snarky bunch at best, and the coffee was actually rather mediocre. In fact, I could think of at least ten places that I'd *prefer* to drink my latte—including one very questionable twenty-four hour gas station. But the one thing that *The Cafe* actually did have going for it was the location. It was exactly eleven blocks between the two biggest objects of my desire, and the beginnings of my plans for a new life.

At block one was the first goal—a studio-style apartment in the ground level basement of an eighty year old house that had been converted into a fourplex. Everything about the four hundred and twenty-one square foot suite was perfect for me. It was at the edge of a residential area, but still urban enough to say that I lived downtown. It was walking distance to a grocery store, ten feet from a major bus route, and far enough away from my parents' house in the suburbs of the Lower Mainland that a weekly visit would be inconvenient, but a monthly one would not. It also had a private entrance, a tiny washer dryer combo, and a countertop dishwasher. There was a six foot veranda off of its sliding glass doors, complete with two potted plants. And to top it all off, the suite was very, very clean. The same thing could not be said of the other four apartments I had looked at this past week. I cringed at the memory of musty walls and sticky stoves. But this place, it positively sang of a new start to me. I had interviewed with the landlord—an older Asian woman named Mrs. Huong—in the morning, and I was confident that I had made a good first impression. I was already planning the perfect spot for my gently used pullout couch and my Tom Waits poster.

And at the other end of the eleven block span centered by *The Cafe* was something that I wanted even *more* than the apartment. It was an opportunity. I had been guided to this unusual possibility by my friend Kristen, who had heard of the program and thought immediately of me. It was a privately funded, decently paid, and totally comprehensive photography internship course. I would gladly trade in my dignity, my patience, and my personal taste in hot beverages for access to the program. The wait list had been a long one, and the short list had been very short indeed. Only twenty students received a first interview. Of the initial twenty, only twelve of those would be short-listed to submit a portfolio. Then finally, six would be selected to work with the three professional photographers who acted as professors, as mentors, and as keys into the business. The program was a unique one, and thanks to my dear friend's interfering ways, I had made it into one of the twenty preliminary interviews. I was eager to impress them, and absolutely determined to secure one of those six elite spots.

I had my camera—a decent but affordable Canon Rebel—around my neck, and my carefully prepared resume in a file under my arm. The only thing standing between me and that dream was the line of people in front of me in *The Cafe*.

I silently cursed my caffeine addiction and sighed again, tossing my long, dark hair over my shoulder.

I heard another amused laugh from behind me and my irritation hit a new high. Although I consider myself to be generally even-tempered, the present lack of coffee combined with the jitters

I had about my upcoming interview put me on edge. I gave in to my irritation and I spun around impulsively, preparing to confront the source of the laugh.

But karma, or my own clumsy nature—or maybe a combination of the two—got the better of me. I turned too sharply, immediately lost my balance and started to fall forward. Instinctively I flung my hands over my most prized possession, letting my resume drop as I tried to keep my camera from hitting the floor. It was an unfortunate decision. With both my arms occupied, I had no way to balance my body, and I completely lost my footing. I realized my mistake too late, and as I let go of the Canon to try to stabilize myself, both my feet slid out in front of me. The strap attached to my camera caught a chair as I went down, and with a loud snap, the whole thing flew out of my grasp and hit the ground with an awful cracking sound. And then, landing as hard on my rear end as I ever had, I found myself staring up at a pair of concerned, compellingly blue eyes.

⇛⇝

After a rush of confused conversation and embarrassed protests, I was appalled to find myself leaning against the blue-eyed stranger in a crowded hospital waiting room. Although the triage nurse had given me a grossly inflated, ring-shaped pillow, I had not been able to find a comfortable way to position myself until my head came to rest on his shoulder. I was reasonably certain that my tailbone was not broken, but I was also sure that it was at least as bruised as my ego. He had wanted to call an ambulance, and it had taken all of my powers of persuasion to convince him that I had banged my bottom but *not* my top. Then he had given in and only insisted on driving me to emergency himself.

The ride over to the hospital had been awkward at best, wedged into the backseat of his car with a cushion pilfered from one of *The Cafe*'s overstuffed chairs keeping my more bruised parts from bumping painfully against the centre console. When he had lifted me gently but unceremoniously from his car into a waiting hospital wheelchair, half of me had hoped that he would just wheel me into the reception area and then disappear. The other half of me was extremely grateful to have him guide my chair into the hospital with my purse slung stoically across his shoulder. Not very many guys will carry a purse for their own mothers, let alone a complete stranger.

Now his arm was draped casually across the back of my wheelchair, and my purse had been moved from his shoulder to a snug resting place between his feet. *The Cafe's* stolen pillow was balanced cozily on his knees, and he was tugging idly at a tassel in the centre of the cushion. I felt like too much of a voyeur when I stared at the other patients in the waiting room, but I also didn't want to make eye contact with my makeshift hero. I examined him from the corner of my vision. He was not unattractive, in the conventional sense. He had an even jawline, and a bit of dark stubble on his chin. His brown hair was shorter than I usually liked on a guy, but the cropped cut was likely indicative of his age, which I judged to be five or six years older than me. Maybe when I was nearer to twenty-five, this would be the kind of man that attracted me. Sensible. Conservatively dressed. Kind to strangers.

I watched his hand as it fiddled with the cushion's tassel. I couldn't help but notice how the dark hair on the back of that hand stood out in contrast against his tanned skin. His nails were clipped roughly short, and as he twisted his fingers this way and that, I noticed also that they were calloused. They were a man's hands, toughened by what? Working outside? Fixing cars? A few hairs were caught in the band of his wristwatch. Before I could stop myself, I reached to adjust the watch to that it wouldn't get stuck and pull on his skin.

He put his other hand overtop of mine, and I instinctively jerked away, embarrassed.

"Over two hours," he said.

"Hmm?" I was too flustered to respond properly.

"You were checking my watch?" he prodded.

I blushed and turned my face away so that he wouldn't see.

"I'm guessing that you don't like to wait too much, eh?" he asked. "You were very concerned with the line in *The Cafe* as well."

He laughed, just as he had at the coffee shop. It was a rich, warm sound and I wondered if I had only imagined that it had been mocking before.

I stared at him. "Who *are* you?"

"Well," he said, still laughing, "I'm Richard Porter Lockhurst. But you can call me Richie, if you like. Everyone does."

∾∾

The hospital visit ended in a mortifying warning from the ER doctor to "not sit on anything too hard for the next week" and also be "a little more careful when standing in dangerous line ups". Richard had insisted on taking me out for dinner, winking at the doctor, saying that he knew of a restaurant with very soft upholstery. I was irritated and embarrassed. But since I hadn't eaten since breakfast, I was also way too hungry to offer up more than a weak protest. Richard grinned when I gave him my grudging agreement, and the doctor muffled a laugh.

I pretended to ignore my rescuer as we drove from the hospital to the restaurant, but it was more difficult than I wanted to admit to sidestep his charm. He was open and friendly, and easily disregarded that fact that I was deflecting all of his small talk. By the time we reached our destination, I was actually having a hard time *not* feeling at ease.

He pulled out my chair in the restaurant, and the old-fashined gesture took me so off guard that Richard had to prompt me to sit down. I smiled to myself.

He talked easily through the appetizer and the main course, telling me about his job as a part-time, seasonal landscaper at his dad's business, and how it fit in nicely with his school schedule. He was majoring in business at SFU, and was hoping to eventually start a finance management company of his own.

"My dad pays me really well," he told me. He stated this as a fact, and managed to sound like he wasn't bragging. "It's a perfect balance, because even though I *am* technically taking money from my parents for university, I'm helping my dad out too. And I never have to feel bad about leaving the job in the fall for school because by October, there's really only enough work for my Dad and his business partner. The work itself is nice, too, because once I get that business degree at the end of next year, I'll be inside all of the time." He grinned at me self-assuredly, and I wondered what it was like to have that much direction and that much drive.

I felt an anxious pang as I remembered that I was supposed to finishing my own life-altering interview right about then. Although I had to admit, so far my life hadn't taken on anything that resembled direction.

In my first year of university, I had changed intended majors no less than three times, dropped out once, been put on academic probation, and then finally decided that maybe pursuing a formal post-secondary education was not quite right for me. With the exception of one enjoyable course the previous summer, I had been on an academic hiatus for nearly a year, and I had started pursuing full-time work just this week. My excuse was that I needed to save some money. But the truth was, I made a lot of plans that seemed to fall short more often than not. I decided not to tell Richard any of this. It was much nicer to just sit and listen to someone who had no doubts and plenty of goals.

"You're a quiet girl," Richard said, stopping in the middle of an anecdote about one of professors.

I smiled. It was true that he was doing all of the talking, but I would never have described myself as quiet. I was oddly happy that he hadn't mistaken my reservation for snobbishness or true shyness.

"I just keep my cards close to my chest. A woman of mystery," I said in a light voice.

Richard smiled back. "Should I assume that you're protecting yourself because you've been hurt in the past? Or just that my charm overwhelms you?"

He was teasing, but I felt a lump form in my throat. I forced the lump, and the reason for it, back down.

Richard assessed my face and made a hasty apology.

"I'm so sorry," he said. "I shouldn't have said that."

"How old are you?" I asked, shrugging. I tried to sound more polite than curious as I turned the conversation back to safer ground.

"Twenty-one. My birthday is at the end of next month," he answered.

I covered my surprise by taking a big sip of my water.

Richard was only two years older than me. And yet, here he sat, comfortable in a restaurant that served wines I couldn't pronounce, wearing a plain navy blue golf shirt and neutrally beige Dockers style pants. I had already felt very conspicuous in my peasant blouse, Doc Martin boots, and corduroy pants. The fact that he was so close to me in age but so many miles away from me in maturity heightened my self-consciousness. And made him more interesting. I felt a little rush of excitement and quickly dismissed it.

I cleared my throat. "And you're in third year Business?"

He started to explain to me that the reason that he was "behind" in his university studies was that he had spent an entire year working for his dad immediately after high school before deciding that he wanted to be on the business management end of things rather than being hands-on.

I realized that I was staring at Richard in a childishly awed way. He had stopped talking and was staring back at me with a half-smile on his lips. He reached out and touched the back of my hand lightly.

"Hi," he said softly. "Your face is so serious. What're you thinking?"

I looked down at my pasta. "Umm. This restaurant really does have soft upholstery?"

Richard's eyes opened wider and he laughed his increasingly familiar and affable laugh. I gave in and let myself enjoy the easy sound of it.

As we shared the decadent chocolate cake recommended by our server, the tone of the meal changed. Richard kept locking his fingers together and then unlocking them. He avoided eye contact, and I started to worry that I had said something wrong. I could tell that he was attracted to me, too, but knew that we were on very different paths. Regretfully, I got ready to thank him for the dinner and excuse myself. I couldn't help but wish for a moment that we had met later in life.

Because I think that I could really like you, I thought to myself.

He was very quiet for a few moments and then he stated, "I'm sorry."

"Sorry?" I asked, puzzled.

He grabbed one of my hands between both of his "Yes. I'm having a great time. I just don't want this date to end." And then he groaned. "That sounded so lame."

I felt an unreasonable moment of panic, and choked on a sip of hot coffee. *A date?* Of course. I'd have to be totally out of of it to have *not* realized that it must be seen that way. Richard watched me, a look of open concern and a tinge of confused embarrassment on his face.

Why not a date? I forced myself to recover. *A lot of people my age went on dates.*

"This is a date?" I asked, teasing him, trying to keep the weird combination of excitement and apprehension out of my voice.

I wondered if the other patrons in the restaurant looked at us and thought that we were on a date. We must've seemed an odd couple, him with his clothes carefully selected to blend in, and me with my outfit designed to stand out.

Richard relaxed, encouraged by something in my face. "Yes. In fact, I think it's our second date. The first one ended when we left the hospital. That was the awkward one where we didn't know what to say to each other. This one is the comfortable one where we get to know a little more about each other."

He kept his face serious, but his eyes twinkled with amusement. I wondered how I had thought for even a moment that he was ordinary looking.

I smiled back at him. "I'm not sure if I even agreed to the first one."

Richard still held my hand between his and as he ran his thumb along my wrist, a slow warmth spread up my arm. I felt like my heart was going to leap out of my chest. I pulled my hand away slowly, uncomfortable with my strong reaction to his touch. I tried to take even, measured breaths and told my heart sternly to calm down.

"That's too bad," he said softly, watching my face searchingly. "Because date number three is the one where we flirt uncontrollably and have our first kiss. I'd hate to have to go through one and two again just to get to that."

Instantly, my heart forgot all about the commands I was giving it, and leaped straight into my throat.

కాడ

I let Richard drop me in front of the apartment building at the end of my parent's block.

"This is me," I said, and if he noticed that I was lying, he said nothing.

I was glad that the worn wooden plaque identifying the building as the Shady Grove Assisted Living Centre was obscured by an overgrown bush and a poorly lit walkway.

"Thank you," I added gratefully as I moved to open the car door. "For everything."

I hesitated, wondering if he would try for that first kiss he alluded to earlier.

"Any damsel in distress is a friend indeed," Richard replied with a smile, and made no move.

I got out a little reluctantly, wincing inwardly at his use of the word "friend". The unreasonable part of my brain wondered *why* he didn't try to kiss me goodbye. As much as I didn't need a kiss from an attractive near-stranger, I couldn't help it if I wanted one. Sighing, I waved as enthusiastically as I could from the doorstep of the apartment building, and then ducked thankfully into the foyer as someone came out.

I pretended to wait for the elevator, watching as surreptitiously as I could until Richard drove away.

Sighing again and closing my eyes, I leaned against the wall of the strange apartment building. I thought about his bright blue eyes, his roughly calloused hands. He had made feel like a regular nineteen-year old girl. And it was such a good feeling.

"Miss?" said a voice. "Are you lost?"

I opened my eyes and nodded at the elderly lady who was watching me with concern.

"A little," I admitted, smiling in a way that made her eye me warily. "But the last thing I need is a complication," I added.

The old woman stepped aside nervously.

I let myself out the big glass doors and walked slowly up to my parent's house, realizing belatedly that Richard hadn't even asked for my phone number.

Dammit.

As I walked down the street toward my parents' house, I was thankful that even if our "date" hadn't led to anything more, it had at least helped boost my spirits. It really had made me feel human again. Having just had to move back in with my parents—a necessary but temporary situation—hadn't exactly been good for my confidence. My steps slowed as I remembered that my mom could very well be sitting in the living room, waiting to hear how my photography interview had gone. When she heard that it hadn't happened at all, I knew that she would say nothing, but that the disappointment would be evident in her face. Worse, I was sure that she was already expecting me to fail. A self-fulfilling prophecy, so to speak.

So much for high spirits, I thought regretfully.

But the house was dark as I approached. I turned the door handle slowly, appreciative of the fact that my dad never let a squeaky door last for more than a day. I snuck carefully into my temporary bedroom and flopped noiselessly down onto my old canopy bed, still fully clothed. I wondered if I would be able to get to sleep as I rolled over the details of my brief encounter with Richard. *Richie.* I resolved to call my friend Kristen in the morning, knowing that she would remind to put myself and my own goals first. Or I would call Isabelle and let her tell me how I was better off without a romantic attachment anyway. Smiling to myself, I slid into a fitfully dream-plagued slumber.

෨෴

I rolled over, groaning at the enormous pain that wracked my whole body.

"Crap," I muttered, remembering my accident in the coffee shop the day before. I blushed a little as my thoughts went immediately to Richie's warm blue eyes, regretting again that he hadn't asked for my number.

I glanced at the digital alarm clock on my nightstand. Almost nine already. My parents would probably be finishing breakfast and heading out the door any second.

If I just stay in bed for fifteen more minutes, I probably won't have to see them at all, I thought, knowing it was childish to avoid them.

My mom knocked lightly, and then opened the door without waiting for me to answer.

"You're awake," she stated, eyeing me skeptically "And already dressed. Or is it still dressed?"

She was wearing her crisp, two-piece nurse's uniform, understated makeup and a raincoat. Her bulky, knockoff designer purse was slung over one shoulder.

I sat up guiltily, and my backside screamed in protest. I yelped involuntarily, and my mom was at my side in an instant, concern replacing suspicion.

"You're hurt?" she demanded in her best clinical voice as she glided to the bed.

"I'm okay," I lied without conviction.

My mother lifted my shirt to examine my lower back. Her hands were cool and professional against my skin.

"Just a bruise," she concluded after a few soft pokes. "A very large bruise."

"I fell," I explained lamely, and for a full minute my mom probed me with her eyes. Finally she stepped away, letting my shirt fall back into place.

"You've had two calls already this morning. And one delivery," she told me, clearly irritated at the interruption to her routine.

"Sorry," I muttered.

But I felt a little leap of puzzled excitement. I waited, knowing that if I started demanding to know who had called and what had been delivered, my mom would just drag it out.

She relented to my silence. "A nearly indecipherable Asian woman called about an apartment. It appears that your lease has been approved."

I couldn't tell if my mom had any feelings at all about my moving out again, so I kept my own pleasure contained. I shrugged as casually as possible.

Yes, I thought with a mental fist pump.

"A *Gregory's Bookstore* called as well. A woman named Carla says that you've got the job if you want it. I took the liberty of telling her that you did," she paused and looked at me expectantly.

"Thank you," I managed to say, unable to keep my grin in check.

"The photographer, however, did not call," my mom told me.

I felt a guilty dip in my stomach. "No?"

We stared at each other for a moment, and she turned to leave the room.

"The delivery?" I reminded her.

"Right." She pulled an envelope with a broken seal out of her purse. "This came, along with a dozen roses. I put those in a vase on the kitchen table."

I stared after her as she exited, too surprised to ask her if she had personally opened the envelope, or if it had come that way. I pulled out the note immediately.

Laura,
My grandmother used to live in that building. Clearly, you do not. Dinner soon? Oh, yeah. I stole your address from the hospital records. I told them I was your husband.
Richie

He had scrawled a phone number across the bottom. I smiled to myself, and wondered if it was too early to call.

Chapter 2
THEN

I stared at myself critically in the mirror, wondering what Richie would be wearing. He made casual look so easy that it was almost a uniform for him—jeans or khakis paired with a collared shirt. We had been out twice already, and each time I felt like an overdressed Christmas tree standing beside him. And to make it worse, he had refused to tell me where he was taking me tonight, saying only that I might want to bring a sweater. The anxiety of choosing an outfit for our date was high enough. Not knowing the venue was multiplying it ten-fold.

"Damn you," I muttered, unsure if I was cursing Richard or my wardrobe.

The majority of my clothes were still in unlabeled boxes, ceiling high in my new living room. I had been tearing through them for an hour, and had located stacks of high school homework and textbooks, a pile of old purses, and my bath towels. But only one box of clothes had surfaced and it was full of stuff I hadn't worn since high school. It didn't help that I was also limited by the fact that my bruises weren't quite healed, and slipping into anything that wasn't stretchy or made of cotton caused me at least a small amount of discomfort.

I finally settled on a pair of black leggings with a small hole in the front seam, and a mossy green sweater dress that was long enough to cover the hole. The dress had an almost unnoticeable stain on the waistline, but I stuck a wide brown belt overtop just in case.

"Fine," I said resentfully to my reflection.

I tried not to be nervous. Earlier, I had called Kristen, and she had confirmed my suspicions that date number three was first kiss material. I had half-hoped that she would come up with an excuse for me to stay home, but she had just encouraged me to go with what felt right.

"Some help you are," I complained.

As I started to lace up my Doc boots the phone rang from underneath a pile of discarded items. I stared at the mess, deemed it hopeless, and let the answering machine pick up.

"Laura," said Kristen's voice, "Are you there? I know you've got that date tonight, and I wanted to give you one final piece of advice."

"What?" I wondered aloud, even though she couldn't hear me.

"Be careful," she admonished, and then added, "Try going out without the boots, just this once."

Sighing, I unlaced my Docs and slipped into a pair of more practical, far less eye-catching flats.

When the doorbell rang, my heart leaped in my chest, and I stomped to the door, irritated with myself. I swung it open, and Richie greeted me with a warm smile. Sighing, I stood on my tiptoes, pulled his mouth to mine and gave him a firm kiss.

"There," I said to his flushed face. "Now we can go."

❧❦

Although Richie quickly made it clear that he wasn't seeing anyone else, he didn't ask me if I was. He hadn't tried to define our relationship, asked me to make a commitment, or even wondered out loud where we might be headed.

So I was taken by surprise when he turned to me suddenly one evening and asked, "What is it that you like about me?"

We were in a crowded movie theatre waiting for our show to start, and I was immediately hyper aware of the girl sitting next to me and how her elbow kept bumping mine, and of the loud popcorn chewing going on in front of me. I felt a tense and unreasonable sweat break out on my upper lip. Even though it was dark, I couldn't make myself turn to meet Richie's eyes.

"What's not to like?" I whispered back glibly.

"Not much," he joked. "But really?"

"You want, like, a list?" I asked.

Richie laughed, and the loud chewer turned around to look at us.

"Isn't this only date five?" I teased, hedging.

"Date seven," he reminded me. "Or eight if we're counting by my standards. And are you implying that there *aren't* enough things to make up an entire list?"

I shrugged. "Maybe."

He grabbed my hand as the previews started, and although I was temporarily relieved from having to answer his earnest question, I suddenly couldn't focus on the movie.

I thought about Richard's question. There really *wasn't* much not to like about him. He was easygoing, often old fashioned, and up until this very minute, a low pressure kind of guy. He was also funny, passionate, and smart. He was attractive in a grown up way, with his goals and his dreams, and his unwavering practicality. He didn't exactly lack spontaneity, but I couldn't picture him walking in a rainstorm for the heck of it either. Probably more because he would never forget his umbrella than because he minded getting wet.

"It's just that…" he trailed off.

"What?" I asked.

He shook his head. "Nothing." His normally open face was cooly impassive, and I felt disturbed by the change.

I wondered suddenly if the reason he hadn't yet tried to define our relationship was because he could feel my own hesitation. That would make sense. I really couldn't picture him doing anything casually—even dating. My breath caught a little bit. Had I been unconsciously holding back? Worse, what if he left me because of it? I tightened my grip on Richie's hand.

"Laura," he whispered, ignoring the loud chewer, who gave us a dirty look, "I think that there's only *one* thing that I like about you."

"Just one?" I asked a little too tensely, watching his face for a sign of what he might be feeling. "What is it?"

"Everything," he answered. The sincerity in his voice outweighed the banality of his sentiment, and my heart beat faster of its own volition.

I watched from the window of Richie's fifth floor apartment until I was sure that he had driven away for his night class. I often accompanied him up to the school on Wednesday evenings, preferring to sit in one of the cozy reading chairs in the student lounge over sitting at home with just the TV for company. But I had begged off, using a fabricated yoga class as my excuse. I had even gone so far as to purchase and put on a pair of unflattering, stretchy black pants and a sweat absorbing tank top. I felt even worse for lying because Richie hadn't questioned my out of character behaviour at all.

I watched *Wheel of Fortune* twice, and tried to make myself read one of Richie's sports magazines with no luck. I dug a tub of cookie dough ice cream out of the freezer and a spoon out of the drawer. I ate in guilty silence, glancing from the window to the phone. I had tried to call Kristen three times at her dorm in Nova Scotia without success. But I desperately needed someone to talk to.

Finally, I picked up the phone and dialed before I could change my mind. It rang eight times on the other end, and I was about to give up when a heavily accented voice answered.

"*Gruezi?*" he greeted. "Hello?"

"Hi," I replied awkwardly. "I'm looking for Isabelle?"

He paused, and I thought for a moment he had hung up.

"Hello?" I said.

"Just a moment."

Isabelle picked up and answered in a breathless voice, "Hey there."

"It's Laura," I told her. "Laura Morgan."

"Hey, stranger!" she said excitedly. "As if there's any other Laura in my life!"

"Sorry I haven't called," I apologized immediately. It wasn't unusual for us to go months without speaking, but I been deliberately avoiding calling her, afraid of what she would say when she found about Richie.

She laughed. "Funny. I was feeling badly because *I* hadn't called *you*."

"We can be equally sorry, then," I suggested. I tried to figure out what I was going to say.

"I have news," we said at the same time.

"You tell me first," Isabelle offered.

"I met someone," I told her.

"You did?" she sounded surprised.

"Not on purpose," I assured her, and I pictured her raising an eyebrow at me.

"Laura, maybe I'm not remembering quite right, but weren't you planning on avoiding a relationship at all costs?" Isabelle was always blunt. "After the way things ended before..."

"Shh," I said to her.

"Is the someone there now?" she wondered.

"No."

"Then why are you shushing me?"

I shrugged even though she couldn't see me. "I'm in his apartment. I haven't actually been home much lately."

"Laura," she said in a cautionary tone.

"I know," I replied. "But this is different."

"Why?"

"We haven't even slept together yet." This statement was met with disbelieving silence. "He hasn't even tried anything," I added.

"You sound disappointed," my friend said.

"He's a grown up," I stated, knowing that it was a cop out.

Isabelle knew it too. "So?"

"He makes me think about things differently," I ammended.

"Like?"

"Well, before I was always trying to live up my parents' expectations, and I never could. You remember what I was like? I did everything to please them, and it never did. And then I tried to pretend that I didn't care, tried to live up to some expectations that I set for myself, and that didn't work either. With Richie, I don't need to live up to any expectations at all," I tried to explain.

"So he keeps his expectations low, and you can meet them?" Isabelle was teasing, but I sensed an underlying worry.

"No!" I said adamantly. "It's just that I can be *me* so much more easily when I'm with Richie."

"But a different you, I think?" my friend asked.

"You're playing the devil's advocate, aren't you?" I accused.

"Yes," she admitted. "I just want to make sure that you're doing this because you want to."

We were both silent for moment.

"And you love him?" she wondered.

I had been thinking about that a lot. Richie hadn't said the words, and neither had I, but I was sure that was where we were headed.

"I'm kind of scared," I said in a whisper. "And I needed to tell someone."

"No kidding," Isabelle agreed. "Do you feel better?"

"No," I said with a laugh.

"Okay, then. Want to hear something that will scare you more than this?"

"Anything to take my mind off of my own fear," I said.

"I met someone, too," my friend told me.

"Oh, yeah?"

"And it's a *man*," she confided.

I burst out laughing. I pictured me friend, with her cute pixie haircut, brash attitude and feminist ideals.

"It's not that funny," she said, pretending to be offended. "I think I fell for him as soon as I started working for him."

"You're in love with your *boss*?" I asked. "Isn't he married?"

"A widower," Isabelle told me. "Which I honestly didn't know before I came over here."

"Is he at least kind of girly?" I teased.

"You could say," she answered, and launched into a detailed description of her employer and his endearing quirks.

When we finally got ready to hang up the phone, I found that I actually did feel a hundred times better.

"Thanks, Isabelle," I said gratefully.

"For what? Being worse off than you are?" she replied lightly.

"That, too," I agreed.

I was sleeping in my usual spot on the couch when Richie got home from school, and he shook me awake gently.

"It's okay to sleep in the bed," he told me in a teasing voice. "I won't try anything."

"Yeah," I said sleepily, "That's the problem." I buried my face in the blanket so he wouldn't see my blush.

"You, um, *want* me to seduce you?" Richie asked, sounding awkward and surprised.

"I didn't go to yoga," I confessed. "Actually, there was no yoga."

"Did it get cancelled?" he asked.

"No. I made it up, so I could call Isabelle." I met his puzzled gaze with a sleepy, sheepish grin.

"Your friend in Switzerland? I won't even ask," Richie said.

"That's why I love you," I said quietly, and he didn't miss a beat.

"I love you, too, Laura."

I stood up, grabbed his hand, and pulled him toward the bedroom.

❧ ❧

I curled the covers on Richie's bed around my body like a protective shell. I had never noticed before how masculine they were—how rough their army green hue seemed compared to my own peach-coloured duvet. Even the fabric felt scratchier against my skin than it should have. I longed suddenly for the comfortable familiarity of my cozy apartment and the things that smelled like home. I felt tears form inexplicably in my eyes, and let them run freely down my face for a minute before quickly wiping them away.

Richie was in the bathroom, getting ready for bed. I felt like grabbing my clothes and running out the front door before he could join me. I heard the water turn off, and wiping my tears again, I quickly tucked myself in and closed my eyes. I pretended to be asleep.

The lights had remained off, just as I requested, and as Richie came out of the bathroom he left them that way. I kept my eyes closed anyway and pictured him silhouetted in the moonlight from the bedroom window, as he rifled through his drawers in the dark, searching for pajama pants. Richie approached the bed, his bare feet making almost no noise on the Berber carpet. I felt him climb in beside me and then sigh heavily.

"I know that you're awake," he said.

I didn't answer him.

"When you're sleeping, you make a funny little whistling noise when you breath," he told me.

"I'm sorry," I whispered, trying to keep the catch out of my voice.

"Don't be. It's endearing," he said, even though I was sure that he knew I wasn't apologizing for snoring.

I lay there silently, half hoping that I would drift off before we could take the next step. No such luck.

"Laura," Richie began hesitantly, "We don't have to do this."

"No," I answered. "I want to." It was the truth, but I still felt like crying.

"Can I turn the bedside lamp on?" he asked, and reached over me to do it before I could answer. I pulled the blanket even tighter around my body.

He gazed across at me, concern playing at his features. I couldn't make myself meet his eyes. "Are you crying?" he wondered.

"I don't know," I said into the pillow.

"Please, tell me what's wrong," he was almost pleading. "Are you worried that I'll hurt you?"

"No, of course not." Richie was as gentle as could be. But I knew that I would be lacking. I would hold back, not trusting myself to give in to my feelings, even though sleeping together had been my idea in the first place. And I worried that he would know why.

"Are you embarrassed?" he probed patiently.

I rolled over, turning my face away while being careful to keep my body covered. "Self-conscious," I said quietly. It made for a good excuse, and was almost true.

Richie was silent for a moment. "Why?"

I thought of my body. I had stretch marks that I knew belonged on a much older woman and lacked the elasticity of a proper nineteen year old.

"Just not perfect," I replied, not wanting to explain or elaborate.

Then Richie laughed softly. "You're perfect for me. Better than any other naked woman I've seen."

I finally met his eyes. "Oh, and there's been a lot, then has there?"

"Not a one." He stroked the side of my face. "I'm not ashamed to say that I'm glad this is going to be a first for both of us."

The lump formed again in my throat. I sighed, hoping that he would take it for agreement. Richie pulled my body close and kissed the back of my neck. His breath felt warm against my skin. He kissed me again, this time on the lips. I fought to keep my body from shaking as he drew himself on top of me. If he noticed my internal struggle, he didn't say.

He was tender, then rough, then quick, and finally apologetic.

"Laura," he started to say, but I silenced him with a kiss that I hoped would pass as residually passionate and forgiving.

"It will get easier, I think," I murmured, not sure if I was telling him, or me.

We both lay there, staring at the ceiling.

"I love you," I finally said for the second time, but Richie was already asleep.

છ૭ન્જી

I slid uneasily into the role of girlfriend once I had let myself be defined as such, and though it wasn't one that I had played very many times before, Richie made it relatively simple for me. He laughed easily at my clumsiness, was patient with my inability to understand the importance of NHL draft picks, and said disarming and charming things to make me blush. I had to admit that it was almost *too* easy to be happy, and I worried sometimes that something was going to come along and burst that bubble.

I tried not to think too much about the photography internship, convincing myself that it had been a long shot anyway. And Richie did make it easy to forget about it. He bought me chocolates and asked my opinion on buying new shoes. He introduced me to his friends, who were all clean cut and easygoing like him, and he didn't force me to make decisions about starting a career or choosing an academic specialty. He made me feel—almost—passable as an adult.

I hadn't even yet replaced the camera that I had broken in *The Cafe*, and with the amount of time I spent with Richie, I had no time to notice photographic moments anyway. I used my little studio suite less and less, and only slept there when Richie insisted that we give it a "turn". His apartment was bigger than mine, and it was closer to my job at the bookstore.

He liked to stop in at *Gregory's* on his way home from working with his Dad and pretend to browse in the gardening section. I could tell that the two semi-retired ladies with whom I worked liked Richard, and he played it up very well. He would bring in bouquets of fresh cut flowers and give one to each of them. Even though I still called them Mrs. Gregory and Mrs. McDougall, Richard was comfortable calling them Carla and Ellie. It made all three of our days each time he came in. The ladies were more than happy to adjust my days off to match his. We joked that Tuesday and Wednesday were our own private weekend, and we were blissfully content to keep it that way.

Tuesday evening quickly became our unofficial couples night. We did cliché things and laughed at ourselves for doing them. When we watched movies that starred Julia Roberts or Kevin Costner, I would sigh appropriately at the romantic moments, and he would squeeze my hand reassuringly during the tear-jerkers.

We had been together for a little over six months, and the summer was just coming to a blissful end. The ladies offered me a supervisory position at the bookstore, and I was promised a dollar an hour raise by Christmas. The idea of being in charge appealed to me, and so I accepted. Richie was going back to school after the Labour Day long weekend, and lately I had been worrying more and more about how the changes were going to affect our relationship. I loved our routine, and was scared to have to change it. Truthfully, the predictability of our life was becoming a comfort to me. But Richie had seemed distracted recently as well, and I felt restless as we settled in for our last movie night of the summer.

We took turns selecting the movie each week, and this time it was Richard's turn to pick. He had chosen an embarrassingly B-grade horror film. I spent the first half the movie with my hand over my eyes, and then fell asleep during the second half. Richard finally woke me up with a kiss on the forehead.

"That was terrible," he told me.

"It was," I agreed sleepily. "Why did you pick it?"

Richard smiled at me in a way that made warm all over. "Two reasons. First, I was punishing you for making me watch *Pretty Woman* last week."

I punched him lightly in the shoulder. "Jerk. What was the other reason?"

"I was distracted..."

"But not so distracted that you couldn't mete out punishment?"

"I'm never *that* distracted." He paused. "Did you know that I have an older sister?"

I didn't know. Richard talked a lot about his parents and quite a bit about his three younger sisters, but he had never mentioned an older one.

"And she's a psychopathic killer, and this is how you wanted to ease me into the news?" I teased.

Richard touched my face. "Well, not quite. She's always been in trouble. Drugs. Suspected personality disorders. Been hospitalized on more than one occasion. Cara's fourteen years older than me and lives up in Whitehorse. My parents kicked her out when she was twenty. I don't remember her very well." He paused, thinking about it. "But anyway. She called me yesterday, out of the blue. She's married. Met a Native man—he's Tagish, she said—who straightened her right around. That was almost fifteen years ago now. Got a couple of teen-aged kids. Kateri and Atian are their names. She just wanted to reconnect. Mom and Dad don't even know about the marriage or about the kids. And it got me to thinking."

I watched his serious expression. Something in his eyes made my heart beat faster with a combination of nerves and anticipation.

"Laura," he said, "I think that you should meet my family."

Chapter 3
THEN

I knew that he was going to ask me before we ever sat down at the table. We had been together for fourteen months when Richie had made an excuse for a late first year anniversary celebration. He had selected a restaurant where the servers wore clip on bow ties and pleated pants. I suppose that someone with more experience in the dating world might have found the place cheesy. To me, it was the exact kind of restaurant where grown men proposed to grown women with engagement rings placed cleverly inside fudgie desserts.

And lately, I had to admit that I been trying to picture myself in a fancy wedding dress, trimmed with lace and pearls. I had never been one of those little girls who dreams of a handsome prince on a white horse or of a domestic life full of kids and home cooked meals. But since Richard and I had started dating, I had to admit that the thought of forever promised at an alter didn't seem like quite so foreign a concept.

He made my life so simple. Even after more than a year, he never pressured me about my on-again, off-again relationship with school. He was happy to talk and fill up the space when I felt like being silent. I could easily see myself living the next seventy years by his side.

I had only been to three weddings in my life. The first had been my mom's older sister's first wedding. Aunt Hilary's vows had taken place at a fancy Catholic ceremony that had seemed austere and frightening to me. The marriage obviously hadn't agreed with her either—it had lasted only a year. The second wedding I attended was another of Aunt Hilary's attempts at marriage—a simple, Hawaiian beach affair. It had been a much more appealing setting, and not as intimidating as her first nuptials, but that marriage had lasted even less time than the first one. The third and final wedding I had attended had been the one I crashed, in what seemed like another lifetime, on a completely different continent.

It wasn't that I was bitter or had a jaded view of marriage. After all, my own parents had been married for twenty-five years. But to put it simply, weddings had always seemed like someone else's life. Or even like someone else's fantasy of a life.

I suddenly remembered my grade nine lab partner. Her name was Tandy Brown, and one day she had confessed to me that her only dream was to have a fairy tale wedding and a happily ever after life. She was a science genius, a math whiz, and her confession had creeped me out a little. Tandy had moved away midway through the year, and I hadn't thought of her in forever. But as I sat there gripping Richard's hand in the fancy restaurant, I wondered absently if she had ever achieved her goal.

"Laura," Richard spoke suddenly, breaking the awkward silence. My heart thudded in my chest. "I have a confession to make."

"Okay." My response was a little too loud.

"Remember the hospital?"

I nodded my recollection. "Hard to forget."

"I told you that everyone calls me Richie?"

I nodded silently again, not really understanding.

"No one calls me that," he confessed.

"I call you that," I replied, feeling confused.

"Except you," Richard amended. "I don't know why I told you that, all those months ago. But I just wanted a clean slate, okay?"

I patted his hand, feeling silly about reassuring him. "Sure. Okay. Consider it clean."

I was trying to think of something to add when I saw both Richard's and my own parents enter the restaurant. I wasn't surprised to see them—the table we were at was too big for one couple, and had been set for six. Richard stood as they joined us, shaking my dad's hand and kissing his mother on the cheek. Amanda gave me a warm hug, and Cole ruffled my hair affectionately. The Lockhursts had welcomed me with open arms in their son's life. Richie reintroduced his parents to mine, and they all made polite conversation that sounded to me like the hum of a far off fan.

The five of them were positively buzzing with poorly disguised excitement. Richard, who was always so self-assured, kept pointing out the same items on the menu and mentioning the expected rain on the weekend. I had to cover my mouth with my napkin to hide my giggles.

Something else had been nagging at me all week, and I hadn't quite figured out what it was. Whatever the thought was, it was an elusive one—like when I tried to picture myself as a bride. I could see the dress, picture the shoes. I could even imagine Richard standing at the altar saying the vows. But as soon as I tried to see *my* face in that picture, the image would slip away. As I attempted to sift through my mind to grasp whatever evasive idea was escaping me, I realized that everyone at the table was staring at me.

"Umm," I said awkwardly.

My mom nudged me under the table. "I think that Richard wants to ask you something," she told me.

Richard nodded, an attractive blush creeping up underneath the beard he had been growing. I smiled at this side of him I had never seen—slightly unsure and maybe even a little shy. For a second I forgot that we had an audience and I ran my hand lovingly along his jawline.

"Laura," he said very quietly.

And suddenly the thought that had been eluding me all week came into sharp focus.

"Oh, my God," I whispered.

"Laura," Richard repeated nervously, "I was wondering if you would please be my wife?"

I looked at him blankly. "Richard. I think that I'm pregnant."

Both sets of parents went still and silent. Mine stared at me, and Richard's stared at him. My dad stood up, his face a vibrant shade of red. For a second, I thought that he was going to hit Richie, and then he grinned.

"I think that was a yes!" My dad almost shouted.

Richard was grinning, too, self-assurance back in place. "Laura," he amended, "Will you please marry me? Soon?"

ॐॐ

Richie and I had our first argument two days before our wedding. In general, of course, he was easy to get along with, and when a potential conflict did arise, I was not eager to rock the boat myself. But by then I was about thirteen weeks along, and still exploring a wide range of hormonally induced emotions. The disagreement had started after a simple phone call from our DJ.

I was in the kitchen of Richard's apartment—about to become *our* apartment officially—preparing dinner when the call came. Now that I was finally past the wanting-to-puke-at-the-smell-of-food stage of my pregnancy, I was starting to really enjoy cooking in our little kitchen. I had onions in one pan, water boiling in another, and a salad started on the cutting board. The phone rang from somewhere in the direction of the living room.

"Can you get that?" I called to Richard, feeling too happily enmeshed in my domesticity to bother to search for the telephone.

"Sure, hun!" He had taken to calling me that ever since the engagement had become official. He had also tried out "dear" and "sweetie", but "hun" seemed to be his favorite.

I heard Richard pick up the phone in the living room, and sighed contentedly as I dumped the tomatoes in with the onions. My pasta sauce was just coming to a simmer when I felt his arms encircle my waist.

"Smells good," he told me.

"It will be," I assured him. "Who was on the phone?"

"Klein. You know, the DJ for our big day."

"Oh, yeah? Please tell me he's not raising his fee?" I cringed at the thought. Money was excessively tight. I had renewed the six month lease on my suite right before Richie's proposal, and for the time being we were paying rent on two places. We had settled on the May long weekend for our ceremony, and even though we were only having fifty guests, the cost of a wedding in prime season was unfathomable to someone making six-fifty an hour like me. And that wasn't even factoring in all of the money we would have to spend on baby items.

Richard laughed and released my shoulders. "No. Just wanted to know what song we wanted for our first dance."

I relaxed. I had been thinking about that myself. I was leaning toward selecting something sappy and traditional like *Unchained Melody*. I had wondered what Richie thought, and figured that in his typically decisive and romantic way, he would surprise me.

"And what did you say?" I asked with careful disinterest as I started to drain the spaghetti.

I didn't want to ruin anything that he was planning, but I was curious to know what song he thought would define our relationship.

Richard shrugged. "I told him to go ahead and pick something. That it wasn't important."

I didn't realize that I had dropped the colander until I feel the hot noodles hit my feet.

"Shit!" Richard shouted.

I had never heard him swear before. I walked woodenly over to the tiny kitchen table.

"Laura? Laura!" he repeated my name several times. "Are you okay? What happened? Your foot? Is it burned?"

I sat down and stared at Richard in amazement. "It doesn't matter," I stated flatly.

He misunderstood me. "Of course it matters! If you're burnt, you need first aid!"

I shook my head stiffly. "Screw my foot. The song. How can it not matter?" I couldn't help it. The emotion brought my voice up several octaves. "It's supposed to symbolize everything in our life together! And you say—to a near stranger—that it *doesn't matter*?! What is wrong with you?" I realized that I was yelling and crying at the same time.

Richard stared at me incredulously with his mouth slightly open.

The words kept coming. "You know, you never even asked me what I was doing in *The Cafe*! Not once! It never even occurred to you that I might have had a reason to be there! You just assumed that I was there waiting for you to sweep me off my feet!"

Richard finally jumped in, visibly hurt and angry. "No," he said quietly, "I assumed that you were there to buy coffee. Silly me."

"I wasn't," I told him vehemently. "I hate their coffee. Hate it! It was a stop along the way to my *life*. The life that I will *never* get back. Because I met *you*. I was going to be something. Now, I'm going to be nothing."

It was a selfish and untrue thing to say, and I knew it as soon as the words were out of my mouth.

Richard looked at me, all traces of anger erased from his face. Surprise and sadness filled his eyes.

"No," he said. "You're just going to be my wife. And the mother of my child."

⮜⮞

I watched with tears streaming down my face as my fiancé wordlessly cleaned up the spaghetti from the floor. Richard scooped the pasta into the dustpan and then into the garbage without looking at me. He left the kitchen and came back with a thick bath towel. He used it to soak up the spilled water. He left the kitchen again and I heard the sound of the washing machine start in the hall. I stared down at my hands, trying to form an appropriate apology in my mind. When I looked up again, Richie was seated across from me at the table.

"I'm so sorry," he said to me.

"What?" I'm sure I sounded as confused as I felt.

"It was insensitive of me. I assumed that having a song—having an 'our song', I guess—wasn't important to you. It just hadn't come up, and with everything else that's been going on, I was trying to make it easier by letting Klein pick it," Richie told me, his voice filled with sincerity. "What song would you like?"

It was my turn to stare with my mouth open.

Richie touched my cheek tentatively. "Okay. You're still mad. What're you three favorite songs?"

"Of all time?" I finally answered.

"Sure."

- 30 -

"My favorites are always changing…"

"Okay, so right now then. Pick one."

"You might not like it." I suddenly felt really awkward. Why was this something we had never discussed before? In eight weeks of planning, it had never come up. Why was it so important now?

"It doesn't matter," Richie assured me, probably relieved that I was no longer screaming like a madwoman. "Your taste can't be *that* bad. I promise to like whatever you pick."

"Okay." I hesitated, and he nodded encouragingly at me. I said the first thing that came to my mind. "Right now I love… Umm. *The Wagon* by a band called Dinosaur Jr."

Richard grinned at me. "I have not heard that song. Sad story."

"Sad story," I agreed, smiling back at him.

"Does it make a good wedding song?"

I shook my head. "Sadder story. Not at all."

"What do you think then?"

"I think that I'm sorry, too," I told him, realizing too late that if the song had really been that important, it would've come up before. "And I think that I'm very lucky to have such a patient man as my fiancé. You were right. It doesn't matter. Let the DJ pick something."

"Wait a minute. Now I *want* to pick something. Just to impress you with my musical prowess. And now I also have something to go on." He winked at me. "But just to check that we're on the same page…I'm guessing that Mariah Carey and Aerosmith aren't contenders?"

I laughed out loud, and got up to boil more water for spaghetti, round two.

––

I wish that I could say that my wedding was engraved firmly in my mind—that I was able to recall small and large details alike—but the truth is that it happened too fast for me to remember more than bits and pieces. If felt like sitting in the eye of flower petal and satin storm.

Richard's mom had to make some last minute adjustments to my dress, shortening the spaghetti straps and letting out one of the gathered areas across the bodice. The morning sickness had left me thinner across the shoulders, but the pregnancy had left me wider across the chest. My mom bemoaned her own inability as a seamstress while she tried to make herself useful by holding Amanda Lockhurst's straight pins. My mother-in-law was just doing her best to keep *my* mom from poking me accidentally.

I sat as still and silent as possible, going over my vows in my head, and trying to keep the names of Richard's sisters, cousins, and friends straight for the thank you speech my dad had made me prepare.

Richard's middle younger sister had just finished a makeup artistry course at the Blanche Macdonald Institute in Vancouver, and she had been eagerly waiting to try out her new skills on my face. As soon Amanda finished her adjustments, Marie jumped in to do her part. The eighteen year old was a tiny person, and she applied the makeup in quick, sharp movements. It was, I imagined, what it would feel like to have my face done by a hummingbird. I closed my eyes as she painted on eyeliner, several different shades of eyeshadow, and mascara. When her flurry of movement stopped suddenly, I was startled into opening my eyes.

Marie's face was right in front of mine.

"Hi?" I said awkwardly. "We're done?"

Marie didn't move for a full minute, staring at me. Finally she nodded and sighed. "A few more minutes. I just wish that you had let me do your hair, too."

It was one of the only things that I hadn't let myself be steamrolled about. I wanted my hair long and loose because one of the benefits of this pregnancy was that it was growing in faster and thicker than it ever had in my life. I shook my head at my soon to be sister-in-law, trying to smile.

Of Richie's sisters, Marie was the one I felt least comfortable with. The other Lockhurst girls were easier to build a relationship with.

Jessie, Richie's youngest sister, was a teenager, still living at home with their parents, and I had gotten to know her sheerly by exposure. She was barely sixteen and was present as often as not when we went to visit the senior Lockhursts. Since she had only recently obtained her driver's license, she also regularly called Richie for rides to and from concerts, movies, and the mall, and I usually tagged along. Jessie was acting as junior bridesmaid in our wedding.

Liz, who was the oldest of Richie's younger sisters, was my age, and we had become quite close over the past year and a half. It was easy for us to connect since she was also expecting a baby, though she was due in November and I wasn't due until January. Even if we *hadn't* been able to bond over our pregnancies, I thought that we would have become close friends anyway. I had asked Liz to be my matron of honour.

I had even developed a written relationship with Cara in the Yukon. Every month or two, she would send a letter and some photos of her family. At first she had addressed them to Richard, but since he was busy trying to balance part-time classes with working full-time for his dad, I had taken it upon myself to answer them. It only took two or three letters, and then Cara's correspondence started coming to me instead. She has a flair for telling stories about her kids and their unusual lifestyle up north. I hadn't been able to talk her into coming down for the wedding, but she had sent us a beautiful, handmade blanket that her husband's grandmother had assisted her in stitching. I knew that no matter what other gifts we received, the quilt would still be my favourite.

But Marie was different. And not just in that she wasn't accessible in the way that the rest of the family was. She had a restless and unpredictable personality that I found unsettling. Richie told me that a year before Marie was supposed to graduate high school she had moved out of their parents' six bedroom home and into her twenty-four year old boyfriend's downtown studio apartment. Two years later, with no explanation, Marie randomly moved things back into her old room at the Lockhurst house and announced that she had enrolled in the makeup program. She completed the nine month course and twelve week practicum, and then moved her stuff back out again.

My comfort level wasn't helped at all by the fact that when I had called her to ask her if she wanted to be in the wedding party, she had not-so-politely declined.

"Don't you have a friend you can ask instead?" she had wondered.

"No," I answered honestly.

"Really?"

"I've never exactly run with a big crowd," I told her.

"But surely you must have one friend? From school or something?" Marie made me feel like I was lying.

"No," I explained, slowly, feeling kind of foolish. "I have a few close girlfriends, but they all seemed to have moved away on me. One is studying law at Darmouth in Nova Scotia. Another is traveling somewhere in South America. Isabelle, my best friend, is in Switzerland and has a baby due any day now, too."

"What about from SFU?" My future sister-in-law pressed.

I started to get uncomfortable. "No one close enough to ask to do this."

I heard her sigh, and wondered why I was still trying.

"Look," she had said, "I'm honoured that you asked me, really. But I just can't."

"Fine," I had told her, and hung up before the tears could start.

Richard just shrugged it off with the explanation that Marie was just Marie.

The free makeup job she was doing now was her wedding gift to us.

When she paused to wash her hands, I stole a quick glance at myself in the mirror.

The hasty dress alterations had clearly been a success. I couldn't detect a flaw in the bodice, and the straps appeared to be glued in place. The empire waist flattered me nicely, and the very small beginnings of a baby bump were hidden under the gauzy depths of the loose skirt. And for all of her oddness, Marie's artistry with the makeup brush was undeniable. The subtle tones she had chosen evened my skin to a porcelain-like texture, and the muted bronze shades on my lids brought out glints of gold in my eyes that were normally drowned in flat hazel.

Marie was staring at me, and lifted a strand of my hair critically.

"Maybe you can do my hair at my next wedding," I finally joked half-heartedly, and she walked out of the room without laughing.

I suddenly wanted to scream that I, too, had once been free and impetuous, and that somewhere buried underneath the bride and mother-to-be, my restless soul still lay waiting.

Chapter 4
WAY BACK WHEN

In spite of my mother's multiple, repeated warnings, I was so ridiculously cocky when I got off of the plane in Heathrow Airport that it never occurred to me that something could go wrong.

I had just put in a disastrous first year at university, and was ready to make up for it by embarking out on my own. My parents really hadn't wanted me to go—especially my mom. And however reasonable my trip had seemed to me, they had practically begged me to reconsider. They wouldn't admit that going straight into my post-secondary career out of high school had been a mistake, even though it was clear that I had been overwhelmed by university life. I wasn't prepared for the responsibility of writing a paper each week, of studying for hours on end, or for the pressure of being continually asked by my professors and peers alike what my intended major was going to be. I had gone through my first semester with the lofty goal of becoming a French teacher. I enrolled in three French courses and tossed in one Psychology class—just for fun. I quickly discovered that French at the university level was an unrelenting series of oral exams, French novels, and advanced verb conjugation. The 'A's I had received in high school quickly became 'D's in university. By the time my first semester had come to a close, my dream of teaching French had evaporated, and my GPA was an embarrassing nightmare.

I had considered immediately dropping out of school, but instead had let my parents talk me into tackling a lighter course. Since Psychology was the only course in which I hadn't met with complete disaster, and was my dad's own area of expertise, I chose another class in that discipline, alongside something I thought would be a surefire grade helper—introductory Philosophy. More disaster. When I received the letter in the mail warning me of my academic probation, I knew that it was time for a mental break.

To appease my parents and my conscience, I registered in one class for the summer at a community college—photography. It became my first successful attempt at post-secondary education. I found the class inspiring. Taking photos and developing them myself was richly and creatively satisfying. The other people in the class were like me. Though they varied in age and experience, they were dissatisfied with the decisions they had made thus far in life, and they were searching for an out.

For my own sanity, and in attempt to at least resemble a responsible adult, I had also taken a part-time job at a local grocery store. It was mindless, paid poorly, and had no prospects for a career. It was perfect. I set up a reasonable savings plan with no specific goal in mind—fifty percent of my earning went straight into the bank, and fifty percent went to my photography supplies. By the end of the summer, I had absorbed a respectable chunk of photographic know-how, and had amassed what my dad called a decent nest-egg. I had also become afflicted with an ever increasing sense of panic in regards to the approaching fall. I knew that I couldn't immediately step back into the academic world. I also knew that my parents expected me to do just that.

And then, on a particularly cloudy August day, when the crushing anxiety of returning to school was weighing on me with an almost physical presence, I walked past a travel agency. Actually, I had probably walked by it a hundred times or more without ever really noting its existence. But this time a sign in the window caught my eye. In bold letters it read, BACK TO SCHOOL BLUES GOT YOU DOWN? FALL SPECIALS ON NOW: EUROPE, MEXICO, CARIBBEAN. I had to go in.

∽∾

Breaking the news to my mom and dad was easier than I anticipated. I just sat them down after dinner that same night, armed with a detailed book of hostels and the step-by-step guide carefully typed out by the enthusiastic travel agent. I smiled at them when

I finished outlining my plan, bracing myself for the inevitable lecture. They didn't let me down.

"Is this something to do with Isabelle?" my mom asked immediately.

I rolled my eyes inwardly, but kept the smile planted firmly on my face. "Of course not."

Isabelle had been my best friend for most of high school, and she had been my parents' favourite scapegoat for every bit of trouble I got into. Immediately after graduating high school, she had packed her bags and left for Europe.

"You've seemed a little lonely since she left," my dad told me, trying to take the soft approach.

True enough, I thought. *It's hard to replace a friend like that.*

"Is that your psychological evaluation, Dad?" I teased.

"Her parents told me that Isabelle ran away to England because she's a lesbian," my mom informed me bluntly.

"So she could *become* a lesbian," my dad corrected.

"Are you a lesbian?" demanded my mother.

I gritted my teeth. "Isabelle left because she got a job as an *au pair* with a Swiss family."

My parents gave me a dubious look, and I sighed.

"And because her parents couldn't accept the fact that she *might* have questions about her sexuality," I added reluctantly.

"We'd still love you," my dad assured me quickly.

Maybe, I thought. "I appreciate the gesture, but I'm not going because I'm a lesbian. Or to become one," I said. "I'm going because I want a vacation."

"You've never had a boyfriend," noted my mother at the same second my dad asked, "A vacation from what?"

This time I rolled my eyes in actuality. I decided not point out that they were the only parents in the world who weren't relieved to have a—not necessarily by choice—celibate teenaged daughter. I also opted not to remind them that *as* an eighteen-year old girl, the only thing I could possibly need a vacation from was my parents.

"What will you do there?" my father wondered.

"Sightsee," I replied, smiling to myself. The photography course had sparked my enthusiasm for capturing life on film, and as soon as I had paid for my plane ticket, an idea had started to form in my mind.

"But you've never even been to a *local* museum," my mom protested.

"I leave in ten days," I told them with a finality that brooked no argument.

And so, less than two weeks later, I had arrived in London with my life in a backpack, blissfully alone and full of self-assurance.

❧❦

As soon as I had collected my baggage, and worked my way through customs, I dug out the four most important accessories for my trip—my camera, my itinerary, my prepaid long distance calling card, and the brown satchel that I would use to carry my smaller belongings around. I found a pay phone right away, and called my parents as I had promised I would. The answering machine picked up, and looking at my watch, I mentally calculated that they had probably both left for work about an hour before. I left a message, assuring them that I was safe and that I would try to call again in a day or two. I then tucked the calling card into my purse with my passport and my traveler's cheques.

I made my way to the busy parkway. Feeling satisfyingly touristy, I scanned my itinerary. *Get to Station Hostel, Kings Cross* was the first instruction. I was going to sleep there for one night, and then make my way into Peterborough the next morning to stay at a place recommended by the travel agent. I was eager to check out the Peterborough Cathedral, and thought that I would spend a few days or more pouring over the Gothic architecture. I also had notes for Nottingham, Newcastle Upon Tyne, Manchester, Birmingham, and finally Portsmouth. On the back of the last page of my itinerary the travel agent had written a list of reliable cab companies based out of the London area.

I stepped out onto the sidewalk, inhaling my first breaths of European air. I scanned the multitude of cabbies waiting for hire, and finally selected one at random. I handed the driver the address for Station Hostel, and he grunted me a quote of forty-five pounds. I did a quick mental estimation of the exchange and reasoned that it was going to cost me a little over a hundred dollars for the ride. I winced, trying to hide my disappointment—that was enough for an entire week at the hostel in Peterborough.

The cabbie looked up at me, and grinned sympathetically. "American?" he asked me in a Eastern European accent.

I shook my head. "Canadian." I showed him the patch sewn purposefully into my army jacket.

"Hungarian," he told me. "Kristof," he added, tapping his cabbie ID.

"Hi," I replied lamely. "Laura."

"Listen," he said to me, "If you ever tell anyone I told you this, I'll call you a liar at the least." He winked and I blushed.

"Whatever it is, I'll take it to the grave," I assured him, drawn in by his conspiratorial smile.

Kristof looked satisfied. "Okay. You can take a train or you can take the tube. Either will cost you less than a quarter as much as my taxi." He looked around as if he expected someone to reprimand him for admitting this. "Most of the young kids like the train. Scenery, you know."

"Thank you!" I exclaimed with genuine appreciation, fumbling to hand him a five pound note. The cabbie waved the tip away.

"Keep it," he laughed. "Buy yourself a pint in the city. Doing a pretty foreign girl a favor is all I need for reward."

I smiled back at him. "One more favor then?"

"Maybe," he teased.

I pulled my camera out of my satchel. "A picture? To show my friends at home?"

Kristof leaned out the window of his cab and posed awkwardly with his hand on his chin. I clicked quickly and then waved goodbye as I headed back into the airport.

The train station was in such an obvious place at the airport that I don't know how I missed it after deplaning in the first place. I stepped up to the wicket, smiling at the girl in the booth. She was young, even by my standards. Her name tag said "Ginger", and her hair was dyed to match.

"Hey, y'all," she greeted me in a surprising American drawl,."Where ya headed?"

I pulled out my itinerary, once again accentuating my tourist status.

"Well," I answered, and launched into my detailed plan of spending a night the Kings Cross hostel, the time in Peterborough, and my tour throughout England. "Can you help me?" I resisted the impulse to tell her that the cabbie had recommended the train as a cheap alternative for my travels. I had promised him confidentiality, after all.

Ginger shook her head at me. "Bad plan," she stated.

I was too surprised to be offended by her criticism of my carefully orchestrated schedule.

"Why?" I asked her.

"Two main reasons," she told me. "First, that hostel at Kings Cross is closed. It's only open between the last week in May and the first week in September. Second, y'all don't really want to stay near Kings Cross at all. That area is only any good if yer a hooker or a druggie." She eyed me up and down. "And y'all don't look like either of those."

I couldn't decide whether to laugh or cry.

"How old are you?" I asked Ginger.

"Sixteen," she answered easily. "Moved here four years ago when my Daddy got custody, been working at the station for almost a year."

"What should I do?" I wondered a little helplessly.

Ginger turned to the screen in front of her.

"Hmm. Should be easy enough to get y'all to Peterborough," she told me and then laughed. "But ya have to make a switch at Kings Cross Station, so at least ya' can say that ya' went!" She grinned at me, clearly enjoying the irony. "Hmm," she said again, typing quickly. "That ticket is eleven pounds. But for twelve pounds, y'all can get the round trip. It's good for essentially anywhere up and down the east side—London through to Newcastle and back. Y'all can use it for up to ten days after purchase."

"Perfect," I said, relieved to have a new, more affordable plan.

Ginger handed me a few sight-seeing brochures, circling her favorite places to visit and writing down a few good restaurants. "Anything else I can help y'all with?" She asked as I thanked her profusely for her help.

I held up my camera. "One for the road?"

Laughing, Ginger grinned prettily for the photo and directed me toward the right platform.

Chapter 5
THEN

You can still run.

I pushed the unreasonable thought down violently. I was standing at the alter with Richie. He gripped my hand in his vise-like fingers. His sisters stood to my immediate left, and their presence weighed on me—like I was trapped by Lockhursts on all sides. I was glad that I had a veil to mask the sudden the panic I was feeling.

You can still run. The thought came again, unbidden. I pictured myself fleeing down the aisle. My mother would probably tackle me and drag me by my hair back to Richie's side. I stifled a giggle, and Richie tightened his grip on my hand a little more. I wanted to pry my hand loose. I could feel sweat beading between my shoulders.

Oh, God. I'm going to faint.

And then I felt it. A little nudge right under my belly button. It came again, light and insistent. *The baby.*

"Hello?" I whispered, panic morphing into giddiness.

Richie leaned in. "Okay?"

"Perfect," I said. "Perfect."

And the minister began to guide us through our vows.

Richie snuck up behind me. I had been staring a blankly out the window of the little hall we had rented for our reception.

"Wondering if it's over yet?" he teased.

"Oh, no," I protested, struggling to keep the exhaustion out of my voice. "Everything has been fantastic. The cake, the food, everything."

"Really? Because I'm ready to be done," my new husband admitted.

I sighed in relief. "Me, too. I just want to start our regular life. I'm so tired of looking at flowers and smiling like an idiot."

Richard gave me his own best fake smile, and I laughed.

"Don't you wish that you'd been able to put that into the vows?" he asked.

I laughed again, but sobered immediately. "Do you think that people know?"

"About the baby?"

I nodded wordlessly.

He shrugged. "Does it matter?"

"Maybe," I told him.

"They might suspect," he conceded as he ran his hand gently along my midriff.

"I don't want people to think that we got married *because* of the baby," I said softly.

"We didn't," he reminded me. "I had this ring here before I had any idea." Richie threaded his fingers through mine and caressed the little diamond with his thumb.

"Kids," called Amanda from inside the main hall. "They need you in here for the first dance."

Richie led me out, and everyone clapped.

I recognized the first strains of the song the instant it started to play, and my face tingled with pleasure. "*Sweet Jane?*" I whispered in my husband's ear.

He kissed the side of my face and dipped me theatrically for a photo. "The Velvet Underground meets your approval?"

I wondered if he knew that it was the very same song that had been playing in *The Cafe* on the day we met. But as he spun me around on the floor, I decided that it was something I would rather leave a mystery.

Chapter 6
THEN

"Mom," I complained loudly from my prone position on the couch, "Bed rest is going to kill me."

She handed me a cup of herbal tea. "Laura, the bed rest is designed to *not* kill you. You only have two weeks left. And I'm beginning to think that the doctor should've forbidden you from talking as well as walking." My mother patted my knee. I knew that she was kidding, but she was also probably right. She had been taking care of me for almost a month, and I was pretty sure that I had tried her already limited patience to its edge. This was the most one-on-one time we had ever spent together.

Three days after Christmas my blood pressure had shot up, and my obstetrician had started tossing around words like "hypertensive" and "hospital". I had already been off of work for a week at the point, and was going crazy from the amount of time that I spent alone in the house. I couldn't stand the thought of being confined to a hospital bed, watching reruns of *Jerry Springer* on a little tiny television, surrounded by other cranky pregnant women doing exactly the same thing.

So I did the only reasonable thing, the most desperate thing—I called my mom.

She came with me to the obstetrician's office, outlined her credentials as a retired nurse, and assured him that she would not leave my side for the duration of my pregnancy. I had worried about my dad, but my mom had assured me that she would stock the fridge with frozen meals, and reminded me that he was perfectly capable of using the microwave. In the end, my trepidation in regards to a lengthy hospital stay won out over my anxiety about how my father would make out on his own. Twice a week, my mom would drop me at the hospital for a two hour non-stress test, and she would head home to my dad to prepare more meals and tidy up whatever mess he happened to have made in her absence.

I sighed dramatically as my mom lifted my legs, sat down, and placed my swollen feet in her lap. "I'm an invalid."

"Just be thankful that it's not summer," she told me. "Do you want a foot rub?"

"I was just getting the hang of being a grown up," I complained petulantly, "And now I have my mom here babysitting me."

She ignored me and started to massage my toes. I pretended not to enjoy it. My legs and back had been aching worse than usual today. And I wasn't done being grumpy anyway. When I heard Richard's key turning in the door, I feigned sleep. His constant cheeriness was irritating.

My husband leaned over my face, kissing me on the cheek, and I could smell alcohol on his breath. I yanked my feet away from my mom's hands and sat up. Richie didn't drink. And the smell of booze made me feel a bit nauseous and irrationally angry.

"What's wrong?" I demanded.

"Nothing. I have good news, actually," he answered excitedly. His eyes were a little too shiny.

"You're drunk," I accused.

"I got a job!" he announced.

"That's fantastic," my mom said.

"A drinking job?" I asked sarcastically.

Richie shook his head. "I had a celebratory beer. Two beers. And a half. With my new boss." He gripped my hand and grinned enthusiastically.

"That's fantastic," my mom repeated. "Where at? Doing what?"

"What about school?" I wondered out loud. Richie had just been approved for a student loan, and had resumed part-time winter classes immediately after New Year's. We were both hoping that he would be able to graduate in the spring.

He ignored my question, and turned back to my mom. She was clearly the more receptive audience.

"B and K Electronics," he said. "You know, that big chain from back east? They're opening a new store in the city. It's just a floor manager position to start, but the money's very reasonable, the schedule's flexible, and there's room for advancement. It's retail, so I'll be doing some evenings and weekends, but I'm guaranteed hours and benefits after six months."

"Manager! You must be thrilled!" My mom beamed at Richard and nudged me under the coffee table. I just stared at both of them. I felt a terrible twinge in my side and an awful sense of foreboding.

My mom and my husband looked at me expectantly.

"I don't know what to say," I managed finally. The twinge in my side amplified. I felt light-headed.

Richie balanced himself on the couch's armrest. "Say that you're happy," he said to me in a quiet voice. "This job is practical. It's stable. It's what our family needs."

I stood up in a more fluid motion than I had made in nine months. My sudden movement knocked Richie off of the armrest, and he landed on the floor with a thud.

"Sorry," I said faintly. A white-hot pain, tight and throbbing at the same time, surged across my abdomen. I moaned a little, and then my mom was at my side.

Richie stared up at me. I nodded at him. "Now," I said breathlessly. "Now."

ॐॐ

I gazed down at the tiny baby wedged between me and Richie on the hospital bed. It was so surreal to me that this little person had been living inside of me only hours ago.

"Wow," said my husband.

"Yes," I agreed.

"Wow," he said again.

I wanted to stare for hours at my new son, hold so tightly that I knew he could never possibly slip away.

"Did you always know that you were going to get married and have kids?" I asked in a whisper, not wanting to disturb the enthrallingly tranquil breathing of our nine-hour old infant.

"Yes," Richie replied without hesitation. "What about you?"

"I don't know." I was too tired to fabricate. "I guess that I hadn't considered it too much before. Maybe I thought that I didn't deserve a family."

My husband stroked my face lovingly. "What a funny thing to think. You're the most deserving woman I know."

"I think that I have a badly developed sense of self," I admitted. "I had only just made the decision to move out of mom and dad's and get out on my own again and I was still thinking about school when we first met. And trying to make sense of everything—" I cut myself off mid-ramble.

Richie looked at me with sudden interest. "You don't talk too much about yourself, or about who you were before we met."

I looked away. "I'm just not that exciting," I hedged. "I was looking for something, I think. Still trying out roles. My role. And then I found you in *The Cafe*."

"Any regrets about that?"

I stroked Jordan's little cheek and smiled at my husband. "None."

"What were you really doing in *The Cafe*?" he asked softly.

"Chasing a dream."

"Which was?"

I thought about it, wondering what to share. "I was getting ready to hand in a photographic portfolio for an internship program."

"Huh," Richard had a puzzled look on his face.

"You're surprised?" I asked. "I *was* carrying a camera and a dozen snapshots."

"I thought it was part of the outfit."

I laughed, and then covered my mouth as the baby stirred a little. "What outfit?"

"You know. The semi-hippie thing." Richie had the grace to look a little embarrassed.

"Oh," I said in small voice. "No. I really used to take pictures."

"Oh," my husband said back. "I truly didn't know."

"It doesn't matter now." I had said that words to reassure him, but realized immediately that it was the truth.

❧

Although I hadn't taken a photograph in over two years, from the second that Jordan was born, I was able to find a renewed interest. It was almost a compulsion, really. I wanted to capture every moment. After our awkward conversation in the hospital, Richard had somehow managed to find and repair my camera. He had snapped a dozen photos in the first days of my son's life before handing my little Canon Rebel back over to me.

I greedily snapped two hundred more pictures over the next eight weeks.

Richard began to joke that we would have to sell our car to pay for developing. But I couldn't stop. I poured over pictures of toothless grins and action sequence shots of first roll overs. I created my own photo cards and sent one to each family member for every occasion that I could think of. Spring cards, Easter cards, Mother's Day, Father's Day and Summer Solstice cards.

By the time Jordan was almost a year old, I had taken so many photos that we had to buy a new shelving unit just to house the albums.

When Richie suggested that I showcase some of my pictures at Jordan's first birthday party, I was struck with an inspiration. I sent out invitations, billing the event as a drop-in open house. I mailed the cards to Richie's siblings, to our parents, to people from the play group we attended every week, and to the neighbours in our building. Then I bought up well over a hundred dollars worth of supplies, and began to prepare. I stayed up after both Jordan and Richard had gone to bed, working on my surprise into the wee hours of the night for over month.

The day of the party, I sent my husband and son out in the morning with strict instructions not to return until the open house was scheduled to begin. I set myself to work, and by the time the first few guests began to arrive, I had decorated our whole apartment with handmade photo crafts. I hung mobiles from the ceilings, and turned blown up negatives into unique, stained glass window art. I made three personalized baby books and set them out on the coffee table for our friends and family to flip through. I crafted two shadow box frames, and wrapped one for each set of grandparents.

The work was satisfying, and the reactions that I got were even more rewarding. But best of all was the response I got from Richard.

Our next door neighbours, Richard's parents, his youngest sister and her boyfriend were crowded around one of the baby books when I heard my husband call out loudly from the apartment door. As he entered the living room with Jordan riding on his shoulders, my husband went completely still and silent.

"Dada?" said our son from up near one of the mobiles. He looked around, trying to grab the art.

Jordan's voice stirred Richie to speech. "Wow," he said softly.

"Wow?" repeated Jordan, and I laughed.

Richie set our son down and hugged me tightly. "If I have never told you before, I must tell you now. You are a very, very talented woman. You know that, right?"

I hugged my husband back, delighting more in his praise than the combinations of all our friends and family's exclamations together, wondering when his opinion had become the one to supercede all others.

🙠🙢

After the guests had cleared out, Jordan had been tucked into his crib, and we had tidied up the last of the leftover food, Richard pulled me to the living room.

"I know that it was Jordan's birthday," he told me softly, "But I got something for you anyway."

"A present? For me?" I asked teasingly.

Richard had remained quieter than usual throughout Jordan's party, staring for long moments at the mobiles and my other craft projects like he was in another world.

"Five presents, actually," he amended, pointing at the couch to indicate that I should sit down.

"But I didn't get you anything," I protested as I sat.

Richie laughed. "That's okay," he said. "Just keep this five present occasion in mind in the future. In case I ever forget an anniversary or a birthday. Wait here a sec."

He got up and I could hear him rummaging around not so quietly in the hall closet. He came back carrying a smallish Rubbermaid bin that I recognized as having been home at one point to our tea towels and wash cloths.

My husband grinned at me. "I hope that you like the wrapping."

Richard handed me the bin. It had five, numbered plastic bags inside.

Raising an eyebrow, I pulled out the bag labelled "1" and held it up cautiously. Richard was still grinning at me, so I opened the bag and reached in. There was a single sheet of paper inside. I unfolded it.

"Advanced Amateur Photography Class," I read aloud. "Registration Confirmation for Laura Lockhurst."

I looked up at Richie questioningly.

"I enrolled you in a course," he told me, his grin growing so big that I thought it might split his face. "Open the next one."

His enthusiasm was infectious. He was like a five year old on Christmas morning.

I pulled out bag number two and opened it with exaggerated flair. I reached in with my eyes closed and gripped a six inch by six inch box. I read the label.

"A camera?" I asked. I looked at the box more closely, realizing that this was the same near-professional Canon EOS that I had been eyeing at Richard's store last week as I waited for him to finish a shift. I also remembered that it cost almost as much as one month's rent.

Richard misjudged my expression. "You don't like it? You wanted one of the new digital ones that are coming out?"

I shook my head. "We just can't afford this."

My husband relaxed again. "Open the third one!"

I couldn't say no. The bag labelled "3" contained an official looking manila envelope. I opened it and out slid a form, stamped with B & K Electronics' letterhead. I scanned it quickly.

"A promotion?" I asked. "No wonder you look so smug."

Richie winked at me. "It's not just any promotion. It's a regional office position. No more evenings. No more weekends. Monday to Friday. Nine until five."

"A grown up job?" I teased.

"A really, truly grown up job," Richard confirmed. "With grown up pay. Now open your last two presents."

I lifted the fourth and fifth bags.

They were light.

"More paper?" I guessed, holding them up with mock suspicion.

Richie just winked again.

I dumped another manila envelope out of the fourth bag. "And more good news?" I asked.

"You'll see," Richard answered, leaning forward to help me open the envelope. It was a stapled stack of papers, and the cover was a real estate listing.

I stared at it. The photo on the listing had clearly been taken in the winter. The house was blue with white trim, and snow dotted the lawn. A white fence was visible beside the curved driveway, and through the slats of the fence, I could see the top of a wooden swingset. "Richard? Did you? I mean did we? Did we buy a house?"

"Almost."

"Almost?"

Richard folded over the colourful real estate photos. "Take a look at the papers behind the listing."

I looked. "It's a purchase offer," I said.

Richard drew my attention to the subject conditions, and asked me to read it aloud. I obliged.

"Subject to financing. Subject to inspection. Subject to wife's approval?"

My husband laughed. "Well. I would never buy a house *without* my wife's approval. Would I? But you're going to love it. It's in the suburbs, so I'll have to commute, but that's a small price to pay for perfection. It has three bedrooms, a basement, a backyard, and one more room that I know you'll appreciate."

I stared at him, understanding for the first time what it means to be dumbfounded.

"Aren't you going to ask me what is is?" Richard prompted expectantly.

I shook my head, unsure if I was answering his question or if I was trying to clear my thoughts.

He took the final bag from where it sat in my lap. "It's to go with this," he told me, drawing out yet again another few pieces of paper held together by a paperclip.

I shook my head again, and Richard took my hand. He pulled off the paper clip with his teeth and fanned the papers out onto the coffee table.

"This," he said very softly, "Is just for you. It's a home business kit, and a small government grant application. I want you to be able to do something you love. Something you're great at. Something you can do while still being Jordan's mom and my wife." He paused, searching my face for encouragement.

I tried to smile back at him. "What's the other room?" I asked finally.

"It's a dark room," he answered with his voice full of pride. "The seller is a photo buff, and as soon as I saw it, I knew that the house was perfect."

I could feel tears start to form in my eyes. It *was* perfect, but I couldn't seem to find the words to thank Richie. And then I heard Jordan stirring restlessly from his room.

I squeezed Richie's arm silently, and went to retrieve our son.

Chapter 7
THEN

I was sitting in the laundry room on top of a pile of dirty clothes when I heard Richard calling me from the living room. I looked at my watch in disbelief. It was after six o'clock. I knew that Richard must have come through the garage door that adjoined the kitchen. I pictured him coming in, setting his keys in their customary spot on the counter beside the coffee pot, and staring around in horror. There was a pile of dishes in the sink from breakfast and lunch. I couldn't even remember if I had put away the cereal or the milk this morning.

"Laura?" My husband called out for the fifth or sixth time. His voice was starting to sound a little frantic.

"I'm here," I answered so softly that I wasn't even sure he would hear me, but his dress shoes tapped against the hardwood floor and then stopped just outside the laundry room.

Richie opened the door slowly, and stood looking down at me with a worried expression on his face. His arms were laden with Jordan's toys, some dirty towels, the mail, and his briefcase. He stared at me.

"I found these in the hall," he said finally.

I stared back. The absurdity of his business suit mixed with the domestic load in his arms struck me as funny, and I started to laugh.

"Where's Jordan?" I asked him between hysterical giggles, and he looked back at me blankly.

"Jordan?"

"Jordan. You know? Your fifteen month old son? It's Thursday," I reminded him, trying to control my laughter. "You pick him up from your mom's on Thursdays."

The arrangement had actually been Richie's idea. On Tuesdays and Thursdays after an early lunch, Amanda would drive out from her house to ours, have a cup of tea, and then take Jordan for the afternoon. Then Richie would grab him midway through his one hour commute and bring him home. At first I had protested the idea, thinking that I would miss my son too much, that it would inconvenience my mother-in-law, and that I would be failing as a mom in general if I relied on someone else to care for my child. But then Amanda had called me directly, almost begging me to let her spend time with Jordan, and I had reluctantly caved.

Now, I relied on the time to myself. My free afternoons gave me an opportunity to catch up on leftover housework, make sure that I had reasonable dinners ready, and return calls for my little photography business. Completing the eight week course had inspired me, and although my goal had started out very modestly— one photo shoot per month—the extra time I now had two days a week would probably allow me to nearly quadruple that goal before the end of the summer. I had been thinking that closer to Christmas I might even be tempted to hire an assistant and turn one job a week into two. But now that was going to be impossible.

Richard was still staring down at me, and his worried expression had been replaced by a guilty one. In two months, he had never once forgotten to pick up our son. Richie sat down suddenly beside me on the clothes pile, and the tears that I had been holding back all day burst through. He rubbed the back of my neck reassuringly.

"It's okay," he said, and I wasn't sure if he was talking to me or to himself. "I'll call my mom and ask her if she'll keep Jordan overnight."

I reached into the my jeans pocket, gripping the object that had been plaguing my mind all day. I yanked it out and proffered it to my husband with my eyes closed. He stopped rubbing my neck, drew in a breath, and then laughed.

"What's funny?" I demanded through my tears.

"I thought that something was *wrong*," he told me. "The way the kitchen looks, the toys everywhere—not that you don't deserve a break, if you want it—but this! This is good news!"

Richard touched my face in his familiar and gentle way. I pushed him away, and ignored the hurt in his eyes.

"Another baby?" I said angrily, grabbing the positive test from his hand and throwing it as hard as I could against the wall.

"What's wrong?" My husband genuinely didn't understand.

"I was just getting used to *this* life," I tried to explain. "I'm not ready to adjust to a new one."

But I could already tell from his face that he couldn't—and wouldn't—comprehend my frustration.

I stood silently and began tossing items into the dryer. After a moment I heard him stand and leave the room.

ॐ

My unexpected pregnancy had been passing in a blur that I couldn't even compare to my experience with Jordan. There wasn't time to dwell on morning sickness, nor to appreciate each fluttery kick, or to obsess over every symptom, wondering if it was typical or abnormal. And everything seemed to happen twice as fast.

Although I had kept to my Easter and summer photography commitments, I took no new orders for the fall. At first I was a little bit sad to be shutting down my fledgeling, home-based business. But by the end of of the summer, a heat wave was in full force, and I was glad to have little to no obligations outside of the house.

I stared at myself in the mirror with irritation. The little black maternity dress was stretched tight across my abdomen. Richie came up behind me and kissed my throat. I turned my irritation on him.

I stuck my tongue out. "This was a bad idea," I told him grumpily.

"This was a great idea," he answered, ignoring my attitude. "In four weeks, we will have this baby. No later, the doctor promised. And there is no way that you will then want to go out to dinner and the movies."

"Stop being so reasonable," I retorted.

Richie kissed my neck again.

I swatted him away. "And I swear that this dress fit me last week," I complained.

"It fits you now," Richie answered, raising an eyebrow suggestively.

"You're gross," I told him. "No one should look that lasciviously at a pregnant lady." But my irritation had already subsided under his admiring eye.

"But you're *my* pregnant lady. And my mom has Jordan for the entire weekend," was his arch reply, and I couldn't help but laugh.

"Richard," I said, suddenly struck by a thought. "Why don't we ever fight?"

"Huh?"

"We never fight."

Richard looked at me, considering. "Do you want to fight?"

"No," I said, feeling a bit ridiculous. "But everyone fights. My parents. Your parents. The other moms I know are alway complaining about their men.They say that their husbands stay out too late with their friends, or that they like hockey better than they like sex…" I trailed off.

Richie was quiet for a moment. "Well," he said. "I always wanted a family. I came from a big one, and I like that," he told me. "My last girlfriend, Trina…" Richie hesitated, searching my face for something, though I couldn't say what.

Previous relationships were one thing we had never really discussed. I knew that it was unusual to not share that part of our pasts with each other. The other married people that I was acquainted with seemed all too eager to divulge those kinds of details to their spouses, but Richie and I never talked about it.

On my part, it was because there wasn't much to discuss. As a teenager, I had been socially awkward and especially shy with boys. Somehow, it would've seemed pretty silly to bring up my first and only high school kiss. A drunk exchange student from Hong Kong had grabbed me at a grade eleven dance, and before I could react, he had pinned me against the gymnasium door and stuck his tongue in mouth. By the time I had recovered enough to either kiss him back or to slap him—I never figured out which it would've been—he had already run off. I found out later that he had done it on a dare, and I was so mortified that I hadn't gone to school for a whole week after the incident.

The only other love experience that I had was pinned so closely to my heart that I could never find the words to share it with Richie.

I figured that it was similar for my husband. I knew that he had been in at least one other long-term relationship before meeting me, but he never volunteered more information and I never asked.

I held very still, wondering if I even wanted to hear what he would say next.

Richie looked down at his hands. "With Trina," he said again, "We always fought. About where to eat, what movies to watch. About who would drive. We dated for almost two years, but we kept it a secret for the first eight months. We fought about that, too. She was embarrassed by our relationship to start out with. She was a year older than me, the older sister of a friend of mine. I didn't care, but I always teased her about it anyway, and she hated it. On her nineteenth birthday we had a big fight—like one that you see on soap opera. It was almost unreal. She tore apart her parents' kitchen, throwing around food and utensils, breaking plates. I punched a hole in her bedroom door. It was pretty ridiculous."

I tried to picture my mild-mannered husband getting so angry that he would turn violent. I couldn't do it.

"Anyway, it turned out that her father had been physically abusing her mom for years, and had recently started hitting Trina as well. I found that out after—from the news. Trina never told me herself." Richard stopped again, and I could tell that he was having a hard time. "So we had that fight, and I left her house so angry. She called me later, apologizing, and I guess we kind of made up. But that night Trina's mom finally had enough of her dad, packed her things, and just walked out. The next morning, Trina was dead."

"And even though I knew that we were just high school sweethearts, and I'm one hundred percent certain our lives would have gone on in separate courses—probably very soon—I felt cheated. And angry. Like I got robbed of a normal heartbreak. When you end a relationship, you move on. You have a choice. When someone dies, you don't get that choice. Her dad and her younger brother left town as soon as the police confirmed that Trina's death was suicide."

I could see the unshed tears in my husband's eyes, and felt my own well up in return. "Why did you never tell me?" I asked, already knowing the answer. It was not a sharing kind of story.

Richie shrugged. "I never tell anyone. I graduated high school the next month, and people in town stopped talking about it before the end of the summer. My parents made me go for counseling. But you have to take away from life what you can."

I could tell that he was looking to change the subject, and I couldn't help but wonder if I would ever stop learning new things about my husband.

"And I knew that it was you. As soon as I met you." He reached out and brushed my arm, making goosebumps stand up along my whole body. He pulled me in tenderly, kissing my eyebrows, my cheeks, and finally my lips. "Always you," he murmured. "It hardly seems worth it to waste the time we have fighting," he cleared his throat. "When we could be doing other things."

"Oh, crap," I answered, pulling away.

"Do you want to fight now?" Richard asked me, sadness flickering momentarily across his face again.

"No," I answered. "But my water just broke."

Chapter 8
THEN

Tori's birth did not affect me as Jordan's had. With my son, the affection was instant, and a kind of euphoria directed equally at the tiny baby and at motherhood itself, had set in as soon as I held him in my arms.

But when the obstetrical nurse first handed my daughter to me, Tori looked up, made an petulantly angry face, and began to cry. She didn't want to feed, she wouldn't take a pacifier, and bundling her snugly the way I had to soothe Jordan only made her cry louder. After an hour of trying lullabies, diaper changes, and rocking, Richard had come to my rescue. The transformation was miraculous. And embarrassing. Within seconds of being in her father's arms, Tori's face went from an unhealthy shade of angry red to a pleasant pink. Her eyelids fluttered and closed. And it was only then that I finally felt a surge of love for this quiet version of my new baby.

❦❧

Bringing Tori home was also a stressful ordeal. I had to continually remind myself not to compare her to Jordan, but it was almost impossible. He had been a quiet baby, coming into our quiet apartment. He had often been content to lie awake in his bassinet with a mobile overhead, or happy to enjoy the soothing vibrations of his battery operated bouncy chair. Tori, on the other hand, used the extra space in our larger home to fully exercise her acoustic abilities.

She cried when I carried her around. She screamed when I put her down. My arms and my head ached, and I forgot what sleep felt like. I found myself unconsciously watching the clock every evening, awaiting Richard's arrival home with an almost feverish anticipation. My husband tried to help me out. He brought home a bottle of gripe water as recommended by a sympathetic co-worker. He bought an expensive vibration device that attached to Tori's crib and was meant to simulate the motion of a car. But the only thing that really settled her was laying directly in her father's arms.

After four weeks of tears—both mine and Tori's—Jordan finally looked at me solemnly across the dinner table and said in surprisingly articulate and intuitive way, "Mama. Baby doesn't like you. We need a new one?"

I made an appointment with our family doctor the very next morning.

෨෨

As I sat in the waiting room of Dr. Whitaker's office my emotions were mixed. I was glad to be getting a professional's opinion, but mildly ashamed that I hadn't been able to cope with my own child. I tried to cover my discomfort by pretending to look around this familiar office.

Harry Whitaker was an openly gay activist who decorated his work space with pride memorabilia. A small but obvious rainbow flag adorned one door, while a large poster lettered with the words "Stop Homophobia" was exhibited on another. A collage of Madonna head shots that I was pretty sure Dr. Whitaker had commissioned as a tongue in cheek project hung on the large wall opposite from the office assistant's desk. Some people, I know, would've felt uncomfortable with the display, but I found it reassuring. With Dr. Whitaker, it was easy to take everything at face value; he put all of his cards on the table and made no apologies for who he was. I liked that.

When the secretary led us into the examining room, my doctor reached for Tori automatically. I winced. She had been sleeping peacefully in her car seat—a rare and agreeable occasion. But as Dr. Whitaker started his examination, making small talk as he went, she just sighed and kept her eyes closed. I watched anxiously from my chair while Jordan flipped through some board books in the corner of the office.

Finally the doctor expertly re-diapered a still sleeping Tori, buttoned up her sleeper, rocked her for a moment and then fastened her back into her car seat.

I gaped at him. "How did you do that?"

"Do what?"

"She cries every time I move her. Every time I put her down. And most of the time even when I'm holding her," I explained in an anguished voice.

"Didn't you get the right manual for this baby?" Dr. Whitaker asked in a teasing voice.

"Seriously," I said.

"Seriously. Everything looks lovely, Laura," he told me in his typically sunny way. "Tori is in perfect health. Ninetieth percentile for height, fiftieth for weight. Great colouring, excellent reflexes, even in sleep."

I continued to stare at him. "She's not sick?" I asked.

"Definitely not."

I felt a combination of irritation and relief. I was very, very glad that Tori was in good health. But if she wasn't sick, what was her excuse for her loud, constantly grumpy disposition?

"Baby cries. A lot," Jordan piped up from his corner. "But not for Daddy."

Dr. Whitaker grinned at my son. "So your Mommy tells me."

"Is it colic?" I asked, dreading eight more weeks of crying, but still seeking a logical answer.

"Could be. But you say she's sleeping fairly well at night?"

I nodded. "For almost six hours," I admitted. "I think that she wears herself out by crying all day so she's too tired to wake for night feedings."

The doctor laughed and patted my hand. "Well, that's something, you know. Most new moms would kill for that kind of rest. And it explains why you're looking so refreshed."

He sounded so sincere that I didn't have the heart to tell him that I was so on edge from the eighteen hours of crying that sleep still eluded me most nights. So instead I laughed politely and said, "Maybe you could tell that to my mirror at home?"

As Dr. Whitaker stood to dismiss us he added, "Laura. Two pieces of contradictory advice. First, if she cries less—even a little bit—when you hold her, just don't put her down unless you have to. Second, in the interest of maintaining your sanity, get some rest."

ɩɪ

That night Richie came home with a grin on his face and a wrapped package under his arm. He scooped a crying Tori from me, and she instantly stopped wailing.

"Open it," he commanded, indicating the present.

I obliged.

I pulled out a long piece of brown fabric, and was unsure of what to make of it.

"A hammock?" I guessed.

Richie laughed. "It's a baby sling. You wrap it around your shoulder like this." He set Tori into her playpen and pulled the cloth on a diagonal across my body.

By the time he had secured it around me to his satisfaction, Tori had started to scream. He lifted her deftly with one hand, stretched open the sling with the other, and then deposited her into the cozy pouch.

Tori opened her eyes, and I could almost see her brain working through anger, suspicion and confusion. Finally, her face settled into a look that I didn't recognize at first—contentment. Blissful, silent contentment.

"Hey," said Jordan, "Baby not cry?"

I giggled girlishly, nodding.

"Okay, good," Jordan nodded back at me with satisfaction. "Where's *my* hammock?"

Richard winked. "No hammocks for us men." He reached into his suit jacket pocket. "But how about a new car?" He handed an unopened Hot Wheels police car to Jordan, who eyed it skeptically and then shrugged.

"'K. Hammocks for girls. Cars for boys."

I stared at my husband in amazement. "You," I told him, "Are the most amazing man I've ever met. Just thought you should know."

Richard grinned back. "I try," he said, reaching gently across Tori to kiss me firmly on the lips.

I sighed, remembering a time when I was able to accomplish things on my own.

Chapter 9
WAY BACK WHEN

I found Platform Seven easily, and waited with a boldness that I did not truly feel for my train to arrive. The kinks in my plan thus far had made me a little leery of my own overconfidence. Still, it was as thrilling as it was intimidating to be standing at the station surrounded by strangers from all over the world. It was amazing and distracting to hear the sound of a half dozen foreign languages being spoken loudly and simultaneously. I recognized words in Greek, French, and Italian. I caught what I thought might be Russian, and several conversations in dialects I had never heard before at all. It was blissfully overwhelming.

When my train arrived at the platform, I rushed forward with the crowd to board. People quickly eased themselves into seats with friends, family, and strangers. I walked through three full cars before finally coming to one that had any empty spots. Each seating area had four chairs—two windows and two aisles facing each other. I scanned for a completely unoccupied compartment, but found none. Sighing, I looked for the next best thing.

It was slim pickings. A mom sitting with her infant in her lap seemed a promising choice until the baby started to cry. I saw a teenaged girl sitting by herself, and headed toward her with relief. I was two rows away when she was joined by a teenaged boy who promptly locked his arms around her waist and pressed his lips against her neck. I considered standing for the duration of the trip, but as the train lurched to a start, I realized that it was not a smooth enough ride to guarantee that I wouldn't end up on my rear end.

I scanned the car again.

At last, I spotted a young man at the back with a foursome of chairs to himself. He had enormous headphones over his ears and appeared to be sleeping.

Sitting with him will almost be like sitting alone, I reasoned as I quickly headed toward the seats.

I placed my backpack as gingerly as possible in the window seat opposite his knees and started to slide into the aisle seat beside my bag.

The young man's eyes flew open. "Naw!" he almost shouted.

I stood bolt upright, banging my head on an overhead bar in the process. I gave the shouter a dirty look and started to grab my backpack.

"Naw," he said again, this time in a more reasonable tone. He leaned over and held my backpack down with one hand. He pointed with his other hand at the seat that I had been about to use.

A large wet spot marked the centre of the chair.

"Oh," I said with embarrassed appreciation. "Thank you." I continued to stand awkwardly between the seats.

He patted the aisle seat beside him and whispered conspiratorially in an Irish lilt, "Naw wan 'as peed on dis wan."

"Thank you," I said again and sat beside him. He reeked of alcohol, and the smell intensified as I sat down.

"Oi'm Darby O'Neil," he told me. "Ballymacarbry, Ireland."

"Laura Morgan," I answered. "Vancouver, Canada."

"'Eaded ter Kings Cross?" he asked me. He reached into his coat pocket and retrieved a flask. After a long swig, he offered it to me and I shook my head.

"For the moment," I said. My mom's multiple warnings forbade me from sharing too much information with a stranger. Especially a drunk one.

Darby grinned at me. "Well t'anks be for dat. Terrible place." He took another drink and quickly pocketed the flask as the ticket-taker came by to check our fares.

"So I hear," I replied, trying to sound nonchalant.

"Ah, yeah. Red light district, yer nu? Oi tink dat a jimmy got offed a few blocks from de stashun last week. Drug scrap, likely." The Irishmen listed off a few other colourful crime related events that had all occurred near or at the Kings Cross train station. A knifing. A turf war erupting in gun shots. A possible human trafficking plot. After each vivid description he would pause, assess my reaction, and then wink. I got more and more nervous as he listed off offense after offense. The contrast of his soft Irish lilt and the horrors he gleefully described made the monstrosities sound all the more frightening. I was going to have to wait for fifteen whole minutes at that train station for my transfer. My stress level hit an all time high and I finally tried to change the subject.

I interrupted him midway through a dramatic recounting of a bar brawl between a six-foot two transvestite lady of the night and her angry Chinese pimp. "Darby," I asked, almost wishing that I had agreed to a sip from his flask. "Where are *you* headed?"

The Irishman switched gears easily. "Home, t'be sure," he told me.

"Ballymacarbry? Is there a train from Kings Cross to Ireland?" I prompted, wanting to keep him from talking about murderous hookers.

Darby laughed. "Nigh dat wud be a round-aboyt an' roi weord 'omecomin'. 'Enny been dare in more than four years. Ma proobably 'as a 'alf dozen American tourists stayin' at 'er guest house roi nigh. Giver a 'eart attack if oi showed up. Oi'm not exactly de prodigal son, 'ey?" He went on to describe his parents and what he called their traditional expectations, as well as his younger sister, who had married at eighteen and already had three kids by twenty-two. "Oi 'av two nieces an' a nephew who ain't even aware av their uncle an' 'is nefarious life 'abits," he told me.

An automated voice interrupted, announcing that we would be arriving at Kings Cross in five minutes. We both sat silently for a moment or two.

"But you said you were going home?" I asked politely.

"Roi," answered Darby. "Oi *are* 'eadin' 'um."

"Oh," I said with a nervous laugh. "And where's home, then?"

"Well, Kings Cross t'be sure!"

I groaned. Of course he lived there.

The train stopped and Darby leaped out of his seat. "Walk yer somewhere?" he asked politely.

I shook my head, pretending that I had to find something in my bag. I sighed in relief as my Irish companion exited the train, and I waved goodbye through the safety of the window.

At the last second, I grabbed my camera from my satchel and photographed Darby's receding firgure right before he got swallowed into the crowd at the train station.

∽∾

I gathered my things and stepped out onto the dreaded Kings Cross station platform. I tried not to look nervous as I scanned the train station for the Peterborough exchange. Did the seats in the waiting area look a little too ratty? Did the lingering passengers look a little too scruffy? Was the guy in the tweed jacket watching me a little too intently? I knew that I was letting the Irishman from the train and the Texan ticket agent feed my paranoia.

I shouldered my backpack and reminded myself resolutely that I was perfectly comfortable walking through Vancouver's downtown east side on the darkest of nights. I looked up at the big clock above the ticketing area. Nine more minutes waiting at a train station in a possibly sketchy area should be no big deal. I took large, falsely confident steps toward my platform, avoiding eye contact with the other people waiting in the same area. I couldn't help but sigh with relief when I heard the friendly female voice announce over the PA that my train was arriving. I tried not to seem too eager as I boarded, and failed miserably as I couldn't hold in an even bigger sigh of relief when I stepped into the passenger car.

The train was much larger than the one from Heathrow, and almost empty. It had sleeper cars as well as general semi-private seating, with each set of four chairs separated from the next by a thin wall. I selected an unoccupied one and opened my bag, choosing items at random to spread out onto the other three seats in order to discourage any guests from joining me.

"No offense, Darby," I muttered under my breath.

As I arranged a few books on one, my jacket on another, and all of my tourist maps and other informative literature on the final one, I felt the train start in a jerking roll. I surveyed my handiwork, hoping that it looked like I was truly using each of the seats, and not just trying to appear that I was.

"Good evening. *Guten Abend,*" I heard a German-accented female voice say.

I looked up guiltily, thinking that my ploy had been figured out.

A svelte, blonde ticket agent in a blue uniform grinned at me. She was about forty, and very pretty, with kind, blue eyes. "Settling in, *ja?*"

"Getting organized," I lied lamely.

"You want private?"

"Too expensive," I admitted, thinking longingly of the comfortable looking cabin with the sliding door I had walked by on the way to my own seat.

"Show me ticket, pack stuff, Elsbeth fix you up." The ticket agent held out her hand and smiled.

Three minutes later I found myself thanking the German woman profusely as I settled into a cozy sleeping cabin.

She waved off my appreciation. "Train *ist leer.* Empty. Ride is much longer in *den Abend.* Almost two hours. More stops. Many stops. Makes work long." She shook her head, muttering something else in German that I took to be a swear word. "Young people like naps. Little *Schlafs. Gut,* " she added, gesturing toward the bunk. "You rest. I put up 'Do Not Disturb' sign, you need something—food, drink, *etwas*—you find Elsbeth, *ja?*"

"You bet," I answered enthusiastically, and the German woman chuckled.

I talked her into posing outside the cabin door for a quick photograph and then she chuckled again as she closed the door to my cabin.

I peeked out my little window, surmised that dusk would soon settle into darkness, and used that as an excuse to close the blinds and stretch out gratefully for my little *Schlaf.*

❧❦

I struggled to pull my eyes open. I could hear the sound of an automated voice repeating an unintelligible message over and over.

So this is what jet lag feels like, I thought vaguely, trying to force my arms out of their folded position. I was balled up on the little bunk. My head was pressed awkwardly against the wall and one foot was wedged in between the foamy mattress and the wooden plank it rested on. I thought about untangling myself and I could already feel an awful ache in my neck and the dreaded tingling sensation in my squished foot as it struggled for blood flow. I kept my eyes closed, willing my body to feel less like that of a hundred year old woman and more like my eighteen year-old self.

Someone began tapping my shoulder gently.

"Ugh," I said. I rolled over, turning my face toward the source of the prodding, and was rewarded with a sharp, stabbing pain in my head.

I opened my eyes.

A pair of dark brown eyes filled with concern were only two inches from my face.

I screamed, and the body attached to the eyes staggered backwards.

I sat up quickly, banging my head against the low ceiling and then toppling out of the bed.

"*Señorita?*" said a muffled and hesitant voice from underneath me. "You okay?"

"Ouch," I answered lamely, and righted myself with as much dignity as possible. My face burned with embarrassment as I realized that I had knocked over a chubby, Spanish-looking ticket taker. "Sorry," I said belatedly. "You're not Elsbeth," I told him.

He looked a little puzzled and then pointed to his name tag. "Marco," he said.

"Polo," I joked, but his puzzled frown grew even deeper. He said something in Spanish, and the only word I caught was *loca*.

"Isn't anyone who lives in England *from* England?" I wondered out loud.

Marco's brow unfurrowed slightly. "Spain," he told me. "Marco. Ibiza."

"Laura," I replied obligingly. "You're still not Elsbeth."

Marco grinned at me in a way that made me sure that he had ascertained that he was dealing with a madwoman.

"Elsbeth off at Peterborough." He rolled every one of the R's.

I grinned back. "I'm off at Peterborough, too."

"You off now."

It was my turn to look puzzled. "Are we at Peterborough?"

Marco shook his head. "Last stop. Edinburgh."

"That's in Scotland."

Marco sighed and pointed at his name tag again. "Ibiza. Spain."

I sighed, too and sat down on the little seat in my cabin. "Marco. Ibiza. Spain. Where's Elsbeth? I thought that she was going to wake me at Peterborough."

He shook his head at me. "No, *Señorita*. Marco wake you. Elsbeth off at Peterborough. You off now. Edinburgh. *Sí*."

I felt a rising sense of panic. I stared at Marco, the gist of what he was saying sinking in.

"Scotland?" I whispered.

The Spanish ticket-taker grinned back at me, sensing that he was finally getting through to me. "*Sí*," he said enthusiastically. "Off now," he added when I remained seated. "Marco carry your bag. Marco off, too."

"Thanks," I answered faintly, and stood to follow him off into the dimly lit train station.

∸∾

Marco led me to the ticket booth inside Edinburgh station, patted me on the back, and started to walk away.

"*Buena suerte, mi hermosa dama!*" he called over his shoulder.

"Wait!" I shouted, waving frantically at him.

He paused, momentarily confused, and then noted the camera I held out in front of me. Grinning, he gave me a thumbs up and I snapped a quick photograph. Marco gave me a comical salute that made me laugh before he finally sauntered off.

I turned to the the ticket agent, who had been watching with interest.

"Hi," I said nervously to the enormous man behind the counter.

"Friend of yours?" the agent asked with an accent I couldn't place. His name tag said, 'Kinji', which I assumed to be African. I tried to smile at him. Kinji was huge, black, and I could feel the skepticism roll off of him as I shared my story. I recounted how I fell asleep on the train, refrained from cursing Elsbeth, and praised Marco for his help. When I had finished, Kinji raised one large eyebrow at me.

"That's embarrassing," he said.

"Yes," I agreed whole heartedly.

He stared at me, keeping the brow raised, and I started to explain myself again. Kinji lifted a finger to silence me.

"And you babble," he told me.

"I know," I answered. "One of my faults."

"And to top it off, I've got bad news," he added. "You're stuck in Edinburgh overnight."

"What do you mean?" I felt as though the longer I stayed in Europe, the less clever I became.

"Well," Kinji said slowly. "The last train back to Peterborough left one hour, forty-five minutes ago. It is now almost midnight. Your little nap was four hours long. And since it is Sunday, the last train to London is leaving—nope, just left. Now. Obviously, I can no longer sell you a ticket. Miss."

I said a swear word.

Kinji laughed, and then became sympathetic. "Miss, I am truly sorry."

"What should I do?" I wondered out loud.

The ticket agent raised the eyebrow again. "Perhaps you could go home with the Spaniard, Marco? He seemed fond of you." Kinji grinned.

I raised my own eyebrow at him.

"Perhaps the joke is too soon?"

"Too soon," I agreed.

"In more seriousness, miss, there is an open hostel only two kilometres from here. Many cabs are outside," Kinji told me. And then he grinned again. "I get to go home, and my Scottish wife would not appreciate me bringing a pretty American girl with me."

"Canadian," I corrected automatically.

"Even worse," Kinji assured me, winking and starting to close his wicket.

"Wait one sec," I said.

The big black man stopped and waited.

"Just a picture," I told him, grabbing my camera and snapping one quickly before he could say no.

"Paparazzi will do anything for a photo," he teased as he went back to closing and locking his wicket.

Chapter 10
THEN

The phone started to ring and I grabbed it quickly before the noise could wake Tori. It had taken me almost an hour to convince my two year old to take a nap. I gave myself a mental pat on the back for remembering to unplug the upstairs extension. I had been having a horrible week—the mom's equivalent of a stock market crash. Jordan had woken up on Monday morning with a fever that had quickly progressed to a full blown flu. By Wednesday, he shared his germs with Tori, and her usually stubborn disposition had degenerated to downright ornery. On Thursday morning we had run out of children's Tylenol, and when I had tried to go out to grab some more, our van had died part way down the driveway. The transmission was blown, and our mechanic had said the engine wasn't far behind. He recommended looking for a newer vehicle rather than wasting money on repairs. A quick assessment of our finances had revealed that I would probably remain vehicleless until the end of eternity. And to top it all off, I was starting to feel a bit nauseous myself.

"Hello?" I said very quietly into the receiver.

"Why are you whispering?" my mom asked.

"Tori's sleeping," I told her.

"And the world shuts off?" she wondered.

"Just our world, Mom." I rolled my eyes.

"Wait until she's a teenager. I remember all the trouble you caused me."

"Mom!" I said a little too loudly, and winced. I waited for the corresponding wail from Tori, but all I could hear was the sound of Jordan's *Lion King* video playing in the TV room. "Mom," I went on more quietly, "I think that I was the best behaved teenager in our whole neighbourhood. Maybe the whole city."

"You ran away from home."

"I took a vacation," I said through my teeth.

"You remember it your way, I remember it mine."

I waited.

She sighed. "Okay, you're probably right."

"Well, thank you," I murmured sarcastically. "Now did you call to chat, to harass me, or to tell me something?"

She was silent for a moment, and I knew that I probably offended her. I had always assumed that me having kids would bring us closer, but somehow it had created a conflict that kept breeding more and more tension. My mom was, and always had been, so orderly. I could only imagine how chaotic my life must have seemed to her. I think it galled her that my laundry sometimes went unfolded for days, and that brushing the kids hair was lower on my to-do list than reading a good book. She and my dad hadn't even driven in for Tori's first birthday. It had made me sad when she had announced that they wouldn't be joining us, but I was relieved that they weren't there when I burned the pizza and forgot to order a cake. We just rubbed each other the wrong way more and more.

"Mom?" I said hesitantly, getting ready to form an apology for my snappishness.

"Maybe all three," my mom finally responded. "But most importantly, I have news."

"Let's hear it," I replied, glad that I hadn't hurt her feelings after all.

"We sold the house," she told me.

"You did?" I wasn't sure what else to say. My dad complained incessantly about the stairs and his bad leg, and about trying to maintain the yard with his weak arm, but I couldn't really picture them living anywhere else. My mom had never even taken the posters down from my walls when I moved out.

"We did," she confirmed. "Put it up for sale last week, got an offer yesterday, reached an agreement today. Possession date in six weeks from tomorrow."

"Wow," I said. "That was fast. But where will you live?"

"Sechelt," my mom told me.

"What?"

"Sechelt," she repeated. "You know, up the coast."

I sat down at my kitchen table. "No, Mom, I know where it is. I just don't understand."

She sighed loudly again. "We found a nice little rancher up there, close to all the small town amenities we need. Low maintenance, no stairs, two bedrooms. Perfect for us."

"When did you even go up there?" I couldn't remember her mentioning a trip.

"Last weekend. You know the Bernards from next door? They bought a place in Gibsons last year and we went for a visit. Your father and I took a day trip to Sechelt and we saw this little house and everything just fell into place," she explained.

It was my turn to sigh. "Okay, Mom."

"Good," my mom said. "Oh, Laura?"

"Yes?"

"Your father and I made some money on the sale of the house, and we'd like to help you out," she spoke in a rush. "I've put a cheque in the mail already so that I can't change my mind. Seventeen thousand, five hundred dollars. But please don't cash it before the fifteenth, okay?"

I was astonished. My parents never gave us money. Ever. "Sure."

"Good," she repeated. "We'll make plans for Easter, okay sweetheart?"

"Aren't we going to see you before you go?" I asked.

But she had already hung up.

I stood there, staring blankly at the phone.

Finally, I put the phone down, grabbed a newspaper, and began circling vehicle ads that suited our needs.

❧

I have heard that adjusting to having a second child in the home is more like ten times the work than like twice the work. In Tori's case, it was more like adjusting to living with one very smart, very opinionated teenaged princess. It was a round-the-clock, sleep depriving, plan canceling battle. On the bright side, there was never a dull moment, and the time passed very quickly.

So, when the day came for Jordan's first day of kindergarten, it didn't happen. Or rather, it happened without him.

My son was dressed in his first-day-of-school outfit—a Tommy Hilfiger golf shirt and matching khaki shorts courtesy of Amanda Lockhurst. His *Pokemon* backpack was ready to go, packed with one of the nutritious snacks suggested in the school's introductory letter.

I was ready, too. My hair was carefully arranged in a casual but tidy ponytail, freshly washed and dyed a neutral sandy brown. I had partnered a crisp new pair of Gap jeans with a pretty, fitted Esprit blouse and my old Birkenstocks. I had agonized over my outfit, trying to perfect a look that said "stay-at-home-mom" but did not immediately add "slob". I thought that I had accomplished it well, and was all in all as prepared as I could be.

Unfortunately, Tori had other ideas. To say that she had woken up on the wrong side of the bed would imply that she had woken up at all. It would also imply that Tori had a good side to get up on.

We were supposed to leave the house at 8:25AM, but at 8:17, my three year-old was still snoozing away the morning. It was not for lack of trying on my part. I had opened the bedroom door at 7:45, and then turned on the light at 7:55. At 8:05 I had pulled back her covers and then opened the lid of her music box and placed it on her pillow beside her head.

She had sighed once and pulled her favourite doll over her face.

At 8:15, I sat down on the edge of Tori's bed and stared at my daughter, willing her to open her eyes without further intervention. Two full minutes went by as I sat there, not daring to whisper her name, not daring to gently shake her into consciousness.

I sighed. 8:18. If this had been Jordan, I would've tenderly kissed his forehead and brushed one of his unruly blonde curls behind his ear. He would've woken up sleepily, grinned at me lovingly, and then let me carry him out to the car or stroller in his pajamas.

Oh, Tori, I thought. *Why did I did not wake you at 7:45 when I should've?*

I was doomed. If I woke her now with only seven minutes to spare, she would lose it. I had no trouble imagining the consequences.

Firstly, Tori would not go anywhere outside the house without being fully dressed. Secondly, she preferred to watch a full *Sesame Street* episode before she even thought about eating breakfast. And thirdly...Well, I didn't think I even needed a third excuse to not wake my little Sleeping Beauty.

8:21.

I stood and crept out of my daughter's room, turning out the light and closing the door as I left.

Jordan was sitting at the bottom of the stairs, backpack against his little knees.

"Little buddy," I said sadly, sitting down beside him.

"Tori sleeping?" he asked me.

"Yeah."

"She sick?"

I hesitated. I was not in the habit of lying to my son.

"Mommy?"

"No, Jordie. She's not sick. Just Tori being Tori." *And me being me,* I added silently.

My son looked up at me.

"No school?"

I swallowed, the guilt almost overwhelming me.

"No school." It took all of my strength to keep the sob out of my voice.

Jordan sat silently without looking at me.

I dropped my head into my hands, making a mental list of ways I could make this up to my son. Play dates. Cake for dinner. Disneyland.

I was failing as a parent. So much for my attempt at being ultra-mom.

Jordan tapped my knee. "Eight thirty yet?"

I checked my watch. "Eight thirty-one," I confirmed.

Jordan grinned at me. "*Power Rangers*, right?"

"You betcha, kiddo," I answered with as much enthusiasm as I could muster.

Jordan jumped up and ran toward the family room, school quickly forgotten.

I took a breath and grabbed the phone. The first call was the easiest.

"Meadowland Elementary," answered a friendly female voice. "This is Jillian, how can I help you?"

"Hi," I said, "My name is Laura Lockhurst. My son, Jordan Lockhurst, is supposed to be starting kindergarten there today, but he's not going to make it in."

"Medical reasons?" asked the secretary.

My heart beat a little faster, but it was much easier to lie to this stranger than it was to lie to my son.

"Yes," I answered quickly. "My daughter—Jordan's younger sister—she's sick and I can't get her out of bed." At least the second part was true.

Jillian was sympathetic. "It's so sad when the little ones get sick. Will Jordan be here tomorrow?"

"Absolutely," I assured her—and myself. "If she's still unwell, I'll make other arrangements."

The second call was much more difficult.

"B and K Electronics." This female voice was not friendly by any stretch.

"Richard Lockhurst please." It came out as a whisper.

"Sorry, what was that?" The voice sounded bored and irritated at the same time.

"Is Richard Lockhurst available?" I said more audibly.

"Yep."

I heard a click and then the inevitable hold music. I tried to tune out the elevator-ized Mariah Carey.

In the four years since Richie had taken the office position, I had never once called him. Not on the morning last year when both kids had woken up with matching chicken pox, and not last month when Jordan had dumped two tubs of pudding into the

VCR before I caught him. I had actually had to use our babysitter's emergency call list to get the correct number to call him now. I took some deep breaths as I thought about what I would say to my husband.

"Richard speaking."

At the sound of his voice, cool and professional, I lost all rational thought and began crying uncontrollably.

"Laura?" he said uncertainly after a moment.

"Richard," I whispered, trying desperately to regain some control of my emotion. I explained haltingly what had happened. "I am a bad mother. I am scared of my daughter, and I put my own needs above the needs of my son," I finally finished.

"Laura," Richie said again, this time reassuringly, "You are a fantastic mother. The best I know. Put your pajamas back on, make a cup of tea, and sit down. There will be three hundred more days of school this year alone. I promise that tomorrow will be better."

"How can you be sure?" I asked him in a small voice, wanting to believe him.

"Because," he answered, "It always is."

ॐॐ

I was still in my pajamas when Richard came home from work that night. Dinner wasn't made, and the dishes weren't done. The three of us—Jordan, Tori, and I—were watching *Toy Story* for the third time that day.

"Hi, Daddy. Woody doesn't like Buzz yet. But he will soon," Jordan explained without getting up.

I avoided making eye contact with my husband, but he when leaned over my shoulder and whispered, "I have presents," I couldn't help but look at him incredulously.

Tori jumped up, squealing excitedly. New things were the easiest way into my little diva's heart.

Richie winked at me, pulling out two brightly coloured gift bags.

"Ladies first," he said, trying to hand the pink and purple one to Tori.

"Wanna go last," she complained instantly.

"Sure, Princess," Richie said, and handed Jordan the other bag.

He started opening it slowly, pulling out each piece of tissue paper individually, while Tori tapped her foot impatiently. Finally, Jordan pulled out a wooden locomotive, engine car, and caboose, with matching train tracks.

"Boring," Tori stated. "Now me."

Richie rolled his eyes theatrically at me, but handed over the present.

Tori promptly tore through the crinkly paper and yanked out a box that she eyed dubiously. Although the package was decorated with flowers and butterflies, it was obvious that Tori couldn't discern exactly what this new toy might be. She handed it over to me, and I raised an eyebrow as I read the side of the box.

"An alarm clock?" I asked.

"Alarm tock?" Tori repeated.

"Clock," Jordan corrected as he began to assemble his train set on the family room floor.

"Tick tock," said Tori, sticking her tongue out at her brother.

"Uh huh," Richie answered all of us. "It wakes you up everyday with music." He crouched down in front of our daughter and dropped his voice conspiratorially. "But it's not just any music. It's princess only music."

Tori grabbed the box from my hands and I surrendered it easily, marveling at my husband's cleverness.

"For real?" Tori demanded.

Richard stared solemnly back at her. "Cross my heart."

Tori grinned. "Hooray! Can we got to bed now?"

My husband laughed and I couldn't help but join him. "Soon. But how about we order some pizza first?" He said, and looked at me for approval.

I gave him a weak thumbs up, and then closed my eyes, letting my self-disappointment overwhelm me and then slowly dissipate.

Chapter 11
THEN

The house beside ours had been vacant since the summer, and I had grown so used to its empty presence that when the moving truck pulled into the driveway, it felt almost like a violation. The sold sign had come up a week ago, so it shouldn't have been unexpected. But I gave the five tonne truck a dirty look anyway as it backed into the driveway.

It was a Tuesday afternoon, and with Jordan and Tori at school until almost three o'clock, I had been been enjoying a solitary cup of tea on my recently enclosed patio. My parents had driven in from Sechelt to visit for three weeks in August—the first time we had seen them in a year—and in order to keep the men "occupied", my mom had suggested that they build the small solarium where I now sat. The project had been the source of many jokes, as Richard was not handy with a hammer and my dad's hands were too shaky now to be of much use in assembling anything. But they had persevered, and I was glad now that they had been so stubborn about finishing it. The eastern exposure warmed the room up enough—even on a cool November morning—to enjoy a full day of coziness. I loved bringing in my laptop to edit my photos, and now that I had both the time and the space to do it, I often spent the better part of my day working there from my favourite overstuffed chair.

So the "beep, beep, beep" of the U-Haul next door was intrusive to say the least. I watched the unpacking with irritated curiosity. At least my view from the sunroom was mostly unobstructed. A pick up pulled in beside the larger truck, and two men in jeans and t-shirts jumped out and began unloading furniture. The U-Haul driver, another man in casual attire, got out and began helping them. I wondered which one of them was the new owner. But they all looked too young for this neighbourhood of kiddie pools and swing sets. They carried in couches and lamps, boxes, and shelves. I saw what looked like crib pieces go in, along with a professional looking easel and several large paintings.

An art-lover with kids? I wondered.

I watched so long that my tea grew cold and not a single photo got edited.

Finally, all three men got into the larger moving truck and drove away, leaving the pick up behind.

Weird. Must've just been the movers. I thought.

"Hello?" called a female voice, accompanied by a tapping on my glass door.

"Oh," I exclaimed, looking over to see a pair of heavily made up eyes peering into my little oasis.

"Sorry, neighbour," she said, letting herself in. "Didn't mean to startle you, but I saw you watching, and I could really use some company! Virgin margarita?"

I realized then that she was holding an icy pitcher, and two glasses on a tray. She was also enormously pregnant.

❧❧

"What the hell?" Richie demanded in a loud but groggy voice, pulling me from a deep and dreamless sleep.

"Huh?"

"What is that?"

"What?"

"That banging!"

I listened for a moment, and I could hear it, too.

"It's banging," I told him.

"Helpful," my husband said as he climbed out of bed. He tossed on his robe—a bright blue terry cloth affair that made him look like a skinny Cookie Monster. The kids had chosen it for him last Christmas, and he used it diligently every evening before bed and each morning after his shower. As he tiptoed out of the bedroom, I wondered sleepily what a robber would make of it.

I had just started to drift off again when Richie shook me awake.

"It's for you," he said.

"What is?" I asked.

"The banging. Cindy's at the door."

"What the hell?" I wondered, echoing my husband's earlier words.

Richie rolled his eyes. "Always full of surprise."

It was true.

In the year since she had moved in, Cindy had insinuated herself into our lives in a most unexpected way. Kindred spirits she called us, though I felt that I could hardly compare myself to her, with her outspoken personality and exaggerated artsy style.

Cindy had bought the house next door for a steal, she confessed, and it had come at just the right time, with her twins due in three weeks. The house was almost identical to ours, with its split level entry and partly finished basement. The spacious master bedroom and two kids rooms were on the main level, while the kitchen, living room and spare room were upstairs. In our place the spare room was the converted darkroom—Cindy was using hers as an art studio for painting and pottery.

I loved Cindy, with her loud personality and put-on artistic attitude. She was always fun, always laughing, and a fantastic friend.

I had never asked her about Lee and Mike's dad, and she had never volunteered the information either. It was the one part of her life that she kept private, and I could respect her desire to keep a few secrets to herself. She knew that people speculated about where or who he might be, and she played it up well. She confided falsely to a mom we met at the park that her husband was serving in the American army in the Middle East. I had also heard her tell a clerk at a shoe store that she was a lesbian who had been impregnated by her gay best friend. I had drawn my own conclusion.

At forty, Cindy was single, with no potential suitors in the wings. I could only assume that her taste was discerning, though I had never seen her with a man. She was attractive, smart, funny, and had a readily disposable income. And I had heard that twins were a reasonably common outcome of artificial insemination.

But I kept my thoughts to myself.

"What time is it?" I asked Richie as I donned his discarded robe.

Cindy was always a source of entertainment. Even in the middle of the night.

"Two minutes after midnight," he answered, pulling a pillow over his head. "Good luck!"

I trudged sleepily down to the door, where Cindy stood waiting, fully clothed and vibrating with energy.

"I'm ready!" she announced.

"Ready?"

"To date again!"

"What? Now?" I gave her my best disgusted look. "Why? Where are the twins?"

My friend shoved me good-naturedly. "They're sleeping, silly. But it's their birthday as of two minutes ago. And I promised myself that I would devote an entire year to them before I even looked at a man. I've done it!" Cindy's eyes shone.

"Crazy much?" I asked, considering whether or not to close the door on her.

"Seriously," she said. "Richard has friends, right? He's always complaining about the single guys at his work—how they don't have families at home so they don't understand him."

"What? Seriously?" I asked, really waking up for the first time. "You want *Richie* to introduce you to someone?" I tried to picture Cindy on the arm one of the businessmen that Richie worked alongside. It was almost laughable.

"Yeah, you know. He's dropped a few names. Steve in accounting who always tries to make Richard go for beers after work, and Kyle, the human resources dude who has a houseboat in the Okanagan."

"What, are you making a list?" I asked.

Cindy laughed and pulled a piece of paper out of her pocket. "Don't worry," she said to me. "It's not that kind of list."

"Good Lord. What *is* it a list of?" I was scared to unfold it.

"Criteria."

"Criteria?"

"Things that make a man dateable."

"Why can't you just date online like everyone else?"

"Just give it to Richard, okay?"

"Okay," I agreed, not being able to imagine his reaction.

Cindy laughed and headed back over to her house at a sprint, giving me a little wave when she reached her porch.

I closed the door and wondered out loud, "Why, oh why can't I just have a normal friend?"

❧

I gave Richie a skeptical look.

"Third time's the charm," he told me. "Besides, it's Valentine's day. The most romantic day of the year. It's a no fail deal."

"But Newton? With Cindy? Even his name is too nerdy for her," I asserted. "He's six inches shorter than she is, meets only one of the requirements on her list, and I'm pretty sure that he has some kind of speech impediment."

Richie turned my own skeptical look back on me. "Didn't you used to be kind of nerdy, too?"

I blushed. "I chose to not follow a mainstream lifestyle. That's different than being nerdy."

Richie gave me a smile. "And it's Charles, the floor manager, who has the speech impediment. Not Newton."

I stuck my tongue out at him. "If it wasn't Cindy..."

My husband straightened his tie and kissed me on the cheek. "The last two guys met each of her criterion. You've read the list?"

I nodded impatiently. Of course I had read it. "Tall. Financially comfortable. World traveled. Funny. But not too funny. Intellectual but not pretentious. Always roses, never carnations. Must have read *The Grapes of Wrath* and seen the Mona Lisa. Over thirty-five but under forty-five. Looks good in orange. Minimal chest hair," I reeled off.

"Right," Richie agreed. "Do you know how hard it is for one guy to ask another about his chest hair?"

I laughed.

"But I did it. And not for Cindy. For you. Finding your friend a husband may kill me, but it will make *you* happy," he said sweetly.

"Are you sucking up?" I asked.

"Definitely."

"Okay, I'm listening."

Richard smiled knowingly. "Who has the best relationship you know of?"

"We do," I answered truthfully.

"Exactly. Now, let's just review our previous experience. I brought Cindy to the office Christmas party as a blind date for Kyle. Who looks fantastic in orange and waxes his chest."

I winced. As soon as Kyle had started talking about his deep love of eighties hair bands, Cindy had tuned him out. By the time he was drunk enough to request that the DJ play tunes by those very same bands, Cindy had feigned a headache and gone home.

"And then I invited Steve over for our New Year's Party. And we know what a disaster *that* was," Richie reminded me.

I remembered it well. Cindy had introduced herself, and immediately demanded to know how Steve felt about White Snake. Steve had laughed it off, but had followed her question with a joke about single mothers putting out. Needless to say, that had sent Cindy over the edge. She ranted angrily for about three minutes and then called him a cab.

Richie went on. "Steve still gives me dirty looks at every budget meeting. So I'm trying my own thing this time. Besides, Newton meets at least *two* of Cindy's criteria."

"Two? I know that he does alright financially. What's the other one?" I asked.

"Oh," Richard said, "I hadn't even counted that one. So he meets three, then. He's a member of Mensa, so he's gotta be bright. And I know for a fact that he vacationed in Paris last year. He mentioned the *Louvre* several times. So…Mona Lisa, check."

"Okay, I'll warily concede those three. But a family dinner with all four of our kids? You're insane. You might as well be tossing him into shark infested waters."

"You'll see," my husband assured me, and was saved from further criticism by the ring of the doorbell.

∂∽∾

Cindy was wearing an outlandish red dress, form fitting and better suited to a nightclub. Typical.

"You look lovely," Richie said as he gave her a kiss on the cheek. She winked at me over his shoulder.

The twins were dressed in matching t-shirts and pants, and I knew that they must've been a gift because Cindy was always adamant about dressing them differently than each other.

"What are you up to?" I whispered to my friend as the doorbell rang a second time.

Newton Green didn't let me down, either, and I could feel my anxiety level rise. Newton's hair was curly in a way that was probably cute a kid, but with each passing year, he lost a little more off the top and grew it a little longer in the back to compensate. He was wearing a pin-striped suit that would've been appropriate on a mafia movie mobster and nowhere else. He had an orange satin shirt buttoned up to his neck, and a clip on bow tie fastened to the collar. He was also grinning from ear to ear and holding a dozen yellow roses.

"For me?" Cindy asked innocently.

"Who else?" Newton answered and handed them over with a little flourish.

I avoided making eye contact. "Food?" I suggested.

I had opted to serve dinner immediately so that any awkward moments could be filled with chewing. As I let Richard usher everyone into the kitchen, Cindy whispered, "At least it's not a combover."

I prepared myself for the worst.

We sat down to homemade macaroni and cheese—a family favourite that even one year old Lee and Mike were able to eat on their own. I was just about to start a safe chat about the weather when Newton pulled a book from his coat pocket and cleared his throat. I read the title as he bent back the cover with an exaggerated motion. *The Grapes of Wrath.* Newton took a folded piece of notepaper from between the pages and opened it up. Before I could ask any questions, he said, "Let's get started, shall we?"

"Um?" I asked, not sure what to say.

"So, Cindy," he looked over at her seriously. "How do you feel about White Snake?"

I kicked Richie under the table. He muffled a laugh.

Cindy started to open her mouth and then closed it again. Her eyes went very wide.

Newton kept an impossibly straight face. "And I should probably be up front about something." He unclipped his tie and began to unbutton his shirt. "My mother is Italian, through and through. So you might not like this." As he reached for the third button, we could all see a little tuft of dark curly hair poking through.

"Funny?" My husband remarked.

Cindy burst out laughing. "Oh, he's funny."

"But not too funny," Newton agreed.

Richard squeezed my knee under the table and sat back in satisfaction while I watched in amazement.

❦❧

My husband came home from work with an odd look on his face.

"What's up?" I asked, immediately suspicious.

"Have you seen Cindy lately?" he wanted to know.

I thought about it. Before we had introduced her to Newton, I had seen Cindy at least every couple of days. She would pop by for tea, or stop in for lunch when Richie was at work. She usually came by at least once a week for family dinner as well.

But now that most of her evenings were taken up by stay-in dates, she needed her days to work on her sculpting and painting. Newton's car was usually parked in her driveway every evening, and often overnight as well. Richie had recently joked that he and Newton were going to have start carpooling to work.

Although Cindy still came by occasionally, her visits had quickly become less and less frequent.

"No, not too much," I answered. "Actually, I kind of miss her. Why, what's up?"

"Well, Newton has missed the last three days of work, and then I got an email from him this morning."

"Oh?"

Richie still had the funny look on his face.

"What does it say?" I asked.

"It's probably better if I just show it to you," he said, and dragged me to the computer.

I waited as he booted it up and typed in the passwords for his work email.

"Oh!" I exclaimed when he opened the one from Newton. And then I started to laugh at the photo displayed on the screen.

Cindy and Newton were standing on either side of a middle-aged Elvis impersonator. She was dressed in a tiny, sequined white dress and a pair of pink bunny ears. Newton was wearing a familiar pinstriped suit and a lopsided fedora. He had Mike balanced on one hip and Lee on the other. He was grinning ridiculously. The caption read, "Nuptial greeting from sunny Las Vegas!"

Chapter 12
WAY BACK WHEN

As I stepped up to the building that was supposed to house the hostel that Kinji had recommended, I knew that something was wrong. It was a tall brick front monstrosity that had probably once been a private residence, and a large colourful sign painted with the words "Happy Traveller Hostel" hung over the gable. But a window was boarded up, and a handwritten note was taped to the door. I walked up the cement stairs, anxiety making me move slowly.

Closed For Renovations.

I panicked, hollering after the taxi cab driver to wait, but his car had already turned the corner. I stared after him, reluctantly acknowledging my situation. All of the things that my mother had told me might happen were happening. What if, God forbid, she eventually turned out to be right about everything in my life? That thought scared me more than all of the cold, empty streets of Edinburgh at midnight and closed European hostels combined. If I hadn't been so nervous, I might've laughed at my own absurdity.

I sank against the large wooden door of the *Happy Traveller* and set my backpack at my feet. I felt an unwanted sob build up in the back of my throat and fought to keep it down.

A plan, I thought. *I need a plan.* Not that plans had been helping me at all.

I could maybe have walked back to the train station—or at least tried to. I had seen some lit shops on the way to the hostel. As Kinji had said, there was little more than two kilometres between the hostel and the train station. I decided to sit for a moment more to collect myself. I took ten deep breaths, counting each one off slowly.

"Hello," said a male voice. "You alright?"

"Heck, no," I answered without opening my eyes.

His laugh sounded like a smoker's dry cough.

"Think I can help?" His "th" was soft, and sounded almost like a "f".

"Are you *English*?" I asked.

"I hope so," was his answer.

"Are we in Scotland?"

"Yes."

"And you're English," I stated.

"Luv, are you drunk?"

"You have a nice accent," I told him.

"Likewise?" It was a question.

I let a hysterical giggle escape my lips with my eyes still closed. "I've been in Britain for about ten hours—give or take. I was in London. Kings Cross. I've been in two cabs. Two trains. Four stations. And now I am in Scotland—accidentally, mind you—and you are the first English person with an English accent that I've talked to all day."

He laughed the coughing chuckle again.

"Not that funny," I said.

"Luv," he told me, "It sounds like the day of my dreams. Intercontinental travel. Strangers aplenty. And now a handsome bloke like me. Well," he amended, "I'd take a pretty bird over a handsome bloke, but otherwise very cool. Did you get some good pictures, at least?"

I finally opened my eyes.

It was hard to tell if he *was* a handsome bloke. He was neither tall nor short. His hair was shaggy and dirty blonde, and it touched his shoulders, but looked more like it had grown out from a shorter cut rather than like he wore it that way on purpose. He was wearing enormous sunglasses that effectively covered the top half of his face, but the bottom half was scruffy with a week or so of beard growth. He was wearing a pink, button front shirt that was only partly done up, a cream-coloured blazer, and a pair of artfully faded jeans. Even if he *wasn't* handsome, he still looked like a rock star after a rough bender.

"Do you stare at everyone this way? Or just Englishmen?"

I ignored his question. "How did you know that I take pictures?"

He shrugged. "Same way I know that you're Canadian. You're advertising."

He pointed first at the flag on my backpack and then at the camera around my neck. Then he bent down so that his face was level with mine. He slid his sunglasses down his nose, and I could see that his brown eyes were thoroughly bloodshot.

"Paul," he said, sticking out his hand.

He smelled like beer, cigarettes, and aftershave. Altogether, the effect was not actually unpleasant.

"Are *you* drunk?" I wondered, turning his earlier question back on him.

"I asked you first." he replied.

"No."

"I stand corrected then. Not my dream day after all. But there's still hope. The pub around the corner has a terribly dodgy owner and a rotten clientele, but they do keep open late," He paused to look at his oversized watch. "For another eleven minutes. Care to join me for a pint?"

And then I had one of those weird moments where even though everything has gone wrong, things suddenly become right. Like missing a left turn, then making three right turns instead, and getting to exactly the right place at the right moment.

I fingered the five pound note in my pocket.

"Yes, Paul. I'd love a pint."

"Brilliant!" he answered, pulling me to my feet and tossing my backpack over his own shoulders. Still holding my hand, he shouted, "Now run!"

෴

When we finally reached our destination, I was laughing and out of breath. I felt exhilarated and exhausted at the same time, and I knew that the combination of stress, jet lag, and the late night air was not helping my giddiness at all.

"Wait," Paul said as I a stepped up to enter the inviting-looking pub doors.

"What?" I asked. "Is this the part where you tell me that you're not who I think you are?"

Paul pulled his sunglasses out of the jacket pocket where he had stored them during our mad dash, and stuck them back on his face. "No, luv. This is the part where I ask you who *you* are, so that I don't look like a fool in front of my dearest mates. I don't even know your name."

I was glad that my face was already flushed enough to cover the redness that crept into my cheeks. I didn't know if I was embarrassed that I had not properly introduced myself, or irritated that I felt so pleased to be used to impress his friends.

"Am a I your own personal Canadian trophy?" I asked.

"Not yet," Paul assured me. "But the night is young."

I folded my arms across my chest. "I believe that the night only has seven minutes or so left," I answered.

"Right. About that. I may have lied."

"Lied?"

"Right."

"About what exactly?"

"The pub may be open a tad later than I initally led you to believe."

"What? Why?"

"Well you *are* a stranger," he told me. "And I didn't think that you'd *actually* be joining me."

"Then why'd you ask?" I wondered with genuine curiosity.

Paul dropped my backpack behind him without any delicacy.

"Hey," was all I managed to get out before he grabbed my arms and pulled my lips against his.

I was rigid for less than a second, and then I felt as though I was going to *melt* into him. I wondered vaguely how his lips managed to be so much warmer than mine in the cool Scottish air. I had one hand against his chest in a half-hearted protest, and I could feel the rapid beating of his heart through his partially unbuttoned shirt. My other hand crept up against his back, pulling him closer. I considered, in the part of my mind that continued to try logical function, whether I was taking advantage of him in his clearly lubricated state.

When he pulled himself away, I felt more out of breath than I had after our haphazard jog.

"Laura," I said in a gasping voice that didn't sound like me at all. "I'm Laura Morgan."

&~&

I was still trying to catch my breath as Paul yanked me in through the pub doors, and the sudden change in atmosphere didn't help.

Loud, vaguely Gaelic music played tinnily over some cleverly hidden speakers, and three very drunk men were doing an enthusiastic but clearly mocking dance on a raised wooden stage. One was wearing a traditional tartan kilt, while the other two were in jeans. All three were topless. My mouth hung open as I stared at them.

Paul jostled me toward two empty barstools. The man behind the counter was having a cartoonish conversation with the serving woman leaning on the bar.

"Oi!" shouted the woman.

"Aye?" said the man.

"I said, oi!"

"Aye?"

"Oi!"

"Naw!"

"Lager and lime, Nathaniel," the woman. "Oi!"

"Feckless half-wit, Englishwoman. Gang back tae yer ain coontry!" he answered, but poured her the drink anyway. His accent was so thick that I almost didn't understand him.

I sat down heavily beside Paul, feeling a little stunned.

It *looked* exactly like the Europe that I had built up in my mind. The walls were decorated with coats of arms, and the furniture was all made of wood that could have been around since the turn of the century. The pub was lit by green glass sconces—probably converted at some point from candle to gas and then later from gas to electricity. A set of flattened bagpipes set into a display case, and hung proudly above the pub's selection of single malt scotches. It had all qualities of the archetypal Scottish pub.

But it *sounded* like the Monty Python rendition.

Nathaniel glanced at me, looked at his watch, then shook his head at Paul. His thick Scottish accent was still hard for me to understand. "Ah ken 'at ah cut ye off nineteen minutes ago, Paulie."

"True, Nate," Paul agreed easily, "But not my friend here."

The bartender took me in, and I felt like a pig being assessed at auction. He curled his lip at my secondhand surplus jacket and sweaty white tank top. I half expected him to lean in for a sniff of my chin length tree-trunk brown hair. I self-consciously tugged on a strand.

"Hi, there," I said weakly.

Nathaniel scoffed, "Toorist?"

"Canadian visitor. A country also conquered against its will by the British Empire," Paul told him. "Do you want her to think that all Scots are as unwelcoming as you?"

"Alrecht," Nathaniel conceded gruffly. "Welcome tae Scootland, and tae *The Bonnie Lass Pub*. Dae ye want a bevy ur nae?"

Paul sighed. "She'll have four pints. And another two at last call."

He lit a cigarette, and handed one to me as well. I took it and let him light it even though I wasn't a smoker. I inhaled and muffled a cough.

"Fine." The bartender lined up the glasses with exaggerated slowness, adding, "But if ah catch ye skitin' them, I'll toss ye it oan yer rear faster than ye can say, "Hail th' Queen," ye kin?" He handed me the first full pint, and gave me a wink. I downed the beer as fast as I could, hoping to shake my jitters.

"An' ye can pay noo," Nathaniel told my companion. "Ye nae good free loader."

Paul winked at me, too. He handed a twenty pound note to the bartender. "Keep the change."

Nathaniel grabbed my empty glass, replaced it with a fresh one, and leaned in to whisper loudly, "Paul isnae sic' a bad guy. Ye coods dae waur. But he's nae as much ay a braw fellaw as he pretends tae be, either."

Paul gave him a dirty look.

I took two big gulps of my second pint, already feeling the warmth of an alcoholic buzz clouding my head.

"I have no idea what you just said," I whispered back.

Nathaniel laughed out loud and went back to polishing his bar.

കൟ✧

Waking up in someone else's apartment wasn't as weird a feeling as I would've thought. Not that it was something I had ever given any real consideration to, but I would've expected some sort confusion, or some disorientation about waking in such an unfamiliar space. The couch where I had fallen asleep the night before was made of cool leather, and could not have been mistaken for my familiarly soft bed at home.

But all I felt as I dragged myself into consciousness was the surety that my mother would not approve of my current situation at all. Nor would she have approved of my behaviour last night in the bar. Although Paul had been sipping on "my" beers each time Nathaniel turned his back, I knew that I had consumed at least four of them myself. I had also smoked several more cigarettes and tried my hand at dancing with the topless Scots. I had drawn the line—barely—at taking off my own shirt.

Aside from the sudden kiss, Paul had been a perfectly frustrating gentleman. When he had offered to let me crash on his couch, I had been half-expecting—and maybe even hoping for—at least a second kiss. But after handing me a blanket and a pillow, my English host had gone off to his bedroom without even a friendly hug. I was both relieved and disappointed. Maybe leaning more towards the latter.

Good thing Mom's not *here*, I thought, blushing a little at where my now sober brain was going.

I kept my eyes closed, taking in my surroundings through my nose and ears. I could smell stale beer and cigarettes most strongly, alongside lemon-scented furniture polish or household cleaner, as well as something delicious. I could hear the sound of food sizzling in a pan, too. Over that, I could hear a familiar Pixies song playing softly, and a pleasant male voice humming along.

Paul, I thought. If I had spoken his name aloud, it probably would have been an embarrassing sigh.

His humming became low singing, and then suddenly erupted into a full out karaoke of *Here Comes Your Man.*

A giggle escaped my lips.

"Whoops!" I heard Paul exclaim. "Didn't mean to wake you!"

But the music volume suddenly became quite a bit louder, and the smell of food immediately became close.

I opened my eyes.

Paul was standing front of me with a frying pan in his hand and a lit cigarette in his mouth. He was wearing the same pink shirt from the night before, now unbuttoned all the way, and a pair of boxer shorts embossed with the Corona logo.

"Here comes your food!" he sang from behind the cigarette, grinning at me.

"Are you in your underwear?" I asked him.

"Oh, bugger. You noticed," he said as he pretended to cover himself with the frying pan.

I narrowed my eyes.

"Are you giving me a plate? Or am I expected to eat my breakfast from *there*?" I inquired dryly.

"Cheeky this morning, aren't we?" Paul put his cigarette out in an already overflowing ashtray on the coffee table. He shoved my legs off of the couch and sat down.

"Hey, ouch," I said half-heartedly.

Paul reached around my body. For an instant, the intimacy of the pose overwhelmed much as the kiss the previous night had. This strange, British, almost naked man was pressed against me in my prone pose. I inhaled his musky, cigarette-laden scent and tensed in anticipation. My heart beat in a disconcerting way. I wondered if he could feel it. I half hoped he could.

And then he yanked the pillow out from underneath my head, placed it on his knees, and balanced the frying pan on top. He reached into his shirt pocket and pulled out a plastic spoon.

"Only clean utensil in the flat," Paul told me.

"Men!" I said teasingly.

I grabbed the spoon out of his hand and went straight to eating the breakfast out of his lap.

❧ ❦

We took turns with the spoon, accompanied by the sounds of Paul's favourite music. The food was absolutely delicious and I told him so.

"Cooking is hobby of mine," he responded as he chewed.

"But I did think that hangovers were supposed to make you sick, not hungry," I said as I waited for my turn with the spoon.

Paul grinned at me. Damn but he had a charming smile. "Are you hungover, then?" he asked me.

I stopped mid-bite to consider it. My throat was pretty sore, probably from all the random smoking and the attempts to out sing Paul's pub friends. My head didn't hurt and I didn't feel the least bit queasy.

Paul was watching me, still smiling.

I shrugged. "No. I guess not. But then, I've really got nothing to compare it to."

Paul laughed. "Have you never been drunk before either, luv?"

I shrugged again, feigning a lack of embarrassment. "My parents did let me have a glass of champagne last year at Christmas. I got a bit light-headed."

"They let you?" Paul looked offended on my behalf. "Your mum and dad?"

I poked him with spoon. "Well I do live in their house. And in British Columbia the legal drinking age is nineteen. Which I won't be until the end of the month."

Now he looked incredulous. "And what? You've never been out on a piss-up with some mates?"

"Even though I'm not entirely sure what that means, I'm going to have to say no, I haven't," I answered. "And you should know that I don't smoke, either."

"Huh. Could've fooled me, luv." He lit another one and handed it to me. "I'm a bad influence, am I?" A hint of pride entered his voice.

"Pleased with yourself?"

Paul grabbed the spoon back from me. His fingers rested against mine for a second too long, and I thought again of the kiss from the night before. "I should feel guilty, shouldn't I? But instead I just feel a little devious. Makes me wonder how else I can corrupt you."

I stood up quickly, trying to cover my blush. "I may not be hungover, but I am quite thirsty."

He nodded toward the kitchen. "Help yourself to anything you'd like. But hurry back, or I'm going eat the rest of breakfast myself."

I walked slowly down the hall, counting off breaths to calm myself down. I wondered if the alcohol I had consumed the previous night was still working its way through my system, because I didn't seem to have full control over my mind or body.

I stopped at the kitchen doorway, leaning against the frame, still breathing deeply. I looked in.

Paul's kitchen was not how I would've pictured it. Where the living room was crowded with evidence of my host's personal preferences—classic vinyl records, framed posters, and eclectic pieces of art—the kitchen was pristine. It was obvious that it had been entirely remodeled to meet a cook's dream.

So much for cooking being his hobby.

A state of the art stainless steel stove was the focal point of the room. It was built into an enormous, drawer filled island. Every imaginable cooking utensil, pot, pan, and spice was housed in open faced cupboards that lined the walls. I had expected dirty dishes and old appliances—not evidence of an experienced and fastidious chef. I grabbed a glass from inside of one of the cabinets and poured some chilled water from the fridge tap.

A thought struck me, and I opened each drawer on the island until I found the one I was looking for. The fifth one revealed it—a shiny set of very clean utensils, spoons included. I stared at them in puzzlement.

"Laura?" Paul called from the living room.

I didn't answer him, and in a moment I felt his presence at my side.

"I think that you should know that I am considering dumping this water over your head," I told him.

"Why?" he asked, and then caught sight of the open drawer. "Ohhhhh," he drew the word out.

"You are a terrible person," I said.

"There's a logical explanation," he answered.

"For lying about cutlery?" I was afraid to turn to look at him, knowing that if I moved even a little bit we would be close enough to touch.

"Okay, it's a lame excuse and entirely illogical," he admitted. "But do you want to hear it?"

"Sure. Why not?" I said with an exaggerated sigh.

Paul grabbed my hand and pulled me out of the kitchen, back down the hall and onto the couch in the living room. He didn't let go when we sat down, and I didn't pull away. I continued to avoid looking at him. I was unbearably conscious of his bare knee against my own. I was afraid to breath.

"Explain," I commanded with false confidence.

"Are you going to believe me?" he asked, teasing but sounding genuinely unsure.

I finally forced myself to look up at him, and I realized that his face was as red as mine. Interesting.

"I would probably believe anything you told me," I admitted, pleased to see his blush get even deeper. "But don't let it go to your head. I consider that English accent of yours to be a form of mild duress."

It was weird and empowering to have this kind of influence on the changing colour of a man's face. It helped me to feel a little more control over my reactions to Paul's presence. Experimentally, I pushed my thigh closer to his, and my heart still raced. Not that much control. I wondered if he could feel the quick throb of my pulse through my femoral artery.

"The spoon?" I pressed in an embarrassingly ragged voice.

He cleared his throat and avoided my eyes. "It seemed like a good way to create some intimacy?"

I wanted to giggle. "That *is* illogical. Don't most guys just dim the lights?" I replied.

Paul's other hand crept into my lap and he threaded his fingers through mine. "I don't have much practice in the art of seduction," he admitted.

"Define much."

"None." I wanted to believe him.

"And what exactly does 'braw fellaw' mean?"

Paul laughed. "It probably translates best as 'cool guy'."

"I see."

"Do you think that I'm a braw fellaw?" he teased.

"You're something," I answered.

He rubbed his thumbs against mine and a warm tingle spread involuntarily up through my fingers, across my arms, and into my chest. I felt heat rise up through my face. Paul smiled, and as I stared into his milk chocolate brown eyes, I sensed that my minimal control of the situation was slipping away.

"I figured if my lips had touched the spoon," he said, pulling my arms over his neck and resting his hands on my waist, "And your lips had touched the spoon," he leaned toward me and I held my breath, "Then our lips touching each other wouldn't be too much of a stretch."

And then he pressed his mouth gently against mine.

I gasped, realizing a little to late that my self-control had really only been in my head.

❦❧

I watched Paul from the corner of my eye. He was inhaling a cigarette in slow, even intervals, and blowing smoke rings toward the ceiling above his head. His eyes were closed peacefully, and if he hadn't been smoking, I might've thought he was sleeping.

I admired his rockstar-esque profile, enjoying the companionable quiet we'd been sharing. As an only child, silence was like an old and comfortable friend. And somehow, that calming stillness was even more agreeable with Paul beside me. It was solitude without being solitary.

"What's your nicname?" he asked suddenly, breaking into my reverie. "Laura," Paul added without opening his eyes, "Is a name that you can't really shorten. That's unfortunate."

"Sorry," I apologized, and then pointed out, "Paul's not exactly a name that gets any shorter, either."

"Paulie," he said.

"That's not shorter. That's longer," I told him.

"Still a nicname," he answered, and went back to his silent smoking. He lit one cigarette off of another. I waited, but he said nothing else.

"Is this what it's like, then?" I asked.

He laughed. "You're going to have to be a bit more specific, luv."

"All this," I said, making a grand gesture around the room.

"Which part? Passionate sex? British men?"

"All of it," I said, not the slightest bit embarrassed by the teasing directness of his inquiry.

Paul was silent for a minute, and I wondered if he had been trying to deflect my question with his glib responses.

He smiled at me, blowing another practiced smoke ring above our heads. "It's my experience that most British men are alright blokes when it comes to each other. Right good mates. But with a bird or two involved? Well, you've heard of James Bond?"

I laughed out loud. "You realize that you've just compared yourself to fictional British spy, right?"

"A fictional, *womanizing* British spy," he corrected.

"Right," I agreed.

"I do like to be as realistic as possible," he told me, still grinning.

"Right," I repeated, taking the cigarette and inhaling slowly. I enjoyed the rawness of it as it pulled through my throat and into my lungs. It burned pleasantly before I exhaled.

"The rest of it," he paused, thinking. "No. It's not like this. I haven't felt like this...well, even with the birds I've been keenest on. What about for you?"

I felt a pang as I pictured him with some faceless English girl, doing excessively English things together. I brushed off the feeling, reminding myself to be more adult, more European.

I kept my voice casual as I admitted, "I have nothing to compare it to."

Paul sat up, staring at me with new eyes. "I'm sorry," he apologized, and he ran his fingers down my face.

"For what?" I asked lightly. My body warmed automatically at his touch.

"I didn't know," he said awkwardly.

"It doesn't matter," I told him.

But I could see in the rigidity of his form that it did matter to him. To Paul. I leaned into his caress.

"This has been the best two days of my life."

He brightened, and I had to laugh at how easy he was to please.

"Do you mean that, luv?"

"Mmm hmm."

He continued to run his fingers through my hair and I drifted off to sleep.

కళ్ళ

When I pried my eyes open again, the apartment was dark. Paul was watching me intently, an unlit cigarette hanging from his lip. He pulled it from his mouth and kissed me lightly. He sat back and continued to stare at me.

"Morning," I said sleepily.

"Evening," he replied.

"Not everyday that I wake up with a handsome stranger staring me down."

"Am I still a stranger?" Paul made a sad face.

"The emphasis was supposed to be on the handsome part," I informed him.

"Well, then tell me what you usually wake up to," he prodded.

"Rain," I replied. "Vancouver is very wet."

"Pets?" he wondered.

"My parents have a cat named Joey," I answered. "But I think he hates me. Pees on my pillow sometimes."

Paul laughed. "Favourite food?"

"Chicken quesadillas. You?"

"Curry," he told me. "Best holiday?"

"This one, of course."

He leaned over and kissed me again. "First kiss?" he asked.

"No, I've had one before," I teased.

He raised an eyebrow.

"Todd Yang," I amended. "Eleventh grade. Altogether an unpleasant experience."

Paul smiled and lit his cigarette. "So," he said, "Not so much strangers anymore, right?"

"But you're still very handsome," I answered agreeably.

I realized then that Paul was holding my itinerary in his hands. He lifted it up examine it.

"Don't hold it so close the the light. You might burn it," I warned, trying to grab it back from him.

He swatted my hand away. "You really want to do all of these things over the next three weeks?" he teased. "You *want* to be a tourist?"

"Twenty days," I corrected. "Since we haven't left your apartment in almost forty-eight hours, I'll probably have to skip a castle or two."

Paul ran a finger along my naked thigh with easy familiarity. I marveled at that. It should've been so much harder for me to talk while so exposed physically. I should've been scrambling to cover myself up with a sheet, but I just watched his knuckle as he moved it up my body, shivering a little when he reached my hip. It was easier—almost too easy to share my thoughts with him like this.

"Are you complaining, luv?" he asked.

I rolled over on his bed and kissed him.

"Nope," I said.

Paul pulled away.

"*Now* I'm gonna complain," I teased.

He held my face between his hands. "Are you open to trying some new things?"

"Excuse me?"

He laughed at the look on my face. "Not like that! I want you to trade in your itinerary for my mine."

"Spend the next three weeks together?" I asked, not bothering hide my excitement.

"Twenty days," Paul reminded me.

"When do we start?"

He kissed my cheek. "Tomorrow. And I have the perfect thing for us to do."

I pulled him closer, dragging my lips across his throat.

"Well, maybe the day *after* tomorrow," Paul said, and we both laughed.

Chapter 13
THEN

I curled my tired feet underneath me on the couch.

"I think that was a success," Richie said to me, and seated himself beside me.

"Yes," I agreed. "Exhausting. But successful."

We had just finished celebrating Newton and Cindy's two year anniversary. The party was still going on next door, but we had finally bowed out close to midnight.

My husband grinned. "I'm glad it was at their house and not ours."

I groaned, thinking of the mess that was going to be left behind by Cindy's artsy friends.

"I'm sure that she'll call me in the morning to help," I said.

"At least Mike and Lee will never be able to complain about having a dull life," my husband observed.

"But they still seem well adjusted," I replied. "I think that Newton's turning out to be the perfect dad for them."

Richie nodded, nudging me. "And the perfect husband for Cindy?"

"Yes, oh wise husband," I sighed. "You were right." I paused. "Do you think that it will matter later, that he's not their biological father?"

"Not at all," Richie said with conviction.

"You sound awfully sure about that."

It was his turn to sigh. "I guess that I've never told you that Cole Lockhurst is not my own biological father?"

I sat up, looking at my husband in shock. "No. That, I'd remember."

"My dad left when I was four," my husband explained. "I only remember vague details about him. He was tall, and rarely laughed. My mom's told me that he suffered from depression. That's why there's such a large age gap between me and Cara. They were try-ing to work stuff out all that time. I learned years ago that he died of a heart attack."

"Wow," I said. "That must've been hard."

Richie shrugged. "Cole—who I've always thought of as my dad—came into my life about a year after my biological father left. Liz, Marie and Jess are all Cole's natural children, but he's always treated us equally. So I guess I've got some insight into Mike and Lee's situation."

I watched my husband's face, and he broke out into a sudden grin.

"What?" I asked.

"I was going to say that I turned out a-okay," Richie told me.

"But?"

"But then I remembered that I stole something. Recently."

"What?"

"A giant piece of cake from the party," he said. "Want to share it?"

He jumped up before I could answer, and left me staring af-ter him incredulously.

❧❧

I was sitting on a park bench, while the kids played at the lit-tle enclosed playground at the end of our block. I had been watch-ing with concern for about five minutes as Jordan encouraged Tori to climb up the complicated plastic structure that led to a twisted yellow slide, when I felt someone sit down beside me.

"Good afternoon," I greeted without glancing at the newcomer.

Tori was hanging by one hand from a metal rung. I cringed in anticpation of a fall, but she got her footing almost immediately.

"Good job," I called.

Suddenly I felt a hand land familiarly on my knee.

"Hey!" I yelped in surprise and looked over.

"Sorry," Richie chuckled. "I was just trying to surprise you."

"You succeeded," I told him. I checked my watch. It was only just after one in the afternoon. "Why aren't you at work?"

My husband shrugged. "I had an early lunch meeting with an out of town client, and thought I'd cut my day day short."

"Since when do they give you clients? Don't you just boss people around and decide which TVs go to which warehouse?" I teased.

He smiled back. "Something like that. It was just someone looking to sell something that we're not interested in buying. They needed an outside opinion."

"Well. At least you picked a beautiful day to come home early," I said.

It was a unusually warm for December, and it hadn't rained all week. I hadn't even had to bother with mittens or hats for Jordan and Tori.

Richard and I watched the kids silently for a moment. Tori had made it to the top of the ladder and Jordan was already at the bottom of the slide, yelling at his sister to come down, too.

"And why aren't the kids at school?" Richie asked.

I gave him a look. "Professional day? I distinctly remember telling you about it this morning."

"Right," he said. "I guess that means we can't do what I had wanted to this afternoon."

"And what was that?" I wondered.

This time Richard gave *me* a look, and I flushed a little.

My husband leaned over and gave me an emphatic and enthusiastic kiss.

"Oh. That," I breathed when he finally let me go.

Jordan and Tori came running over, finally realizing that their dad had joined us. They clamoured up into his lap.

"I guess we'll have to settle for second best," Richie told me over top of Tori's head.

"Second best what, Daddy?" Jordan asked.

"Hot chocolate," my husband told him, and was met with a chorus of excited delight.

Jordan had been morose since the second I had picked him up from school.

Tori was unusually cheery, and she took advantage of Jordan's quietness. While he scuffled along dragging his feet, she bounced happily beside me. A new girl had started in her third grade class that morning, and Tori had a lot to report about the novelty.

"Her name is Aashna. With two 'a's', not just one," my daughter gushed excitedly. "She comes from India, and she was late because her parents had to immigrate. That's a funny word for moving to Canada."

I smiled down at her. New words were her current obsession.

"Jordie," Tori said, "Do *you* know that word?" One-upping her brother was another favourite pastime.

Jordan didn't take the bait.

"Everything alright, buddy?" I asked him.

Jordan mumbled a response that could have been intended for both of us or neither or us.

When we got home, my son headed immediately for his room, and when I peeked my head in through his door, he was focused on his spelling worksheet.

"Tough words this week?" I asked, coming up behind him.

"Naw," he answered without looking up.

"Okay," I told him, not wanting to push it. "Dinner in an hour, alright? You can play your Game Boy if you want. As a treat." We usually didn't let him play until homework was done, but his serious little face had me concerned.

"It's a Game Boy Advance, Mom," Jordan corrected me.

"Well, you can play it."

"Naw."

I hesitated at the door. "Are you sure?"

"Yeah.

"Okay."

My concern grew a little bit, but I went back to getting dinner ready while Tori filled me in on the facts about India and her new friend. I half-listend, distracted by my worry for Jordan.

"In India money is called *Rupee.*"

"Yeah?"

"And Aashna speaks Hindi *and* English. Mommy, can I learn another language?"

"Sure," I agreed, knowing that she would bug me until I actually did find a way for her pursue the request.

"Aashna told me that she's a Hindu. Can I be one, too?" Tori asked right as Richard walked in.

My husband laughed, and our daughter frowned at him. "It's not funny, Daddy. It's multicultural."

"Indeed, it is," Richie agreed. "And I'm sure that you can be whatever you want to be. When you grow up."

That answer didn't ease Tori's frown, but before she could ask another question, I commanded her to go get Jordan for dinner.

As soon as she left the room, I turned to Richard.

"What's wrong?" he asked, immediately sensing my worry.

"Something's bugging Jordan," I told him, positioning myself in the doorway so that I could listen for the kids' footsteps.

"Jordan?" said Richard, sounding surprised. Then we both laughed. Usually when something was up, it involved our daughter rather than our son.

"Yes." But before I could say more, Tori skipped into the room, followed her brother, who looked a little pale.

In typical mom fashion, I put my hand against his forehead and then against the back of his neck. "No fever," I murmured.

"Hamburgers!" Tori announced with delight as we all took our places at the table.

"Everyone's favourite," Richie agreed.

But Jordan just played with his food, and then pushed away his plate.

"What is it?" I asked, trying and failing to mask my anxiety.

Jordan answered with his head down. "We had our farm field trip today."

I waited, but he didn't add anything else. "Are you sad that I didn't get to drive you this time? You knew that I had to take the Halloween pictures for Aunt Liz's baby, right? You seemed enthusiastic about riding with Brian, Jake and Jake's mom this morning."

Jordan shook his head, and whispered something that I didn't catch.

"Pardon me?"

"Did you know that they make meat from *cows*?" he said, his face getting paler.

"And pigs, and sheep, and chickens," Tori added helpfully.

Tears welled up in my son's eyes. "It's gross, Mom. How can we eat them? They were alive!"

I looked at Richie helplessly. He was chewing a burger bite guiltily.

Tori gave her brother a disgusted look. "We're at the top of the food chain. Duh."

"Don't say, 'duh', Tori," I scolded.

"But it's true, Mommy. People are the rulers, so we can do what we want. And we want to eat meat. Besides, it's a food group. My teacher told me." Tori found her own logic infallible.

"Some people are vegetarians," I informed both her and Jordan.

"What's that?" they asked at the same time.

"Someone who chooses not to eat meat, and gets protein in another way," I explained.

Jordan pushed his plate even further away. "I'm going to be that," he announced.

"More meat for me!" Tori, ever the opportunist, grabbed her brother's untouched burger and took a big bite. "I will be a meat-a-tarian," she said with a full mouth.

"Carnivore," Richard corrected automatically. "We can look that word up later in the encyclopedia."

"Yay!" Tori loved an excuse to research something new.

"Maybe we can also look up soy products," I sighed and got up to make my newly vegetarian son an animal-free, peanut butter sandwich.

Liz Smith-Lockhurst and I were sitting in my living room, enjoying that fact that the kids were entertaining each other, leaving us virtually alone. Jordan and Darren had holed themselves up Jordan's room. They were pouring over a *Marvel Comics* guide on my laptop, and pretending not to be playing with my son's expansive action figure collection at the same time. Tori and Nina had taken three-year old Callie downstairs and had built her a complicated chair/couch/blanket fortress. When we had checked on them a few minutes earlier, they had spotted us on the stairs and issued a loud protest.

"Princess Callie is *not* taking any unauthorized visitors!" Nina shouted.

Tori had added, "Give us the secret password or back away slowly!"

Liz and I had wisely chosen option B, and gone back to our tea, low-fat muffins, and complaints about other people's kids.

"I miss this," she told me.

"Whining about our lives over tea?" I joked.

"We should never have moved out of the city," Liz said.

"I agree, for entirely selfish reason," I told her. "But you really don't like it at all?"

She took a little sip from her mug and didn't meet my eyes. "I'm struggling," she admitted. "*We're* struggling."

"It does kind of cramp our style, having you so far away," I agreed lightly.

My sister-in-law smiled at me weakly. "Not *us*, you goof. Jeremy, the kids and I."

"It's not what you expected?" I asked.

She shrugged. "Getting out of the townhouse and into a place with enough room for everybody was good to start out with. But I feel like the extra space has done something to pull us apart. I don't know. Maybe living like a can of sardines was all that kept us so tightly bound before."

"That doesn't sound good, Liz." I patted her knee sympathetically, worried about where the conversation was leading.

"Was it hard for you and Richie? When you moved from the city to the suburbs?" she wondered.

I thought about it, knowing that she was looking for comfort.

"You know," I answered cautiously, "I think that it *could* have been hard. At the time, I believed that I belonged in the city. I had actually moved out of suburbia to get away from my parents' life. Maybe for me it was more like moving back to something familiar than moving away from something that I loved."

Liz eyed me speculatively. "And you don't resent that?"

"Sometimes," I admitted.

She looked a little relieved at the admission. "I always had you pegged for a free spirit. Even after you got pregnant and then you and Richie got married, I assumed that your foot was only halfway in the door."

I laughed uneasily. "Now *that*, I resent."

She went on without meeting my gaze. "I just always thought that it would be you who struggled, not us. I know that it's selfish. But Jeremy and I, we did everything the right way. We were good friends before we dated. We fell in love slowly, and we had all the same long-term goals. So we got married, we bought the town-house. We waited a year and then got pregnant. We got better jobs and more money. But we never got any happier. It's not right."

She paused, and I said sadly, "I'm sorry."

"Aren't you ever lonely?" she demanded.

"No."

It wasn't entirely the truth. Sometimes I felt lost in my own life, like I was so busy being a wife and mother that I didn't have time to be *Laura*. During quiet moments alone, I wondered what would happen to me if my family suddenly disappeared. Would I disappear, too?

Sighing, I said, "I don't think that I ever stop long enough to let myself be lonely. What mother does?"

"I've been lonely for a long time," Liz half whispered. "When we moved out of the city, I lost my friends. I'm too far from my family. All I have is the kids. And Darren and Nina are outgrowing me."

"Callie's still little," I reminded her lamely.

"I don't expect you to understand. You or my brother. You didn't do anything the way you were supposed to," she said bitterly. "You have nothing in common as far as I can see. You got pregnant before you got married, then lived in that tiny apartment with no money. Neither of you finished school or followed through on your goals. And yet, here you are, happy as ever." By the end of her speech she was almost yelling.

"I didn't know that you felt that way," I said in a wounded voice.

"My brother is easy to love, and I know why you picked him," she told me, focusing her eyes on a spot above my head.

"Are you saying that you don't know why *he* picked *me*?" I asked softly.

She nodded.

I looked at Liz with new eyes. I would've counted her among my closest friends, and was shocked by her admission.

"Liz?" I felt myself choking up.

"No. Yes. I know why he picked you. I like you. You're a good friend. A good mom. I wish that I could say that you're taking advantage of him, but you're not even aware of how you are," she smiled sadly at me.

"How am I?"

"You're *that* girl. Like a bird with a broken wing. You won't ever fly again on your own because no matter what, it will never, ever heal properly," she said to me.

I stared at her. I wanted to deny her cruel words, but I couldn't force any sound to come out of my throat.

My sister-in-law finally looked directly at me. Her eyes were feverish and filled with tears. "Jeremy and I separated last month," she confessed. "I feel so lost."

And then she crumbled against me on the couch.

Chapter 14
THEN

"I got a job," I announced to Richie, Tori, and Jordan without preamble.

We were all seated at the dinner table, enjoying the vegetarian lasagna that I had been preparing all afternoon.

Jordan stopped mid-chew. "*Why?*" he wanted to know.

"Are we poor, Mommy?" Tori demanded.

"We're not poor," my husband told her, and looked at me inquiringly.

I met his eyes and gave him a bright smile. Although I hadn't mentioned it to him, my conversation with Richie's sister had been eating me up. Over the last month or two, I had been trying to assess mine and my husband's relationship as objectively as possible. I knew that Liz's feelings on my marriage must be clouded by her own looming divorce, but I couldn't shake the idea that she had to be coming from somewhere.

It was true, I had concluded, that Richard did seem to tread lightly around my emotions. He gave me space to play out my frustrations with the kids, and brushed it off when I wasn't able to return a passionate advance or a loving gesture. It was true, also, that I guarded my feelings and my thoughts more often than entirely necessary. I was often content to let Richie take the lead in lovemaking, financial matters, and major decisions. But did our dynamic make our relationship an uneven one? I couldn't answer that question properly, but lately I had begun to feel like I needed to prove myself as a partner.

"Mommy needs something to do now that everybody's at school all day everyday," I said. *As close to the truth as I'm going to get,* I thought.

"Doing what?" Tori wondered. "You don't know *how* to work."

"Mommy works hard all the time," Richie explained to the kids. He smiled at me. "Being your mom isn't an easy job."

"But she doesn't know how to do a *real* job," Tori argued.

"Don't worry, Tori, it's something very easy, and something I already know how to do," I told her.

"What is it?" Jordan's curiosity was piqued.

"Well, Cindy actually found the job ad in the paper," I explained.

"Cindy found it?" Richie asked. "Can I take a guess?"

"No," I told him.

"Exotic dancer?" he whispered anyway.

"What's a hypnotic dancer?" Tori wondered.

I gave my husband a dirty look.

"Never mind your Daddy," I said. "That little copy and print shop in the mall needs someone twice a week to help run their photo development machine, so I'm going to do that every Tuesday and Thursday."

"Will you be dancing there while you do it?" Jordan asked.

"No!" Richie and I answered together.

৵৽

"Is this what you want?" Richie wondered suddenly.

We had been in bed for over an hour, and I had thought he was sleeping.

"Yes," I said firmly.

"You need to do something for yourself, and I totally understand," he told me. "But is it this?"

"It might not be this forever," I replied. "But it's something for now, and that's all I need."

৵৽

If I had taken the time to think about it, I should've expected a call from Tori's school before fourth grade. But I hadn't, so when the number came up on the call display, my first assumption was that one of the children was hurt, or sick.

"Hello?" I answered the phone, trying to keep the worry out of my voice.

"Is this Mrs. Lockhurst? Tori's mom?" asked a gravelly, vaguely familiar voice.

"Yes."

"Mrs. Lockhurst, this is Janet Smyth. The school librarian." She coughed into the phone and cleared her throat.

I pictured the older woman at once. She had given a brief speech on the importance of home reading at the kindergarten information session we had attended for Jordan years before. Mrs. Smyth was whip thin, wore her hair in a stereotypical librarian's bun, and smoked liked a chimney.

"Is Tori okay?" I asked.

There was a brief pause and I wondered if my daughter had gotten sick in the library, or fallen through a book shelf.

"Yes, Mrs. Lockhurst. Tori is fine. But I have some concerns. Would you like to discuss them in person?" the librarian asked me.

I couldn't tell from her tone if she *wanted* me to come in, or if she was making the offer for my sake. I wracked my brain for any mention Tori had ever made of the librarian. My nine year-old was an avid reader, and I knew that she was testing more or less off the scales academically. I knew also that once a week her class attended a group session at the school library. But I couldn't recall Tori—or Jordan for that matter—ever mentioning Mrs. Smyth specifically.

I must've been silent for too long. The librarian coughed into the phone again.

"No," I finally answered. "Why don't you go ahead and tell me your concern now? I guess I can come in if I think it's serious."

"I'm comfortable with that." Janet Smyth paused again. "Mrs. Lockhurst, I'm sure that you and your husband must be aware that Tori is a voracious reader?"

"We are," I agreed. "Last year we signed off permission for her to take out books above grade level."

"Yes. That's as good a place to start as any. Are you aware of her reading selections?"

I considered the question. It seemed to me that Tori had a different book on the go every few days. I told the librarian as much, and waited for her to come to the point.

"On the positive side of things, Tori makes varied choices in her reading material. I have her checkout history in front of me. She's been reading the *Harry Potter* series, and she's checked out every Farley Mowatt and every Judy Blume book we have. Some twice. She doesn't limit herself to fiction, either. Tori has selected books on martial arts, horseback riding, and even horticulture."

I was getting impatiently confused. "That's all great, Mrs. Smyth. But I'm not sure why any of this is a concern."

"It's her most recent selection that brings me to concerning issue. Last week Tori checked out a book called *Human Anatomy and Reproduction for Pre-Teens.*"

Uh oh.

"Now, I'll take some responsibility for this," the librarian continued. "I was away ill last week, and the substitute wouldn't have thought to check. Tori does have parental permission to sign out books designed for kids in grades six or seven, so it wouldn't have been flagged in our electronic system."

"Okay," I said, closing my eyes against the the beginnings of a headache.

Mrs. Smyth wasn't finished. "In and of itself, the reading of this book is not my biggest concern. It is the sharing of the information contained in the book that concerns me. One of the lunch monitors overheard a very animated conversation on the playground at recess today. After questioning the children, the monitor ascertained that Tori had started the...Err...Discussion."

"I'll speak with her," I assured Mrs. Smith.

"Much appreciated, Mrs. Lockhurst."

As I hung up the phone, my nagging headache graduated into throbbing pain.

Oh, Tori.

INTERLUDE
NOW

She tackled the stack of cream-coloured envelopes first, knowing that they would be the hardest. There was eighteen well-wishing cards altogether—the same number of years she had known Richie. She wondered absently if this was a coincidence or it it had a more significant meaning. Some, like the one from a cousin in New York, contained a heartfelt note and brought genuine tears to her eyes. Others, like the one from an estranged uncle, seemed to have been scribbled in a thoughtless moment and made her bristle with unreasonable anger. She wanted to throw them all into the garbage immediately, but worried that it might be an insult to those who sent them. Would an old boss be truly insulted if her generic sympathy card got tossed into the trash?

She had never lost someone close before, and didn't know if there was an etiquette to go along with the grieving process.

She flipped through the cards. They weren't the kind you could showcase on the fireplace mantle alongside birthday and anniversary cards. She hovered over the garbage can, but in the end she wedged the stack in between the microwave and the wall. Not quite out of sight, not quite out of mind.

The pile of bills in their business envelopes actually took longer than the sympathy cards. And, she felt, were more genuine. The threats to cut off the phone, or the cable, and the curt reminder that the Mastercard went unpaid for the third month in row—those were more real than all of the "Sorry For Your Loss" cards in the world. She felt comforted by their lack of flowery language. She stroked the final notices lightly with the tips of her fingers, and placed them gently beside the computer, ready to be paid as soon as convenient. She knew that when she called the creditors to explain the situation, she would be met with disingenuously sympathetic people on the other end. But for now, these demands without pleases, without thank you's, or any other courtesies, were the most *real* thing in her life. For that she was thankful.

She next sifted through the small piles of pinks, blues, and yellows. She found two more sympathy cards, a party invitation for someone's thirtieth birthday, a birth announcement, and finally, a belated birthday card containing a handwritten note from an old roommate. She wondered how it was that the roommate hadn't heard the news. She checked the postmark absently; it was over eight months old. She wondered if he had since learned the truth, and if he then felt guilty for sending the birthday card. She hoped that he didn't. She even hoped that somehow the roommate hadn't heard the news—that somewhere, in someone's mind, *he*—her mind didn't want to form his name—was very much alive. She hung the birthday card on the fridge.

At last, each envelope, with the exception of the small black one, was open, read, and given what she hoped was an appropriate place in the kitchen.

She realized suddenly that she was very hungry. The little black envelope sat temptingly in front of her, but her stomach grumbled insistently. She reluctantly set the card onto the centre of the table and pushed her chair out.

The house was quiet except for the sound of her stomach. The usual noise that accompanied her life, the sounds teenaged children—fighting, laughter, and a variety of technology-based chatter—was missing. Richie's mother had graciously agreed to take the children, for a week or two, at Laura's own vague request. And Laura hadn't cared if the agreement came from a genuine desire to ease her burden, from a sense of family responsibility, or even from pity. The relief she had felt immediately upon accepting the offer was almost embarrassing. She couldn't bear to look into Jordan's face—such a remarkable replica of his father's—and see her own tortured grief mirrored there. And Tori's anger was too close to Laura's own feelings of guilt.

Silence was eerie to one so used to a place full of sound.

So she hummed loudly and awkwardly to combat the stillness as she stared disconsolately into the refrigerator. It was full. Probably fuller than it had ever been before the day of the funeral. It was another show of people's good will. Flowers, cards, and casseroles. She picked at the tinfoil lid on one of the dishes. Tuna noodle. Perhaps for some people this was comfort food. It made her want to gag.

She closed the fridge and wandered to the pantry, where a box of *Lucky Charms* caught her eye. She started to fill a bowl and then realized that she couldn't recall if there had been any milk wedged in between the macaroni and the meatloaf. Shrugging her shoulders to herself, Laura grabbed the entire box and headed into the dark living room to eat in front of the silent television.

∾∿

It had been so long since she had really slept that she was completely surprised to find herself waking from such a dreamless state. Her hand was still in the box of Lucky Charms and her head was hanging at at awkward angle on the back of the couch. She stretched stiffly and settled herself into a more comfortable position.

Although she had heard that often after the loss of a spouse, the living partner would awake with the feeling that his or her loved one was still there, she did not feel that now. She had been going to bed by herself for so many months that it probably would have felt more unnatural to wake beside someone else than it did to wake alone.

She wondered absently what time it was, and then suddenly remembered the small black envelope. An eagerness gripped her. She stood up abruptly, and resisted the urge to run from the living room to the kitchen. She inhaled deeply and counted off nine small, quick steps from the couch to the hallway, and another twelve smaller, quicker steps from the hall to the kitchen table. With shaking hands, she grabbed the envelope from its resting place and pressed it to her chest. She forced her hands to be still, to breathe normally, to conquer her sudden fervor to rip the card open. After a moment or two, a sense of self-control returned and she was able to place the envelope back onto the table so that she could examine the writing on the outside more carefully. It was only then that she realized to whom it was addressed.

"Laura Morgan," she said aloud.

It had been almost two decades since she had been Laura Morgan. She picked up the envelope and considered what that implied. She read it and reread it. The card was definitely and purposely addressed to her maiden name.

Only one way to find out what that means, she thought.

She slid her thumb under the seal of the envelope, starting when the crisp, black paper gave her a stinging cut.

"Tori would say that this is a bad omen," she stated to the envelope.

But she was past bad omens. The worst had already come and gone with Richie's accident.

She pulled the contents of the envelope out gently. *A letter.* She unfolded it carefully, resisting the urge to scan to the bottom and reveal the identity of its author. There were so few people left in her life who had known her when she was Laura Morgan. She would read slowly, savoring each word as a tribute to here past.

Chapter 15
WAY BACK WHEN

Walking into a train station with someone who knew what he was doing was a totally different experience than going it alone as a tourist.

Paul walked casually and confidently to the correct line, not needing to ask directions or to look at one of the handy, hanging signs that indicated which ticket booth sold for which destinations. He waited patiently with his hand in my back pocket, kissing my neck every now and then as if he had been doing it for years rather than days.

The ticket agent cleared her throat and Paul smiled apologetically at her as he peeled himself off of me. I blushed.

"Two rail passes to Darlington via Newcastle," he told her. "Open return."

"Private car?" the ticket agent asked with a raised eyebrow.

I buried my face in Paul's shoulder. It was one thing to feel comfortable privately with our intimacy. It was a whole other thing to have it exposed to the public like this. But Paul didn't seem to mind at all.

"Not necessary," he said, laughing comfortably.

"Eleven pounds, please."

We held hands as we entered the train, and I felt a little thrill as we took our seats.

We stepped off of the train into cool mountain air. I was thankful that Paul had insisted on lending me a warm, plaid jacket.

"Welcome to Darlington," he said, pulling me into a hug.

"What's in Darlington?" I wondered.

I had desperately wanted to stay in Newcastle when we changed trains there, but Paul had ushered me along, pretending not to hear me as I listed of all the points of interest in that city.

"*We* are," Paul said teasingly. "Oh, and a museum. And a castle. But neither of those is our destination."

He flagged down a cab and whispered into the driver's ear.

Paul winked at me. "Enjoy the scenery."

"Is that your polite way of telling me to quiet down?"

He grinned innocently, but said nothing.

And it was a beautiful, beautiful countryside set in rolling, rocky hills. I watched it unfold from my window in awe. Eventually, we drove past less open land and more whitewashed farmsteads, and then finally into a little village. The cabbie stopped in front of seemingly random building. Paul paid him and we stepped out onto the sidewalk.

I looked around in amazement. Tidy lawns and ancient trees framed each house on the street. The homes were varying sizes and colours, but uniformly antique. The only indications of modernity were the telephone and electrical poles dotting the street.

"Gainford," Paul told me. "Circa ninth century, I think."

"*Ninth?*"

Paul nodded. "Ninth."

"Wow." I was astonished.

"See? I'm not completely uncultured. Or entirely immune to my country's history," Paul laughed. "I want to take you on a hike up the River Tees. It's unbelievable. But first, let's check into this bed and breakfast?" He indicated the unmarked building where the cabbie had dropped us off.

"Sure," I nodded, not knowing what to expect next, and loving every moment of it.

❧ ❧

The proprietress of the bed and breakfast greeted Paul with warm familiarity. She was in her mid-sixties and dressed in a terry cloth robe dotted with appliqué kittens. She had a universal grand-motherly appeal, and I liked her instantly.

"Paul!" she shouted, yanking him tightly into her ample em-brace. "Let me look at ya!" She pushed him out again, pinching his cheek comically. "I did not expect ya so late in the season! Your usual room is booked. Big to-do happening in town." She looked over and noticed me. She looked back at Paul. "But I clock that ya will be needin' a bigger room, anyway, yeah?"

Paul gave me an apologetic smile and spoke to her. "We will, Ma Kay. Or at least a bigger bed?"

The older woman chortled. "I can 'elp ya out, nah problem."

"Great," said Paul, "And my girlfriend likes tourist pamphlets. Oh, and a phone for her to call home?"

I warmed inside at being called his girlfriend.

"Do I 'ave pamphlets? Cheeky boy! Phone's on the table in the hall. Do I 'ave pamphlets!" Kay kept muttering to herself as she rummaged through an antique desk.

I ducked into the hall and dug out my calling card. I felt nom-inally guilty about the fact that I hadn't made an effort to reach my parents since my initial unsuccessful call. I glanced at my watch. It was three in the afternoon, making it seven in the morning at my parents' house. There was a possibility that I could catch them before work. I dialed, not sure if I was hoping that they answered, or if I hoped that they didn't.

The answering machine picked up.

"Hi, Mom. Hi, Dad," I tried to make my voice sound as smooth and bright as possible. "Wish I could talk to you. Keeping so busy here. Meeting great people. I'm in Gainford at the moment—don't panic I know it's not on my list, but I'm heading out for a world fa-mous hike—Oh, hey!" I cut off suddenly as Paul squeezed my rear end. "Gotta go, Mom. Love you both!"

I hung up and rounded on Paul, shaking my finger. "Excuse me. But as your 'girlfriend', I think I should warn you that my par-ents are worriers. Who knows what *that* message is going to make them think."

He chose to ignore me. "I have pamphlets," he said, waving them in my face. "I took our bag up to the room. Let's go for a walk before Kay ropes us into weeding her garden or hanging her laundry."

❧❧

Paul held my hand tightly as we walked through the quiet Gainsford streets.

"Do you believe in love at first sight?" he asked without turning his face toward me.

"You want the truth? Or for me to tell you what I think you want to hear?" I teased.

He stopped suddenly without letting go of my hand. I stumbled a little and he pulled me forcefully to his chest.

"Hey," I said breathlessly.

"Can't they be the same thing?" His eyes held mine. "The truth and what I want to hear?"

I broke my gaze from his and we started walking again.

"I'm not really a fairy tale kind of girl," I answered finally.

"That's evasive," he said.

"I'm just realistic," I told him.

"And realism doesn't include love?"

I shrugged.

"Soul mates?" he asked.

"No."

"That's depressing." He looked genuinely disappointed.

"Do you believe in that stuff?"

"Yes." He kissed me on the mouth, running his hands up and down my arms. He didn't pull away until my breath was coming in short gasps. "You didn't feel that? That spark?"

I nodded my head because I couldn't form a coherent sentence.

"But wishes can't come true?"

"I'm not a total cynic," I protested.

"Good," he said, "Because you're about to get one of *your* wishes answered." Paul pointed to a cardboard sign hung from a lamp post. "You're going to see that castle after all!"

த∾௫

"I still can't believe we're doing this," I shook my head at Paul.

"Shh," he said in a whisper. "They'll hear us. We need to find an opportunity to blend in without drawing too much attention to ourselves."

"Do you often crash weddings?" I whispered back.

"No," he answered, "But I'm sure one of the tricks to doing it successfully is *not* getting kicked out before the drinking starts, luv."

"I'm sure."

He ignored my sarcasm.

"Looking the part helps, too. I'd call that step one in the wedding crasher's handbook." He indicated our attire.

As soon as he had spotted the placard announcing the nuptials of Darla Small and Timothy Parker, Paul had rushed me back to the bed and breakfast and dumped out my bag of clothes. He searched through them hopelessly.

"What kind of girl brings only jeans, t-shirts, and trainers to Europe?" he had implored.

"The kind that doesn't expect to be doing things that will likely get her arrested," I answered. "Besides. Those aren't 'trainers', they're vintage AllStar Cons."

I didn't tell him that the other half of my wardrobe, left lying on his own bedroom floor to make room for adding Paul's clothes to my bag, was equally unsuitable for anything but casual sightseeing.

He had dragged me out to a formal wear shop in town and helped me select the dress and heels I was now wearing. It was a gown, really, and it was nothing that I would've chosen on my own. The dress was satiny, purple, and dotted with yellow flowers. The neckline plunged in an alarming way and the hem hit my calves. The dress had been expensive, but Paul had negotiated it down to thirty-five pounds, and had even talked the sales clerk into adding a teardrop shaped amethyst pendant for next to nothing. Paul himself wore a deep black suit, rented from a place beside the dress shop, with a yellow shirt and matching tie that he said went perfectly with my dress.

"Okay," I said. "Step one is complete, but is getting very wrinkled. Is it absolutely necessary that we continue to crouch behind these bushes?"

"I think we're almost good," he answered, laughing and standing up. "The processional is complete, photos will be next. And then right quick the guests will be making there way to that open area over there with the tables and fancy little lights, you see?"

I stood up, and finally got a full view of Raby Castle and the grounds it sat on. It was an amazing sight. I knew a little of what to expect from the pamphlets provided by Ma Kay, but nothing could have prepared me for the breathtaking reality. The outside of the castle looked untouched by the ages, with it's pale stone front and high turrets. I could almost picture medieval knights standing along its tower walls, or turn-of-the-century horse drawn carriages entering the courtyard through the enormous front gate.

"Wow," I said.

Paul grinned at me. "Stop that. You sound like a tourist."

"I *am* a tourist," I reminded him. "Can we go inside?"

"Maybe. Depends on what the bride's family paid for, I reckon."

"Please?" I asked. "And then have a look around the outside, too?"

The sprawling grounds called to me as much as the castle itself. From our vantage point I could see hills, and forest, and roaming deer. I knew that the wide brick wall I saw housed countless flowers, shrubs, and manicured trees. The wedding guests were making their way into the garden area to watch the bride and groom get photographed. I saw some servers in white jackets handing out glasses of champagne.

"Let's go down there now," I urged Paul. "There's so many people that they won't even notice us."

"So now *you're* the instigator?" he teased.

I blushed and pulled his arm a little, pointing to a break in the crowd of people. "There's a good spot."

"Do you have a boyfriend back home?" Paul asked me suddenly.

"No!" I answered as vehemently as I could in a self-conscious whisper. I forgot, momentarily, the castle and the wedding. "If I did, why would I be here with you?"

He shrugged. "I dunno. Maybe. European vacation. Distance. I'm not judging, luv."

A worrying thought occurred to me. "Do you have a girlfriend?"

Paul didn't answer me.

"Do you?"

He shook his head. "Why don't you have a boyfriend?" he asked.

"I'm shy," I told him.

"Liar."

"Okay, maybe not so much shy," I amended. "But I'm definitely more comfortable in a crowd of two than I would be at a party. And that's the truth." I turned to look at Paul. "You make me feel different, somehow. Back home, I don't have a lot of friends. I live with my parents, and I'm okay with that. I spend a lot of time reading, and walking in the park by myself. The wildest things about me are my taste in music and the way I dress. And if I could make myself like classical or Barry Manilow or feel comfortable in clothes that blend in, I'd do it."

Paul stared at me. "I love you," he said sincerely.

"That's crazy," I answered.

"Tell me that you don't love me, too."

"I can't," I sighed.

"Why?"

"Do you still want to crash this wedding?" I asked, not really caring, but desperate to change the subject.

"That's not an answer."

We stared at each other.

"I love you, too," I whispered finally.

"Good," he said. "Good."

"The wedding? The castle?" I prodded.

"I have something better," he smiled at me. "Let's go back to Kay's."

"What could be better than this?" I wondered sincerely.

"Tomorrow, I'm going to take you to meet my mother."

I laughed. "I don't think that many guys would trade in an open bar for their mothers."

Paul turned and looked me very seriously. "It's not every day a guy meets the girl of his dreams."

I turned away to hide my blush.

"Let's go," he said.

I sighed a little forlornly at the castle, but felt a surge of different excitement as Paul led me away.

❁

It was going to be very late when we finally arrived in Brighton. The one o'clock train from Darlington was supposed to get us there by supper time, but it had been delayed at the Derby station. The conductor had offered his personal apologies, blaming "technical problems" and adding that we would likely be stuck where we were for three hours. We were waiting not too patiently at a coffee shop just outside the train station. Paul said that the delay likely had to do with a dead body somewhere.

"You're making that up," I had said disbelievingly.

"A jumper or a dead old codger," Paul assured me knowingly. "Seen it before."

I had given him a dirty look and pretended to read one of the free newspapers as we waited. He had finally sighed and asked, "You wanna go 'round the pub? Derby has some fine ones. Right famous for 'em, you might say."

"No," I said irritably.

"Okay, okay." He sighed again. "There's probably no dead bloke."

"And?"

"Are you exploiting my guilt?" Paul asked.

"What do you have to feel guilty about?" I responded sweetly.

"That I tore you away from that lovely old castle out of Gainford, and now we're stuck here."

"And?"

"And do you want to go somewhere that's not a pub?"

"Like?"

Paul thought about it for a moment. "I'll be right back."

I watched curiously as he jumped up and ran back in the direction of the train station. He disappeared around the corner for about a minute and a half, and then came jogging back, out of breath and grinning.

"Hi there," I said.

He bent over with his hands on his knees, breathing a little hard.

"Are you going to be alright?" I asked.

"Out. Of. Shape," he answered. "Just. A. Minute." Paul reached into his back pocket and pulled out a brochure, as his breathing slowed. "Your favourite. A tourist pamphlet. Want to go see a really old church?"

I laughed. "Sure."

"Thank goodness. I got us some free bus tickets and vouchers for sandwiches at a shop up the street from St. Peter's." Paul said. He lowered his voice to a whisper and added, "But I can't *guarantee* there won't be any dead bodies there."

I laughed and let him lead me to the bus stop.

かーぐ

"Wait!" Paul said suddenly, stopping in front of a brick structure about half a block from where the bus had dropped us off.

A large glass door, tinted to near blackness, seemed to have caught his eye.

"What?" I wondered. I squinted at the neon sign that blinked lazily above the frame. It indicated that the building was open, but not what might be inside.

His eyes were twinkling a little bit too much, and I was immediately suspicious.

"Come in here with me," he commanded with a smile. "Before I change my mind."

He pulled on my hand and I followed him with exaggerated reluctance into the shop. My senses were assaulted by unfamiliar sights. A single low wattage bulb, covered by a sheer purple lampshade, hung suspended from the ceiling. It cast an eerie glow throughout the room, making it hard for my eyes to adjust to the darkened setting. I blinked a few times and tried to take in my surroundings.

The walls were the same brick as the exterior, and they were posted from floor to ceiling with graphic art. Some of the pictures were artsy, some cutesy, and others bordered on pornographic, making me blush. A large chair was mounted to the floor. It was reminiscent of the kind I'd seen in my dentist's office back home, but this one was made of chrome and had a black pleather seat.

"Is this a medieval torture room gone bad?" I joked, trying to ease my own tension.

Someone cleared his throat loudly from behind us, and I turned to see a very large, very bald man in full-on biker gear standing on the other side of a display counter. He was smoking a pungent smelling homemade cigarette and reading a comic book. There was an enormous shelf behind him, and it was full of colourful bottles, stacked binders, and bizarre-looking tools.

"Can a torture chamber get any worse than it already is?" the strange man wondered as he exhaled a thick stream of smoke. "Welcome to my shop."

Paul laughed, and pulled me close to him. "We want something in a matching set," he said.

"Does *she* know what she's buying into?" the man asked.

I narrowed my eyes, and suddenly I recognized the shop for what it was. "Tattoos?" I replied, turning to look incredulously at Paul. "You want us to get matching tattoos?"

He grinned at me in a charming way. "I was going to get you a postcard, luv, but I was worried that you'd just lose it."

"But tattoos?" I said again. "Of what?"

Paul shrugged. "I'll get your name, you get mine," he suggested.

I shook my head, picturing my mother's face. "Seriously? You don't think that's a bit..." I trailed off, searching for the right word. *Permanent? Preemptive? Impulsive?* I thought. "Crazy?" I said out loud.

The man behind the counter watched our exchange with mild amusement. He had picked up a pen and seemed to be doodling idly on the notepad in front of him. "What *are* your names?" he interrupted.

"Paul and Laura," we answered at the same time.

He made a few more quick movements across the paper, and then held up his handiwork. Two circles, each full of interlocking swirls and barely more than an inch long, adorned the page. The designs were almost identical except for a few subtle difference in the loops near the centre.

"Pretty," I stated admiringly. "Beautiful, actually. But what are they?"

"They're love knots," Paul told me softly. "See how you can't tell where the loops start or end?"

The tattoo artist set the paper down on the counter. Paul traced his fingers along the lines of the love knots. "And these ones are unique," he noted, pointing. "This one has a little 'L' in the middle, and this one has a 'P'. See?"

I looked more closely, following his fingers as they outlined the nearly indiscernible letters.

"You're very talented," Paul said to the man who smiled modestly. "They're perfect."

——

The tiny spot on my hip where I had been branded with Paul's initial burned pleasantly as we stepped back out into the crisply sunny afternoon. I covered my eyes against the sudden onslaught of bright light and clean air. The world looked different. Vibrant. New. We both stood there silently, inhaling the cool summer breeze.

"Dammit," Paul said, breaking the spell. He was rubbing the spot on his own hip that matched mine.

"Does it sting?" I asked. My own felt good. It reminded me of the nagging pain of loose tooth.

"A bit," he told me. "But that's not the problem. That old church is going to have to wait until our trip back. If we don't hop on the bus right now we're going to miss our train to Brighton."

"Why am I actually not surprised by that at all?" I sighed.

Chapter 16
THEN

Each of the kids' teachers had requested conferences via their final report cards, and as Richie and I stepped into Jordan's classroom, it was hard not to feel intimidated. I gripped my husband's hand tightly and he squeezed back gently. Mr. Lee and Mrs. Chancer were sitting together as we entered, and I greeted them uncomfortably.

"Uh, hi?"

Mr. Lee, Jordan's sixth grade teacher smiled at me reassuringly.

I did not feel reassured.

"Sorry to tag team you like this, Mr. and Mrs. Lockhurst," apologized Mrs Chancer. "But we really thought that it would be easier to discuss this with you together."

My unease grew.

"Jordan and Tori are both very bright children," Mrs. Chancer continued. "I had the pleasure of teaching your son last year, as I'm sure you remember."

I nodded.

"And I've had Tori in my advanced math tutorial as well as my gym class this year," Mr. Lee added.

"Have a seat," said Mrs. Chancer, "And we'll get right to the point."

Richard sat down on the edge of the chair that the teacher indicated and I hovered beside him.

"We'd like to send Tori up to grade seven next year," Mrs Chancer told me.

"Oh," I said, as partial understanding set in. "What does this have to do with Jordan?"

"Well," explained Mr. Lee, "We almost always consult with a team of people before considering placing a child ahead of his or her peers. On the academic side of things, that team usually consists of the child's teacher, the school principal, and our district psychologist. But it also usually includes a consult from the child's parents and other family members."

"Usually a sibling isn't too affected by this kind of upward movement, though we do need to be sensitive to feelings of inadequacy or other emotional needs that may arise as a result," Mr. Lee went on. "I wouldn't consider that a problem in a boy like Jordan. Not usually, anyway." He looked to his colleague for input.

Mrs. Chancer smiled at us. "The only reason we're so concerned is that this will place Jordan and Tori in the same grade. And we have no interest in fostering any kind of unhealthy competition between the two. But Tori really needs a challenge, and I'm sure you'll agree that she hasn't been getting one. And Mr. Lee does tell me that Jordan's grades and study skills are impeccable, nearly perfect. So Tori would be unlikely to surpass him on that front. The two would certainly not be placed in the same class."

"Fantastic," said my husband enthusiastically, and the two teachers grinned.

I sat silently, looking at the three of them. Their smiles faltered.

"Do you have any thoughts, Mrs. Lockhurst?" Mrs. Chancer finally asked.

"I'm a little overwhelmed," I admitted. "I think that we'll have to discuss it as a family."

"Of course," Tori's teacher said, smiling again. "But we'd like your permission to start performing the psych testing with Tori now. It's just to assess how well she will adjust to working with older students, having to move out of her peer group, etcetera. I have no doubt that she will sail through it, but with only two weeks of class left, time is of the essence." She looked at me eagerly.

"Do it," I replied with as much false enthusiasm as I could muster. "And if everything goes well, consider this my agreement for her placement in the seventhth grade next year."

I tried unsuccessfully, to assess where my feelings were coming from.

"Good!" Mr. Lee said. "And have no fear Mrs. Lockhurst, we don't make this kind of decision lightly."

"Thank you," I answered.

But when Richie and I climbed back into our van, I began, inexplicably, to cry.

☙❧

A polite knock at the door interrupted me as just as I sat down to sort through the dreaded Tupperware cupboard. It was on my list of least favourite things to do—trying to find lids to match each bowl, and tossing the rest into the recycling bin. I had been putting off the task for a few months, and I was regretful to stop again just after I got started. The knocking became insistent.

"Fine," I muttered to my Tupperware. "I will deal with *you* later."

I peeked through the spy hole in our front door, and was surprised to see Cindy standing there.

"Since when did you start knocking?" I asked as I swung the door open widely.

"Since you started locking it," she replied, breezing by me. Mike and Lee trailed grumpily along behind her.

"I didn't lock it," I told her. "Must've been Richie on the way out this morning."

I followed Cindy into the kitchen, where she rummaged around in one of my high cupboards until she found a bottle of Baileys. Ignoring the Tupperware strewn all about, she poured the liqueur and some old coffee into a mug, and then sat down heavily at the kitchen table. The boys dug into the plastic containers and began to build a tower. I watched my friend sip on her drink, make a face, and then take another sip.

"Something wrong?" I wondered. My friend's hair was sticking straight up and her make up was only applied to one half of her face.

"I have a business proposition for you," she told me.

"I don't like the sound of that," I answered. "I already have one job that I hate."

"So quit." Cindy took another big swig, and grimaced.

I sighed and poured the last of the coffee into my own mug. Cindy held out the Baileys and I shook my head.

"Suit yourself." She shrugged and topped up her cup.

"You know I don't really hate my job. It's just Karen," I informed her. "The woman doesn't like me. I don't know why she hired me."

"Maybe no one else applied."

"Thanks," I said sarcastically.

"It's been what? Over four years?" Cindy laughed. "If the woman really didn't like you, she would've found a reason to fire you by now."

"Weren't we talking about *your* problem?" I retorted.

"Business proposition," she corrected.

"Right," I agreed. "Business proposition. Hit me."

"Well, it's really for Tori," my friend explained.

Cindy went on to tell me how she had agreed to a curate a few exhibits for our local art museum. She was going to be needing someone to pick up Mike and Lee from school two to three times a week and then keep an eye on them at her house for about an hour.

"You think Tori would be interested?" she asked me. "Ten bucks a day?"

I shook my head, making a face. "Tori? With kids? I don't know if I *want* her to be interested. And she's only just going to be thirteen."

Cindy laughed. "Everyone starts somewhere. She might surprise you. Why don't we ask Tori herself."

As if on cue, my daughter came clattering through the backdoor into the kitchen.

"Ask me what?" she demanded and plopped herself in between Mike and Lee on the floor.

"If you want to make a hundred bucks a month to build Tupperware towers," Cindy told her, and my daughter's face lit up.

"Paid? To take care of these little dudes?" Tori grinned. She turned to Mike and Lee. "You guys want me to boss you around and feed you junk food?"

"Yes!" they chorused.

"Wonders never cease," I said.

"Are you really that surprised?" Cindy asked me. "Tori is exactly like you. And you're a great mom, so why wouldn't she be great with kids?"

"Alike?" Tori and I said at the same time, and Cindy laughed.

"Quit trying to butter me up," I joked.

I sipped my coffee thoughtfully. Tori was loud, outgoing, and all raw emotion. I shook my head. Whatever Cindy thought, we were about as dissimilar as could be,

ॐ✺

Jordan, on the other hand, had always been solitary, more like me in personality, *I* thought, than like his amiable dad. So I was a little surprised when he approached me right before his fourteenth birthday to ask, "Mom, I need a favour."

"Sure," I said automatically without looking up from the bills I was sorting. With Tori, I would've waited until she'd described the favour in detail before agreeing to it. My daughter had a new plan each month. This year alone I had been coerced into paying for a professional grade make up kit, a sewing machine, singing lessons, a Whistler ski trip, and briefly—to my absolute delight—a children's photography course. She was good at everything she tried, and each new undertaking had lasted only as long as it was challenging, and then Tori moved on to the next thing.

But Jordan rarely asked me for anything except comic books and computer games.

He sat down beside me at the table, and I finally took a look at him. There was a funny sparkle in his blue eyes and a sheepish grin on his face.

"Anything you like," I said enthusiastically.

"Well, I'd like to have a party," he told me, looking down at his hands nervously.

"A *birthday* party?" I asked, surprised.

His ninth birthday party had been his last by his own request. We had pushed him into pool parties, bowling parties, and laser tag parties until he had looked at me solemnly one day and said, "Mom. No more parties please. It's not that I hate them. But I don't want them. I'd rather just hang out with Jake and Brian. And you and dad. And Tori if I have to."

So each year we just let him do a pizza dinner, and a movie outing with his dad and two best friends while I stayed home with Tori. It was actually so much easier than throwing a birthday party for twenty-odd kids that I was totally happy to stick with the semi-private celebration.

"Really?" I asked. And then something in his face made me add, "What kind of party?"

Jordan grinned awkwardly. "A boy-girl party?"

"Really?" I was even more surprised to hear this. Jordan never mentioned girls, not in a general sense, nor anyone in particular from school. He didn't even remark on pretty actresses or singers, and I had a hard time picturing him involved in the kinds of activities that took place at a mixed, teen party.

"Yeah," he said, looking more and more uncomfortable.

"But you don't like parties," I reminded him.

"I know," he answered. He waited silently.

"Okay then. A boy-girl party. With music and stuff?" I asked. I did my best to sound as disinterested as possible. "We could do that. Set stuff up in the rec room, buy some chips and snacks, maybe order some pizza. We'll make sure that Tori is on a sleepover or something."

"Yeah?" he sounded relieved.

"Absolutely," I said.

"Awesome!" he exclaimed, and got up to leave. He hesitated at the kitchen door. "Mom?"

"Uh huh."

"Nothing," he said, but kept standing in the doorway.

"Okay," I answered patiently, waiting. I knew he was struggling to get something out.

"I like this girl," he finally confessed.

"Okay," I said again.

"Her name's Tessa," he told me. "She's smart and pretty, and even likes comics, too. And really, I just wanted to ask *her* to do something with me. But I told Jake, and he told me not to tell Brian because Brian would make fun of me. So I didn't. And then Brian asked me if we were going to the movies like we usually do and I said we were doing something else. And..."

"You panicked?" I asked sympathetically.

"I guess, yeah. And I told Tessa. That I like her, and wanted to hang out for my birthday," he added. "And she told me that her dad probably wouldn't let her go alone to the movies with me anyway, so then I came up with the party idea. You know, spontaneously. By accident."

I looked a my son with a new respect. He obviously had a confidence that I lacked at that age. I wanted to ask him how he told her but resisted. "It's a good plan," I said instead.

"Thanks, Mom." Jordan came over and to give me an appreciative hug. "And it's okay if Tori wants to come," he added. "Tessa's in her class anyway."

"Very generous," I said, smiling into his shoulder. "Just one thing," I whispered, not being able to help but play the mom-card. "No spin the bottle."

My son wriggled loose of my grip and almost ran from the room, leaving me grinning down at my bills.

જી્જી

"I'm only going to greet the guests as they come through the door," I assured my son and daughter as we waited for the first kids to arrive.

Jordan rolled his eyes, an uncharacteristic gesture for him. "You just want to know which one's Tessa, Mom."

"I want to know who everyone is," I told him.

"Riiiiiight," said Tori, dragging the word out so that it had four syllables.

I was saved by the first knock on the door. "Why don't you guys go downstairs and I'll let people in," I suggested. "I won't do anything to embarrass you, I promise."

"Your definition of embarrassment might be different than ours," Tori informed me, and Jordan nodded with a worried expression on his face.

"I'm glad to see you two finally agreeing on something," I teased. "Go on downstairs so that you can pretend you don't know me."

I tried at first to keep track of the guests' names as they came through my door, but after four or five, they all started to blur together. The kids came mostly in little groups, mumbled their names and then ran as fast as they could towards the music in the basement. There was a girl named Ryan and two boys named Cody. A tiny Asian kid told me that his Canadian name was Troy. A giggling trio of girls came through, and between laughs said that they were Georgia, Mackenzie, and Hayley, but I didn't know which one was which.

One girl's mother actually accompanied her to the door. The poor thing stood in silent embarrassment as her mom grilled me for details of the party. I hoped for Jordan's sake that this wasn't Tessa.

"How many kids?" the woman asked nervously.

"Forty-six were invited. All of the kids in the eighth grade," I smiled.

"That's a lot," she told me.

I gritted my teeth and made a mental note to remind Tori and Jordan how lucky they were to have *me* as their mother.

"Is it?"

"Are you here alone?" the other mom asked.

"I've got my husband for back up," I assured her. And then added, with a hidden smile, "And my neighbour is a very accessible."

She narrowed her eyes, but looked momentarily satisfied. "Fine. Go in, Dee."

Not Tessa, thank goodness, I thought selfishly.

The mom stood on the porch until her daughter scuffled off to join the other kids in the basement. "I hope you know what you're getting into," she warned before turning on her heel and stomping away.

"I think I need a drink," I said out loud as I closed the door behind that one.

After about an hour, I was so tired of greeting kids that I almost didn't notice Tessa's arrival. I had propped the door open and was just waving people silently toward the party as they sauntered in.

"You're much cooler than my mom," one of them commented as I gave him and his buddy a cursory glance from behind my laptop.

"Yeah," the other one agreed. "My mom would be hanging around asking everyone's name and stuff."

I rolled my eyes. "Thanks, guys. C'mon in."

A girl came in behind the two boys and lingered when they went downstairs.

"Hi," I said uncertainly when I saw her standing there.

"Hi," she sounded just as uncertain.

We stared at each other. She was cute in a bookish way, with little round glasses, mousy brown hair, and a plump figure.

"I'm the mom," I announced.

"I'm the Tessa," she said, and then we both laughed.

"Welcome." I smiled at her, glad to see that my son hadn't selected a girl with too much makeup, over-styled hair, or high maintenance appeal.

"I think this party is my fault," she confessed.

"Really?" I asked, wondering what Jordan had told her and what she had pieced together herself.

"I told Jordan that my dad wouldn't let me date?" she made it sound like a question.

"So you did," I agreed.

"I like him. Jordan." Tessa blushed a little and it made her little face turn from pretty to beautiful. She adjusted her glasses and smiled at me. "I'm not ready for a relationship," she added earnestly. "But he thinks that we might get married one day."

"Is that right?" I replied with careful indifference.

"I'm a smart girl, Mrs. Lockhurst," she told me. "And I know that most people don't meet their future spouses at thirteen-going-on-fourteen. But I think that Jordan means it. He's very serious."

"He usually is," I said, unsure how else to proceed.

Tessa brightened. "Okay, then. Just thought you should know. Nice to meet you. I'm going down to the party now."

Tori came up and brushed by Jordan's love interest as Tessa went down the stairs.

"More chips, Mom," she said. "Was that 'the one'?"

"It sure was," I answered, grabbing the chips from the cupboard.

Tori rolled her eyes. "Can you believe she's gonna be my sister-in-law?" She took the chips, rolled her eyes again and walked away.

"Somehow," I said to myself, "I don't have too much trouble believing that at all."

Chapter 17
THEN

I sighed as I walked in the front door, arms full of groceries. "Boys!" I called out half-heartedly. "Little help?"

I wasn't really expecting a response. After a lot of begging and pleading, Richie had finally got me to relent and he and Jordan had hooked a PS3 to the television in the basement. I had been against the idea, worried that Jordan, Jake, and Brian were going to be spending every spare second in our basement abusing their access to a variety of virtual worlds.

"Don't be such a mom, Mom," Jordan had complained.

"Wouldn't you rather have the game system here?" my husband had asked. "Then you'll know where they are and what they're up to."

Tori had rolled her eyes. "Just let them do it. It'll free up more computer time. *And* stop their whining."

Three against one.

"I know you're here!" I said as I set down the groceries onto the counter. "You can't hide down there forever!"

Brian's enormous boots in the front hall had been a dead giveaway. Somehow, in the last six months, the gangly fifteen year-old had gone from skinny nerd to hulking young man. There had been an awkward moment last month when I had caught all three boys eating the cupcakes I had baked for a bake sale. I had started reprimanding them, realized suddenly that I was yelling *up* at them rather than *down*, and I had been unable to finish my lecture. They had all stared at me with crumbs hanging from their mouths as I stomped away, giggling.

I sighed again and went back to the car for my second load. I moved Brian's boots to the side as I began unpacking and hoped that Jake and Jordan hadn't worn their shoes downstairs. Berber carpet can only take so much teenage traffic. Their ability to destroy is both amazing and appalling.

A loud blast of music suddenly pulsated through the heating vent. "What is going on down there?" I muttered.

Looking for an excuse to investigate, I grabbed a bag of potato chips, a bottle of pop and a stack of plastic cups. I stood at the top of the stairs, listening. I couldn't hear anything but the music.

"Coming down!" I called politely, knowing that they wouldn't hear me anyway.

I walked down the stairs in deliberate, heavy steps, keeping my fingers crossed that the loud music was not accompanied by PlayBoy magazines or worse, internet porn.

"Oh my god," I said said loudly and slowly as I rounded the bottom of the staircase. I dropped the pop bottle.

Brian's large frame leaped from the couch, and a smaller, topless, female figure tumbled to the ground. His face was a crimson mask of horror, as he struggled to buckle his belt and straighten his shirt so that it covered his stomach. I took a moment to digest what was going as the girl on the floor righted herself, grabbed her sweater, pulled it over her head and plopped down onto the couch. Then I recognized her.

"Tori?" I managed to say, going almost as red as Brian.

"Mrs. Lockhurst," Brian began, "I'm sorry. I tried to tell her it was a bad idea, coming here, like this. I wanted to..." he trailed off.

"Sock," I told him, pointing at the wayward article of clothing on the coffee table.

He grabbed it and worked to put it on without sitting beside my daughter.

"Geez, Mom," Tori said in a irritated voice.

I cut her off with a look.

"Out." I tried to smile in a forgiving way at Brian, but must've failed miserably because he bolted wordlessly for the stairs.

I waited until I heard the front door slam shut. Then I powered off the stereo, and rounded on my daughter.

"Don't even start," she said to me.

"I was going to say exactly the same thing," I retorted.

"What're you going to tell me? That my behaviour is unbecoming? That I'm not old enough? Or that Brian is *too* old?" Tori demanded.

I sat down. "Yes. To all of those things," I sighed heavily, anger slipping from my body. "And I'm sure that you're going to tell me that you two are in the same grade, that you're not doing anything different than anyone else your age and that I don't understand because I'm too old to get it."

"So now what?" Tori asked without looking at me.

I examined her profile. She was so different than I was at fourteen. Bold, daring, already possessing a self-riteous sense of being and a style all her own. "You're more grown up now than I was at twenty," I told her.

Tori looked at me with surprise. "You're not mad?" she asked.

"I'm plenty mad," I said. "And disappointed. And embarrassed that I didn't see this coming."

She tried to interrupt, but I held my hand up to stop her.

"I want to talk to you like a grown up, in a way that will make you understand my point of view and not get your back up," I continued, "But I'm not sure that I know how."

"I'll to try listen," my daughter told me, probably hoping that her acquiescence would stop her from getting grounded for life.

"Good," I answered, feeling relieved. "Now do you even like Brian? From what little tabs I manage to keep on your social life, he doesn't seem like your type."

Tori shrugged. "Not like that," she admitted. "He's alright and stuff. Smarter than most guys my age. He's kinda cute in a dorky way. Better than a jock, but maybe not as good as a punk."

I couldn't tell if she was joking.

So what the hell were you thinking? I wondered silently. Aloud I said, "So why choose him?"

"It's hard for me, Mom. I'm only fourteen. I won't even be fifteen until November. Some of the girls in my classes will be seventeen by this time next year. The boys think I'm just a kid. I didn't wanna be the very last one to kiss somebody." Tori seemed unembarrassed by this confession.

"And Brian?" I pressed

She shrugged again. "Easy target?"

I winced. "That doesn't sound very nice."

Tori rolled her eyes. "Fine. We have three classes together this semester and he sat with me in Biology and behind me in French. I thought he did it because I'm Jordan's sister, but then I noticed that he was always looking at me. Like, *looking* at me looking at me. And he really is kinda nice."

"You took advantage of him?" I couldn't help but say.

"Mom! Don't make me sound like that. I was being scientific about it, not trying to seduce him. Anyway, it wasn't as easy as I thought. Brian is a bit of a prude, it turns out. Did you know that his parents are devout Baptists? He's never come close to kissing a girl, either. Well, he hadn't before today." She laughed a little helplessly.

Good for you, Brian, I thought.

"It took me three weeks to get him to even come home with me. And, I mean, he's here all the time anyway. What difference did it make that *I* invited him here?" Tori explained with irritation. "And then he wouldn't kiss me with tongue. So much for first base. Even after I took my top off and tried to undo his pants."

Thank God for that. "So what does that teach you?" I asked.

I watched my daughter, seeing her for the young woman that she was already. She seemed impossibly beyond her years—so much so that I felt inadequate to dole out this kind of advice

"Not what I was hoping," Tori answered, pretending to pout. "And that not everything I learned about boys on *The OC* is true."

I knew she was being sarcastic, but I answered her anyway. "It's usually far less dramatic, tonnes more stressful, and does not generally involve weeks of plotting."

"Cause you know so much about boys?" Tori asked.

"I did exist before I met you father," I answered guardedly. "And I have had a first kiss."

"And it wasn't Dad?"

"And it wasn't in my parent's basement."

Tori looked at me with a little too much interest.

Melinda A Di Lorenzo

I decided to change the subject. "But we're still talking about you, here."

"How could I forget?"

"Switching back to mom-mode," I warned. "You are smart. You are pretty. It is not fair to use Brian like that. And it is perfectly okay to wait for the right boy, even if it means that you are the last girl—on earth—to get kissed. With tongue."

"Okay, Mom."

"Is there a boy, Tori?" I asked, looking at her carefully.

"Maybe," she said.

"A punk rocker?" I wondered.

She laughed.

"What?" I asked.

"Please don't ever say 'punk rocker' again," my daughter advised.

"You can talk to me about anything. I give pretty solid advice."

"Sure, Mom." Again, I couldn't tell if she was being sarcastic or not.

"Even condoms, when it comes to that."

"Gross, Mom!"

I could tell that she was starting to tune me out again.

"All I'm saying is that there are better—and more appropriate—ways to attract a boy than taking off your shirt," I told her.

"Like what?"

"Try a bit of makeup," I suggested. "Maybe a pretty outfit. Show off your brains. Find someone who's style you admire, and emulate them."

Tori looked at me like I was from another planet, and I realized that the spell that let me have this brief and tenuous connection with my daughter was broken.

She rolled her eyes, standing up. "Are we done?"

"Sure."

"Thank God," she said, and ran up the stairs.

છ✍

-150-

Jordan sauntered into the kitchen with a grin on his face.

"What's up?" I asked suspiciously.

He grabbed a granola bar and an apple—his preferred breakfast—and sat down at the table.

"Nothing," he answered without meeting my gaze.

"Uh huh," I said, sitting across from him with my coffee. I pretended to start a crossword puzzle.

My son and I often sat this way in the morning after Richie had left for work and before Tori had crawled out of bed. I watched Jordan out of the corner of my eye. He was tapping his hand against his thigh in time with some beat in his head as he examined his math textbook. He had started to change lately, trading in his comic books and using the money to buy guitar magazines. He had also been adding items to his standard jeans and t-shirts wardrobe. This morning he was dressed in fitted pinstripe pants, a short-sleeved black dress shirt, and a gray button front, Mr. Rogers style sweater. Jordan had recently adopted a new hairstyle that was as long as his chin in the front and short everywhere else. And although he hadn't mentioned it, and I hadn't asked, I was pretty sure that he had been using gel to keep his unruly locks in perfect place over his forehead. When we had gone to the mall together the week before, I had caught a young clerk checking him out in none too subtle way.

"Mom, stop staring at me," Jordan complained.

"Sorry," I said. "But I know that something's up."

"Nothing's up," he insisted guiltily.

"Jordan, unfortunately for you, you're an open book," I told him.

"Should I be apologizing for being a bad liar?" He tried to look irritated but failed as his mouth turned up at the corners.

"You could at least fake some teen angst," I suggested.

"Tori was sure out late last night," Jordan answered.

"Are you trying to change the subject?" I asked.

"Nope." His face was back to a full cat-that-caught-mouse grin. "Merely suggesting that someone else has already laid claim to every bit of teen angst available in the neighbourhood."

As if on cue, I heard a crash from upstairs, followed by Tori's door slamming loudly and a string of emphatic swear words.

Jordan leaped up a little too quickly. "See you, Mom." He stuffed his math book into his backpack and flew out the door.

I waited at the table, prepared with a reprimand regarding Tori's creative language. But as my daughter entered the room, the words caught in my throat. She was dressed in form-fitting, midnight black, stretch jeans tucked into lace up boots and a shiny black corset that left little to the imagination. Tori's eyelids were painted with silver and black makeup, and a horseshoe shaped piercing dangled from the centre of her nose.

"Hi, Mom. Bye, Mom," she said, rolling her eyes at me as she grabbed her shoulder bag and sauntered out the door.

I started at her, thinking that maybe hair gel didn't seem like such a big change at all.

The phone rang suddenly, interrupting my thoughts.

"Yes," I answered.

"It's me," Cindy said. "I meant to tell you. Last night Tori came by and asked for some advice."

"About?"

"Impressing a boy," Cindy told me. "Clothes and makeup, that kind of thing."

"Is that right?" I asked.

"Just wondering if she took any of my advice?"

"Oh, she took it alright," I replied. "Maybe a step too far."

"Pardon?"

"Nothing. Yes, she took your advice."

"Good." Cindy sounded please.

"One thing though," I said.

"Sure."

"Make sure that the second Mike and Lee are looking for some input on impressing girls, they come directly to me."

My friend laughed, and I hung up the phone.

Chapter 18
WAY BACK WHEN

I stretched groggily, wondering why it was dark.

"What is it with you and trains?" Paul teased.

"Did I sleep through the whole trip?" I groaned.

"Yes, luv, you sure did," he informed me as he grabbed my backpack from the storage compartment and led me out of the train and into the station.

"Is it a long walk to your parents' house?" I asked, feeling exhausted in spite of my nap.

"Not long," he said. "But I wanted to make a little stop first."

"Ugh," I replied, and just then we rounded the corner and I caught sight of Brighton Pier. The lights took my breath away. I was suddenly wide awake.

"Not bad, right?" Paul smiled.

"It's no centuries old castle, bit it *is* quite pretty," I conceded.

"So you don't want to check it out?" he asked.

"Yes, please," I said without even trying to conceal my delight.

"Perfect," he said.

৵৵

By the time we actually stepped onto Brighton Pier, I had already downed the two cans of Shandy that Paul had purchased at a corner store, and was feeling pleasantly giggly. Paul was sipping his own drink slowly, and pretending to object as I insisted on swilling a bit of his raspberry flavoured vodka myself.

"Please don't chuck up," he teased.

"I'm not drunk," I told him, and promptly tripped over a loose board at the edge of the pier.

"Oof!" I said as I landed on one knee.

"Not at all drunk," Paul agreed. He leaned over to help pull me to my feet, but tumbled down on top of me instead.

"You did that on purpose," I accused.

"I swear that I didn't," he protested. "I've *already* seduced you, remember?"

"Oh. Right," I agreed.

We stood up together, laughing.

"Let's go on the ferris wheel," Paul suggested.

"I thought that you didn't want to get thrown up on?" I asked.

"It might be worth it in exchange for the romance," Paul told me. He pulled me forward a few steps.

"Eww," I replied. "Romance?"

"That's a problem area for you, isn't it?" he joked as he kept walking.

"Wait," I said, stopping as I spotted something purple and shiny from the corner of my eye.

"You want candy floss?" Paul asked, misinterpreting my curious gaze.

"No, not that booth, silly," I said.

Paul groaned, shook his head and stood in front of me, blocking my view. "Oh no. Not that."

"What is it?" I asked, trying to push around him.

He sighed and let me pass.

A tall, narrow box made of wood planks with a plexiglass front stood up against the railing. It was wedged between a prize booth and a snack stand. A life sized female mannequin sat behind the smoky plastic. Her dark hair was pulled into a bun at the nape of her neck, and her eyes were an unnatural turquoise. One painted eyebrow was raised in an inquiring expression, and her mouth was set in an a half-smile. Her hands rested on her knees and her feet were hidden beneath the soft folds of a dress that was vaguely Arabian. I leaned in curiously, and jumped back when she suddenly raised one of her hands and pointed right at me.

"Too-rist," Paul said in a phony Scottish accent.

I gave him a dirty look. I put my hand at level with the mannequins and pressed against the plexiglass. As I leaned in again, I could see that her hands and jaw were both jointed.

"She's quite stunning, isn't she?" I whispered.

Paul slid his arms around my waist. "If you like creepy. Here, put a quid in that slot on the side of the box." He tried to hand me a one pound coin.

"You do it," I said with a little shiver.

He laughed his coughing laugh. "Fraidy cat."

"You're the one who said she was creepy," I retorted.

Paul rolled his eyes and reached down to stick the coin into the little slot. The mechanical woman blinked twice, and her other arm came up beside the first one. Her wrists made a clicking noise and her hands spun so that the palms faced upwards. Her mouth opened and closed several times as a breathy, recorded voice intoned, "Lady Jasmine knows all. What is said can not be unsaid. Your fortune is told."

The mannequin's hands flipped back over and her arms came down to rest on her knees. One eye closed in an exaggerated wink, and I heard the whirring of some internal gears. After a moment a little card slid out from beside the coin slot. I reached for it, but Paul was quicker.

"Hey," I protested.

"No way," he told me. "The Lady's fortunes only apply to those who pay for them."

It was my turn to roll my eyes. "Are you at least going to tell me what it says?"

He read the card aloud slowly, in a mockingly ominous voice. "This. Is not your destiny."

"That's what it says?" I asked.

"Think you can do better?" he responded, quickly sticking the card into his pocket.

"Hmm." I dug through my little brown satchel until I found a one pound coin. I stuck it into the machine and watched as Lady Jasmine repeated her performance. I grabbed my fortune before Paul could and laughed as I read it.

"What does it say?" he wondered.

I showed him.

"Your future happens later," Paul read, and then grinned. "How enigmatic," he said. "But you should know that her fortunes always come true."

"Is that right?" I asked, trying to look serious. "You're a regular user then?"

Paul met my eyes. "I got my first fortune when I was twelve, but it never made sense to me until now."

"Okay. I'll humour you. What did that one say?" I asked.

"No way," he said.

"Please?" I begged.

He gave me a contemplative once over. "You won't believe me anyway."

"I'll try," I promised.

"No."

"Please?" I repeated.

"Fine," Paul conceded. "But no laughing or teasing. It said, 'A foreign girl will break your heart'."

I stared at him. "Really?"

He laughed. "No!"

I punched him lightly in the shoulder.

"Hey," he said. "It said a foreign girl would break my heart. Not my arm."

"Jerk. Liar."

"But I did prove something," Paul told me.

"Oh, yeah? What's that?" I asked.

"That you have at least one romantic bone in that cynical body of yours," he grinned. "Isn't that right, luv?"

I groaned. "I think that I just got tricked into a ride on the ferris wheel."

&∞&

The view from the top of the Brighton Pier ferris wheel made me a little breathless. I could see straight out across the ocean from one side, and I could see the twinkle of the city lights from the other. I didn't even realize that I was leaning out of the little swinging seat until Paul grabbed my arm to restrain me.

"Whoa," he said, pulling me into the warmth of his body. "This isn't exactly how I want to lose you."

I leaned closer, drawing his scent. Cigarettes, alcohol, and cheap cologne.

"I'm not going anywhere," I laughed.

"Do you promise?" he asked, suddenly tense beside me.

I could feel each one of Paul's fingers pressed against the muscle in my upper arm. I stared at his hand, trying to figure out how such heat could come from those five tiny points on someone else's body. Gooseflesh crept from my exposed shoulder down to the crook of my elbow and along my forearm. Paul's nails were chewed down halfway to the quick, and the tips looked very red against my pale skin. I shivered against the cool air and dragged my gaze up to his face. The fiery energy in his eyes matched his grip perfectly.

"Where would I go?" I replied seriously.

"Anywhere but here?" he retorted with such a shattered look that I felt my own heart freeze.

What would happen when I had to go home? The thought caused a panic, sharp and painful in my chest. I gasped, startled at my response.

"I won't," I said fiercely. "I won't go. Anywhere. But. Here."

                                  ॐॐ

When we had reached the street he said was his, some of the fervor had worn off. Paul still held my arm possessively, but we were laughing again and the raspberry vodka was almost gone.

Paul held the bottle up, scrutinizing it in the street light. The equivalent of a few shots was left in the bottom. "Too much to drink now," he said thoughtfully. "I'll put it behind that bush for tomorrow night." He took a step toward an overgrown shrub in front of a pinkish house, tripped over his own feet and landed right in the middle of foliage.

I tried to hold in a giggle as I yanked him to his feet. "Will your mom be mad if you bring it inside?"

Paul looked at me like I had sprouted a third eye, shaking his head. I touched my forehead self-consciously. "What?"

"You have mummy issues, luv," he told me.

"I don't," I protested and giggled again.

He raised a disbelieving eyebrow. "My own mother may not think I'm a grown up, but she has no choice but to admit that I *am* old enough to purchase alcohol."

"My mom will never let me buy alcohol. Not even when I'm sixty. Not even cooking wine," I laughed at my own joke.

"Insight into your psyche is fascinating, luv. But I really must pee. And I can't climb up there with a bottle in one hand and your knapsack in the other." Paul pointed at a large, latticework trellis behind the bushes. It was covered in thick vines from the ground up, and it looked to be over twice my height. Twelve feet, I estimated.

"You're kidding, right?" I asked, forgetting all about both of our mothers. "We can't just go in the front door?"

Paul shrugged. "Left my key in Scotland. Parents aren't exactly expecting me. Sorry. Us. And I'm not going to ring the doorbell in the middle of the night. Unless you want me to?"

He made a move toward the front door.

"No!" I almost shouted.

"Best plan out your attack, then," he said with a grin.

I gave him a dirty look and then purposefully grabbed ahold of the piece of latticework that looked least likely to collapse under my weight.

"It is a damned shame that you are wasting all your charm on being so devious. You should really consider using your powers for good," I muttered as I pulled myself up reluctantly.

Paul reached his hands up and pushed helpfully on my rear end. "I'll be sure to put some thought into that," he said.

I pulled myself up slowly, alternating with my hands and feet. The muscles in my shoulders burned as I forced my ascent higher.

"You're almost there," Paul called softly from right underneath me.

"Assuming that I don't fall off and land on your head," I answered through my gritted teeth. But as I reached up one more time, my hand met with a solid slab of wood.

"That's the deck," Paul told me. "If you lift your left foot up about eight inches and a little to your right, you'll be stepping on a cement brick. It should give you enough leverage to get onto the patio."

"You've done this before?" I asked as I followed his instructions. I heaved myself onto the deck and then lay there panting. Paul was beside me almost immediately.

"Good thing my parents haven't thought to fix the railing. I pulled it off when I was about fifteen so that I could get up and down," he laughed.

"You're crazy," I stated between breaths.

"C'mon," he said, holding out his hand. "Welcome to my childhood home."

He slid open a glass door and I followed him in, my heart still beating crazily in my chest. We collapsed together, in the dark, onto his bed.

Chapter 19
WAY BACK WHEN

I could hear someone knocking persistently on Paul's bedroom door. I reached over to the other side of the bed, hoping to shake Paul awake. His spot was empty.

"Oh, great," I groaned. The room was pitch black. I fumbled around at the bottom of the bed in search of my jeans.

"I know you're in there," called a harsh, British female voice.

Paul's mom, I was sure. *Is she angry?* I wondered. *Where the heck is Paul?*

"I know you're in there," she said again, more loudly. "And I've run you a bath."

"Um, just a second," I called back, feeling more than a little awkward about making this woman wait in her own home.

Paul had said nothing the night before about leaving me here alone. I dug through the blankets and pillows, sighing in relief when I finally located my jeans. I grabbed them and yanked them on. My head was throbbing and my throat felt dry and scratchy. Nausea overwhelmed me as I finally stood up.

Hungover, I thought, placing the feeling. *Great. Just what I need.*

I grabbed the nightstand to steady myself. A shirt—not my own—was draped over the lamp. Deciding that I didn't care, I pulled it on quickly. Better to be caught wearing Paul's shirt that to be caught shirtless altogether. As I unlocked the door, I wished for a ridiculous moment that I had a mirror to check my hair.

"There's our Canadian girl," said a short, very stout woman from the doorway. She stepped into the room. "It's dark in here and it smells terrible. Paul been smoking inside again?"

I struggled to remember. "Probably," I said helplessly.

"I'm Aggie," she informed me. "Paul's mother. Anything he told you about me is a lie." She chortled at her own joke, and the sound was a barking cough that reminded me of Paul's own laugh.

Aggie strode past me and gripped one of the heavy blue curtains that lined the room. She flung it open, and then stalked around to pull back the rest of them.

"Oh!" I said as the light hit me. My head pounded in response.

The room looked different when it was completely lit. The curtains had hidden windows that wrapped around two of the walls, as well as the sliding glass doors we'd snuck in through last night. I walked over and squinted against the sun, blinking at the panoramic view of Brighton Beach.

"Oh," I said again, stepping to the window and resting my forehead against the cool glass.

"Much to drink last night?" Paul's mother asked. She laughed again. "That bath I run you and some tea will straighten you right out."

"Umm. Okay," I agreed unsurely.

She led me out of Paul's bedroom, through a hall decorated with old photographs, and down a wooden staircase so narrow that her hips rubbed against the walls as we descended.

"Old house," Aggie grumbled as the stairs creaked under her weight.

She showed me into a tiled bathroom where an old fashioned claw foot tub stood full of sudsy water, and then she handed me a big fluffy towel.

"And don't forget to wash your hair. Those Dunhills my Paul smokes really stink up a girl," she told me. "Tea in twenty minutes."

❧❧

I sat awkwardly across from Paul's mom, munching self-consciously on the biscuits she had provided. I was also wearing the satin robe she had given me—a flowered deal that was two feet too long and two feet too narrow to belong to Aggie herself. I tried not to wonder where it came from. My hair was still damp from the bath and the cool breeze coming off of the ocean made me thankful for my hot tea.

Each time I stopped chewing, Aggie asked me another question about Canada, about my family, and about my life back home. She also told me the details of the seamstress business she ran from home, and filled me in on some of Brighton's history. If my mouth was full, she seemed content with nods and vague murmurs, so I tried to chew each bite slowly, and ate twice as many cookies as I should have.

"You're an only child?" she asked.

"Mmm-hmm," I answered, mouth full.

"Spoiled?" she wondered.

"I hope not," I replied truthfully, swallowing the last crumbs of my biscuit. "Over protected, maybe."

There was only one more cookie left on the plate to shield me from her questions, and Aggie grabbed it herself and bounced it on her palm a few times.

"Bit young still?" she asked.

"Almost nineteen," I told her. I did my best to keep a defensive note out of my voice, but also knew that claiming to be *almost* an age made me seem even younger.

She grunted a response that I didn't hear, and her eyes suddenly became sharper, focusing on my face. I felt the butterflies in my stomach churn up into a flurry. Even though her questioning hadn't been so much of an interrogation as a polite and rambling conversation, I got the feeling that Aggie had been leading up to something. She took the whole cookie, put it into her mouth, chewed it thoughtfully, and then took a long sip of her tea. I couldn't pull my eyes away from hers.

"Paul's near to twenty-four," she told me.

It was the first time she had mentioned her absent son directly, and I struggled to keep my face impassive.

Aggie appeared to be gauging my reaction. "Met him 'round the pub, I'm guessing?"

I nodded wordlessly, not really trusting my voice.

"He's a right charmer, our Paulie," she told me. "Nice boy."

I blushed, and tried to pull my gaze away. I couldn't. Her eyes held mine thoughtfully, assessing my face. I prayed that she wasn't going to launch into a description of all the girls Paul brought home.

Finally Aggie said, "But you know, our Paul never does bring girls home. Last one was—oh, a year ago? No. Almost two years. That was Jane. We thought that—Well, never mind what we thought." She eyed me curiously. "How are you with international marriage?"

I choked on my tea and tried to cover it with a fake sneeze.

"What was that?" I asked.

"I'd much prefer it if you settled here, I'm sure," Aggie said. "But I wouldn't want to upset your parents, neither."

I stared at her incredulously. I wondered what Paul had told her that had made her leap immediately to marriage.

"Where is he?" I managed to get out.

"Paul? Oh, I forgot to give you this note," she widened her eyes innocently and reached into her pocket.

She handed me folded piece of lined paper.

Laura,
Not exactly a love note! Though I will admit that I spent a good ten minutes staring at your beautiful face this morning before I ran out. Sorry to abandon you for an hour or two, but my stepdad needs some help round the shop this morning. I've got a right headache happening! You? If my mum woke you up (and I know she did) she probably forgot to mention that Will (my stepdad) runs a breakfast stand down by the pier and that his cook is on holiday this week. Be suspicious if she makes you tea! I'll be home by lunch and I promise to take you for fish and chips and sightseeing.
Much Love,
Paul
PS Mum, if you didn't want to hear it, you shouldn't have read someone else's mail.P.

Aggie grinned at me without shame. "Would you like a wee bit more tea?"

I was still drinking tea uneasily with Aggie when Paul and his stepfather arrived home.

Will was a perfect match for Aggie, at least physically. He was short, squat, and hairy everywhere except his head. Blonde tufts stood out on his neck, and a bushy beard covered his round face.

"Perfect day," he told us as he seated himself across from Aggie. The plastic patio chair squeaked in protest.

Paul yanked me to my feet, wrapped his arms around me, and gave me an embarrassing kiss.

"I missed you," he said.

Aggie and Will both laughed as I tried unsuccessfully to cut the embrace short. Paul sat in my newly unoccupied chair and then pulled me into his lap.

"Whose robe is this?" he asked, rubbing his hands disconcertingly against the satin on my thigh.

Aggie shrugged. "Your aunt sent it to me last Christmas. Apparently forgetting that I'm not a super model."

"She has good taste," Paul said appreciatively. "I like it."

"I bet you do." His stepdad smiled and waggled his ample eyebrows.

I looked down at the table with my face getting redder by the second.

"Are you through tormenting Laura, Mum?" Paul asked.

"Her face wasn't near so red 'til you got home," his mom retorted.

Paul raised an eyebrow.

"I'm done. For now," Aggie told him with a sigh.

"Good. I'm sure she'd be more comfortable in her clothes?" Paul suggested.

"Do with her what you want," Aggie said, waving us off dismissively.

I mumbled an embarrassed thank you and then followed Paul back to his bedroom in disbelieving silence.

"What's wrong?" he asked as soon as he had locked the door behind us. "Was my mum that hard on you? She's overwhelming and no one knows it better than me."

"Hmm. Well. No. She fed me."

"Doesn't sound like torture," Paul said as he wrapped his arms around me. "But *something's* wrong."

"If *my* mother found a strange foreign *guy* in my room, she would've called the police," I informed him.

"That wouldn't be very hospitable," Paul noted, a small smile playing on his lips.

"And if you had been able to convince her that for some reason you *did* belong there, she would certainly not have allowed you sit around half naked after running you a bath. And cookies and tea would be utterly out of the question," I concluded.

Paul laughed. "Are all Canadians so uptight?"

I shook my head. "Just the parental ones."

He kissed me and started to untie my robe. I swatted his hands away. "Speaking of my parents," I said, "Is there a phone here I could use?"

"Now?" Paul asked, making a pouty face that got me giggling.

I looked at the alarm clock on the nightstand. It was just after three o'clock, making it seven in the morning back in Vancouver. "This is my best chance to catch them both at home."

Paul sighed, shook his head sadly and sat down on the bed. "Down in the front room."

"Past your parents, of course," I stated.

Paul grinned.

"Fine," I said. "But I'm getting dressed first."

"Suit yourself," Paul told me with a wink.

I quickly grabbed a fresh pair of jeans and a clean t-shirt from my backpack and stuck my calling card in my pocket.

"Be right back," I whispered as I opened that door and snuck down the hall. I ignored Paul's laugh.

I made my way carefully past Aggie and Will, holding my breath as I tiptoed in front of the open patio door. I stoically disregarded that fact that they were arguing about the affordability of flights between England and Canada.

I sat gingerly on the plastic covered couch and cradled the phone close to my ear. I dialed as silently as I could.

"Hello?" Mom answered on the first ring. She sounded tinny and crackly.

"Mom?" I said.

"Hello?" she repeated.

"Mom, it's me, Laura," I spoke a little more loudly, still trying not to draw any attention from Paul's parents. The last thing I needed was to try to explain *them* to my anxiety prone parents.

"Laura?" my mom asked.

"Do we have bad connection?" I wondered. *All the better to deceive you with*, I thought, a la big bad wolf. "Should I call back, Mom?"

"Laura?"

"I'm in Brighton, Mom," I told her.

"What?" She added something else that I couldn't make out.

"Mom?"

"You need to come home," my mother stated, suddenly sounding very clear.

"What are you talking about?" I answered irritably. Could she have found out about Paul already? Could she sense something via mother's intuition? "You can't honestly believe that I'm going to come home?"

"It's your dad," she said, breaking up again.

I realized suddenly that her voice didn't sound funny because of a bad connection. My mom was crying.

"What is it?" I asked, all irritation melting away into concern.

"He's had a stroke. Please, Laura, come home."

"I'm on my way," I responded automatically.

All thoughts of Paul evaporated until I collided with him on the stairs.

Chapter 20
THEN

I'm not sure what stirred me, but I woke with a strange feeling of disorientation accompanied by a craving for something cold to drink. I shook of the dream-induced confusion and sat up. I glanced over at Richie. He was slumbering peacefully on his side of the bed. I could see in the dim moonlight that he had fallen asleep with his newly acquired reading glasses on his nose and a computer magazine on his chest. I smiled fondly at his restful pose.

The glasses had been a big step for my husband, who seemed to be having a hard time admitting that he was getting older. I reached over, gently removed the glasses and his magazine, and set them on his nightstand. Richie stirred slightly, murmuring and turning onto his side.

God, I'm thirsty, I thought suddenly, and stepped gingerly out of bed. I wriggled into my robe and crept out the bedroom door.

I was surprised to see a soft glow of light from the living room.

"Hello?" I called softly.

"It's just me, Mrs. Lockhurst," Tessa whispered back. "Sorry if I woke you."

"I don't think that you did," I answered, stepping into the room.

Jordan's girlfriend was seated at our coffee table in her pajamas and rain boots. She had one of our old family albums in front of her.

"Do your parents know where you are?" I asked automatically.

Tessa avoided my question. "These are very good," she said, pointing to the photographs. "Have you ever thought about going professional?"

"All the time," I admitted with a smile. I sat down beside her, thirst all but forgotten. "Since I was a teenager."

"Why don't you?" Tessa wondered.

I shrugged. "I've actually tried to start a home business twice. But life has a way of deciding things for you."

"I *hate* that," she informed me, and I held in a laugh.

We sat silently for a few moments and then she turned to me and said abruptly, "Jordan won't have sex with me."

"Good," I replied automatically, taken aback by her candor.

"I just spent the better part of two hours trying to convince him," she said a little sadly, and with no shame. "I know you're his mom and probably don't want to hear about it."

I shook my head, unsure if I was disagreeing or disapproving. "I suppose I'd rather not be in the dark."

"I tried everything I could think of," Tessa went on, apparently encouraged by my answer. "I even threatened to break up with him if he wouldn't do it."

"Oh," I said helplessly. "Did he say *why* he wouldn't do it?"

It was Tessa's turn to look unsure. Then she blurted out, "He says that he doesn't want to end up like you and Mr. Lockhurst. To have his choices taken away from him by getting pregnant too young." She stopped and looked at my face searchingly before continuing. "I told him that you guys are the happiest married people I've ever met. And then he said that you *are* happy as a married couple. But maybe not so happy as individuals."

She went quiet again, and I sensed that she was waiting for me to say something, maybe to refute Jordan's claim.

I'm not unhappy, I wanted to protest loudly. But instead I just asked, "And is that why you're down here? Looking to see if me or Richard is unhappy?"

Tessa blushed guiltily. "I couldn't figure out why Jordan would think that. I can see now that you might have become a professional photographer, and I know that Mr. Lockhurst wanted to go into business, but does not doing those things make you unhappy?"

"Are *your* parents unhappy?" I countered evasively.

Tessa shrugged. "My mom died when I was two."

I struggled with the unexpected disclosure, searching for something sympathetic to say, but all I managed to get out was, "How could I not have known that?"

She shrugged again. "I don't tell very many people. It makes them weird. Or makes them think that I'm weird. I don't actually even remember her." Tessa didn't seem disturbed by the admission. "Do you have any hot chocolate, Mrs. Lockhurst?"

"Sure." I headed into the kitchen, my mind trying to wrap itself around everything Tessa had shared with me. My son was more sensitive than I had given him credit for, and impossibly level-headed for his age. I stirred the hot chocolate slowly and brought it back in to Jordan's girlfriend.

"Thanks," she said gratefully. "Look, I don't expect you to help me convince your own son to have premarital sex."

"No, I won't be doing that," I agreed, sipping my own hot chocolate thoughtfully. "I'm not even sure that I can give you any unbiased advice."

"What would you tell Tori?" Tessa wondered.

I laughed before I could stop myself. "I know from years of experience that Tori would never ask for my advice." I thought at once of poor Brian and his wayward sock.

"Okay, that was a bad example," she conceded. She started to laugh, too, and we giggled together for a few moments.

"But I guess that first thing I would do is ask you what makes you think that you need to have sex in the first place?" I asked finally.

"I don't have a lot of friends," Tessa told me, and I raised a questioning eyebrow.

"By choice," she assured me. "I have Jordan. I have Tori, and a few other girlfriends at school. But my point is, no one is pressuring me to have sex. It's not like I'm caving to peer pressure."

"That's not an answer," I replied.

"I think that Jordan and I will probably get married," she admitted. "So I'm not trying to sow any wild oats, or anything. He'll probably be my first and only."

I waited.

"I know, that's not an answer, either," Tessa said.

"So what's the rush?" I prodded.

She looked me straight in the eye. "I want to have sex for the same reason that Jordan *doesn't* want to do it. I want the choice to be mine. I don't want it to happen because we get married and then are obligated to have sleep together. I don't want to give fate a free ride."

I stared back at her.

"It sounds absurd, I know," she said. "But I also know that as soon as I'm a grown up, every choice will be taken away, and my life will be ruled by obligation."

I weighed my next words carefully. "You know, sex can be great. But it always has consequences."

"Like babies?"

"Not just that," I told her.

"You're not talking about you and Mr. Lockhurst, are you?" she asked.

I shook my head. "Tessa, I'm going to tell you something that my own children don't know. Do you promise not to tell them?"

"Sure," she agreed, leaning toward me.

"Grown ups are people, too," I confided, and she grinned.

ॐ∘ॐ

"Richie," I said, "Are you awake?"

"No." But he sat up anyway, groggy and puzzled. "What's the matter?"

"How important is sex?" I asked him.

My husband looked immediately alert. "What?"

"To teenagers," I amended. "Unmarried couples."

"Is there something you need to tell me about *our* teenagers?" he wondered.

"No. They're just a strange breed is all," I stated, and my husband relaxed.

"What makes you so equally wise and curious, now, in the middle of the night?" he teased.

"I just can't remember what it's like to be so...I don't know," I said.

"Young and stupid?" Richie filled in.

"I worry sometimes," I admitted.

"About Tori or about Jordan?" he asked.

"Both," I replied. "You know, on the one hand Tori is a concern. She competes obsessively with Jordan, has no patience for her peers, and can barely tolerate us."

"But?" my husband prodded.

"But she's been babysitting religiously for Cindy for three years. She's reliable, punctual, and treats the twins like gold," I said.

"You sound like you're more concerned about the good stuff than about the normal teenager stuff," Richie noted.

"I just wish that she's let her guard down sometimes. I feel like I can't relate to her at all," I complained.

He smiled. "It's only because you're so much like each other."

"Me and Tori? I don't think so," I disagreed. "I've always thought she's so much like you. Outgoing. Self-confident."

"With all that mysterious intensity and burning creativity?" he teased. "There's no way she gets *that* from me."

"And Jordan's already too much of a grown up for his own good," I said, changing the subject. "Thinking about things he has no reason to be thinking about for another five or ten years."

"At least he's got Tessa to keep him in line," Richie said, and I was glad that it was dark enough in our room for me to hide my amusement.

"There is that," I agreed blandly.

Richie lay his head back on his pillow. "But back to your original question. I guess I'd say that sex is always on a teenager's mind. Especially a boy teenager. But he doesn't have to act on it. I didn't. *We* didn't."

I kept silent, sensing that the time for me to come really, truly clean had long since passed.

"Speaking of sex," I said instead, and my husband pulled me obligingly down beside him.

స్రా

I smiled at Richie as I clutched the thick envelope that I had found on the kitchen table this morning. I had waited patiently all day for this moment alone together. Tori had gone over to babysit Mike and Lee, and Jordan was doing some volunteer work at the library. I had eaten dinner quietly, afraid that if I spoke, I would burst with the excitement of my news.

"Okay," my husband said finally. "I give up. What've you got there that's making you grin like a madwoman?"

"This?" I said innocently, and unwound the red string that kept the fat envelope sealed. "Just these."

My husband took the contents from me. "They look like business cards."

"Not just any business cards. *My* business cards." I took the stack and fanned them out on the table.

"Really? I didn't realize that you had any business," he teased.

I grabbed his hand, refusing to play along. "Tessa made these for me. She thought it was a good idea for me to have something formal and professional-looking to hand out to potential clients. She thought up the name, too."

"*Snapshots by Laura?*" he read off of one of the cards, and then smiled at me.

"Cute and clever, right?" I grinned back at my husband. "And easy to remember."

"Jordan's Tessa made these?" Richie asked. "You two seem to have become close lately."

I avoided replying to that comment. Ever since our late night heart-to-heart, Tessa had made it her personal mission to help me fulfill my dream of becoming a professional photographer.

"She's been working on them for over a month," I answered. "What do you think?"

"I love it."

"Me, too," I said. "And they're working."

"You've got some calls already?" Richie sounded as excited as I felt.

"Last week I put the prototype that Tessa designed up on the community board in the photography shop," I explained. "And this morning I got a call. Maybe *the* call. From a newspaper editor. The paper's contract photographer is on maternity leave, and they need someone to fill in immediately. The editor checked out my website, and thinks that I'm perfect for the job!"

"You have a website?"

"Tessa again," I laughed. "She posted dozens of my old photos and made me sound better than I am, I'm sure."

"You couldn't possibly be any better than you are," he replied. "This is amazing news. I'm going to married to a real professional."

"A part-time professional," I reminded him.

"Still, I think that this calls for a celebration," Richie said.

"Way ahead of you," I told him, and got up to retrieve the bottle of champagne that I had chilling in the refrigerator.

I poured, and we raised our glasses.

"To dreams fulfilled," my husband toasted, and I glowed with the exciting truth of his words.

ৰু৵৹

I strapped myself contentedly into the front seat of our minivan and adjusted the radio until I found a song that I recognized. It was classic Marvin Gaye. My husband grinned at me from the driver's seat.

"Setting the mood?" he asked.

I smiled back. "I would be," I said, "But you insisted that we make this a family celebration."

The kids were following behind us in Tessa's new Volkswagon Beetle.

"I could always try to lose them in the city," Richie suggested, and I laughed. "It wouldn't be that hard. Find a seedy motel somewhere…" He trailed off suggestively.

"Right." I rolled my eyes. "As if Tessa couldn't keep up to you. But romance aside, you were right to include them. It might be *my* birthday, but it's really a celebration of all of our lives, isn't it?"

Richie leaned over the console and kissed me on the cheek. "I love you. And I'm so very glad that you think so."

"Uh oh," I said. "I suddenly get the feeling that I should be asking you for more information, but I'm going to restrain myself."

My husband smiled and turned up the Marvin Gaye.

৵৶

We pulled into an underground parking lot and stepped out into the cool air. Richie wrapped his arms around me, rubbing my back to keep me warm. Jordan, Tori, and Tessa pulled up a minute later, and hopped out. I couldn't help but admire my family. Jordan was wearing a navy blue suit jacket overtop of a crisp white t-shirt and some dark wash jeans. I resisted the urge to straighten the tousled mess of hair on his head. Tessa's ensemble complemented his outfit perfectly—it was a fifties style dress, dark blue with large white polka dots. Tori was dressed in her usual sombre apparel, pairing a long black skirt with a sleeveless gray tank top. But she had added a shimmery black scarf, large hoop earrings, and had even traded in her big black boots for a pair of ballet shoe flats.

"You guys look great!" I said enthusiastically.

Tori rolled her eyes theatrically, but then smiled and said, "You too, Mom."

I patted my utility-use little black dress. "This old thing?" I joked, but I was glad to be having conversation with my daughter that wasn't an argument.

"Oh, and you'll love this," Tessa added. She reached into her purse and pulled out a yellow bandana.

"Should I be worried? I'm beginning to think that this is more than a birthday dinner," I said, and everybody laughed.

"Maybe, Mom," answered Jordan. "*That* is going to be your blindfold." He helped Tessa tie it in place.

My family led me, blindfold securely fastened around my eyes, stumbling and giggling up some stairs and into a building. I could hear the sound of people laughing and talking, as well as cutlery clinking against dishes. We kept walking, and those noises faded into the background.

"Okay," Richie said, stopping me and then letting go of my elbow. "We're here."

I pulled the bandana from my eyes, and tried to orient myself to my surroundings. A roomful of people greeted me with cheers.

"Surprise!" Richie winked at me.

"Oh." I could feel tears welling up in my eyes.

I took inventory of the guests. Richie's parents were seated with his youngest sister, Jessie, her husband, and their brand new baby boy.

"Hello," I said to them, and kissed the baby on his sweet smelling head.

Liz, her three kids, my other sister-in-law Marie, and a pretty woman who I didn't recognize were chatting happily at a another table. Marie stood to give me a cool kiss on each cheek.

"This is Kateri," Liz told me, patting the unknown woman on the hand. She had jet-black hair that was sure to make Tori envious, and beautifully tanned skin.

"Cara's daughter?" I guessed.

"Nice to meet you," she said, and gave me a warm hug.

Tessa's dad and his girlfriend waved to me from their seats. Jordan's friend Jake was at their table too, and he had brought a pretty girl with him. I recognized her from their little circle of friends, but I couldn't remember her name. Brian stood behind Jake's chair. He grinned at me and then blushed as he did almost every time he saw Tori and I at the same time. I smiled and waved back.

Cindy, Newton, Mike, and Lee sat with my prim boss, Karen, from the photography store. I chuckled inwardly at her clear discomfort. The Green family was like its own personal circus. Mike and Lee were building some kind of structure with their forks, knives, cups, and napkins. And rather than trying to stop them, Newton was giving pointers. Cindy was sipping on a margarita while she texted on her cell phone. Tessa murmured to me that she was going to go "rescue" Karen from them, and I waved her off.

My own parents were seated at a table off to the side, and they greeted me stiffly. Sitting with them was a familiar-looking forty-something woman, a man I didn't know, and a little girl, maybe ten years old. I tried to place the woman. She was dressed in a classy pantsuit and low heels. The woman stood, a grin splitting her face, and then I recognized her.

"Kristen," I gasped.

"The one and the same," she replied. "This is my husband, Pete, and my daughter, Hailey."

"I can't believe you're here," I said.

"We'll catch up later," Kristen assured me as Richie pulled me away.

An empty table at the front of the room had clearly been reserved for my immediate family, and as we made our way over there, my husband took my hand.

"Is it perfect?" he asked.

"It's like my whole life in one little room," I assured him.

"Happy anniversary," he said. And then he grabbed me and kissed me with exaggerated slowness, waiting until everyone in the room was clapping before finally letting me go.

Chapter 21
WAY BACK WHEN

Paul was silent as we drove from Brighton to London in his mom's aging Peugeot. I tried unsuccessfully several times to form an apology, but he kept his eyes on the road and his jaw unwaveringly set. Paul finally slipped a tape into the car deck and turned up a techno beat so loud that the car doors rattled. Tears fell freely down my face, but if he noticed at all, he pretended not to, instead just lighting cigarette after cigarette.

Back at his mom's house, I had haltingly explained to him that I needed to get home as soon as possible, and he had become like a different person. I had expected him to cry, as I had. Or to protest that I could not leave, try to force me to stay and to choose him over my dad. But instead Paul had become quiet and still, offering immediately to drive me to the airport. He hadn't let me coax him into bed one last time for a tender goodbye, or really even given me a chance to speak.

On the way out the door, Aggie had gripped my face in her meaty hands and murmured, "I'll have him out to you before Christmas."

Paul hadn't bothered to acknowledge her comment; he just loaded my things into the car and waited for me to get in so that we could start heading north.

When we parked in the Short Stay Lot at Heathrow, Paul wordlessly grabbed my bag and started toward the terminal. I followed his lead, trying hold back my tears. My backpack looked like I felt—deflated and half empty.

I paid for the change to my ticket at the counter, and still Paul said nothing. He walked me to the security area, and I finally spoke.

"When my dad's better…" I said.

"Don't," Paul replied.

"Are you angry?" I asked.

"Not at you," he answered.

"I love you," I told him in an anguished voice.

I put my arms around him, burying my face in his smoke-scented chest. For a second, he gripped me back fiercely, and then pulled away abruptly.

"Don't miss your plane," he advised me gruffly.

"Paul," I pleaded.

He gave me an awkward pat on the back, and I forced myself to walk up to the uniformed female guard and hand her my passport. I looked back once as she glanced at my boarding pass, but Paul was already gone.

Chapter 22
THEN

The shrill ringing of the phone cut through my pleasant dream. I glanced blearily at the clock. It was six twenty-six in the morning. Richie would've left about ten minutes earlier and my own alarm would've gone off in another twenty. *Unknown number* flashed across the call display, and I ignored it.

My feet were icy cold, and I realized that Richie must've left the window open. I pulled the comforter over my feet and shimmied over onto my husband's side of the bed. It was even colder than my own spot.

The phone rang again, sounding more insistent than the first time. *Unknown number* blinked again, angry-looking. Shivering, I grabbed the phone halfway through the third ring.

"This had better be good," I said.

"Is this Mrs. Laura Lockhurst?" said stiff voice.

"It is," I said, a thick ball forming inexplicably in my throat.

"You husband has been in an accident. We need you to come to the hospital right away."

Chapter 23
WAY BACK WHEN

I was surprised to see my mom at the airport arrivals gate. Although I had left my flight information in a message on their answering machine, I hadn't expected that she would be able to leave the hospital long enough to pick me up.

"What are you doing here?" I blurted before I could stop myself.

My mom raised an eyebrow, frowning as she folded her arms across her chest. She was dressed in what I thought of as her non-work uniform—a cream blouse, pleated skirt, and a dark coloured blazer.

"Hello, to you, too," she said. "Is that coffee that you're drinking?"

I held the styrofoam cup out guiltily. "Yes. It was a long flight."

Coffee was high on my mother's list of health no-no's.

"I suppose," she stated, and it sounded more like criticism than agreement.

I tossed the almost full cup into a nearby garbage.

Sighing, my mom leaned in for a hug like it was an afterthought. "You smell a bit off."

"I've just been on a plane for ten hours," I reminded her. I pulled away and tried to change the subject. "Should we get my bag? How's dad?"

In response, she grabbed my chin between her fingers and stared into my eyes suspiciously. It took all of my emotional strength to keep from turning my face away. She moved her hand down to my shoulder, still scrutinizing.

"Mom," I complained. "I'm tired."

"Hmph," she replied noncommittally without releasing my gaze. "Have you been crying?"

"Worried about Dad," I mumbled.

She finally looked away. "I already grabbed your luggage," she told me. "I had time, since you where busy getting your stimulating beverage."

"Oh," I said, only then noticing that my backpack was sitting in a cart beside us. I thought of the other half of my clothes in Paul's Scottish apartment and hoped that my mother didn't notice how much stuff was missing. "I didn't know you were coming."

"No matter. Let's get going. Your dad's in the car," she told me.

"Dad's in the car?" I asked, feeling confused. "Shouldn't he be in the hospital? Did you lie about his stroke?"

"I didn't lie," my mom argued, sounding unconcerned. "He had a stroke. But he's doing fine now."

I felt my body go hot, then cold, then numb. The memory of Paul's painfully rigid face came rushing unbidden to my mind. I stared blankly at my mother, anger combining with exhaustion from ten hours of Gravol-inspired, fitful sleep on a cramped plane, to make my vision blur.

The last sensation I had was the cool concrete meeting the side of my face as I collapsed in a heap on the airport floor.

છ ∼ઉ

I woke groggily to the sound of beeping monitors and a sharp pain in my arm. I opened my eyes slowly and took in my surroundings. Yellow walls and a white ceiling.

Hospital, I thought, and struggled to sit up. My body didn't want to obey my brain's commands.

"Slow down, there Miss Morgan," said a matronly voice.

I turned my head, and immediately recognized the middle aged Indian woman smiling down at me. She was one of my mom's nursing friends.

"Navneet," I tried to say, but it came out as a croak. My throat burned.

She used the buttons on the side of my bed to bring me to a sitting position and then handed me a glass of icy water. I took a tentative sip and felt immediate relief.

"You cracked your melon and have been out cold for almost thirty six hours," Nanveet told me as she took my vitals.

"Is that the technical term?" I joked weakly, pleased to hear my voice come out in a more normalized timbre.

She sat down beside me and put her hand on my head. "You fainted. The doctors call that syncope. You bumped your head and then went to sleep. They call that a massive concussion with resulting loss of consciousness."

"Ouch," I said. "Wait. Thirty-six hours? I lost a day and a half?"

"Any confusion or memory loss?" Nanveet asked.

I thought back, remembering my anger at my mother and then the airport floor. "Unfortunately, no. Bit of a headache is all."

"Good," the nurse said, and watched me hesitantly.

"Where's Mom?" I inquired, trying to keep my fury under a tight lid.

"I sent her home to mind your dad."

"So he was actually sick, then?" I wondered.

"He had a stroke the day after you left for your big trip. A small one though. Your mom brought him in right away. Suffered some minor hearing loss and a bit of numbness in one of his legs. Doc put him on blood pressure medication, I understand. Nothing for you to worry yourself about," Nanveet explained. She stopped and stared at me again, the same unsure look on her face.

"What is it, Nanveet?" I asked.

"When the paramedics first brought you in, the emergency team ran a series of standard tests on you," she said.

"And, what? I'm dying?" I was joking, but something in Nanveet's face caused a hard pit of worry to form in my stomach anyway.

The nurse laughed. "Hardly. But, Laura, when did you start your last menstrual cycle?"

"Pardon?"

"Do you remember when the first day of your last period was?" she repeated.

I thought about it, a new kind of worry crossing my mind. "More than a week before I left. But less than ten days," I estimated. "Why?"

Nanveet handed me a prettily flowered envelope. "This fell out of your pocket when the EMTs brought you in. I figured it was private and you probably wouldn't take very well to your mom opening it."

I turned the envelope over in my hand. It was addressed with a simple 'L', and I recognized Paul's handwriting.

"Thank you," I said faintly.

My mom's old friend put her hand over top of mind, met my eyes and spoke in a low voice. "Laura, the doctors took some blood. And according to their results, you're almost three weeks pregnant."

I stared at her, stunned.

"That's another thing I figured you'd most likely want to keep to yourself," Nanveet said.

"How is that possible?" I demanded.

She gave me a little smile. "In the usual way, I suspect."

"No, I mean. Can someone be only three weeks pregnant? How can they even tell so early?" I wracked my brain, trying to recall everything I could about human reproduction.

"Do you want science, or a yes or no answer?" Nanveet asked me.

"Science?"

She shifted her weight on the bed and gave me a run down. "The pregnancy hormone—HCG—can be detected a day or two after conception, before you even miss a cycle. The amount present gives us an estimate of how far along you are, and the number of weeks is given based on the very first day of your last period."

"Oh," I said in a small voice.

The nurse squeezed my hand. "Laura, you have options."

"No," I told her coldly.

"Laura."

"I don't want options," I insisted.

"But if you're unsure of who the father is…" she trailed off in embarrassment.

"Of course I know who he is!" I snapped, and then apologized immediately. "I'm sorry, Nanveet. I've only been with…Well, there's only one option for who the father is, and he's thousands of kilometres away." I laughed a little hysterically. "Can I please have a few minutes alone?"

Nanveet looked at me uncertainly, and then sighed. "I'll finish my rounds and come back to check on you."

ʒ• ❥

I waited until I was sure that Nanveet had disappeared down the hall before sliding my finger under the flap of the flowered envelope. I pulled out a letter. My heart was in my throat as I read the words.

> Laura,
> I am sorry to tell you this in writing, but maybe it's easier this way. I haven't been honest with you from the start, and I should've been. The truth is, I'm in love with someone else. I thought that maybe—well. If you were staying here. Nevermind.I don't want to prolong this and I think that a clean break is best. We both deserve a life, and it's clearly not together. In time, you'll forget me, as I'm already trying to forget you. Sorry to have involved you in my deception. Goodbye.
> Paul

I set the envelope on my hospital bed, and a business card embossed with a turquoise eye slipped out. I recognized it instantly—Lady Jasmine's fortune. I flipped it over and read the words silently. *She is not your destiny.* Not *this,* as Paul had said on the pier but *she.* He had been lying to me even then. I fought against the nausea that threatened to overwhelm me. The pain in my head and the pain in my heart became indistinguishable as I sat there. I tried to imagine Paul saying out loud the words he had written on the paper, but I kept picturing his face as it had looked on the ferris wheel. I shook off the image, and wondered who the other girl was. I laughed inwardly, mentally correcting myself—it was *I* who was the other woman, actually. A summer fling. I clutched my hand over top of my abdomen. No wonder he hadn't answered my question about having a girlfriend.

For one second I let myself imagine a tiny, faceless baby in a crib beside a stonework fireplace while Paul and I chatted about the weather. And then I blocked it out. The finality of Paul's words made it clear that my brief fantasy would never become a reality. But this baby deserved a life, too. Even if it wasn't one I could ever give.

ॐ◌ॐ

I left a bold-faced note on my pillow before checking myself out. I knew that the nursing staff would make sure my mom got it.

> *mother,*
> *i want you to know that i forgive you. if you don't know what for—well, i'm not going to explain it to you. right now i'm supposed to be walking up the stairs of westminster abbey. i'm going to spend some time away now—maybe a year or so. but don't worry, i'll stay in canada this time. i've learned my lesson, though maybe not for the reason you'd think. i'll send you a post office box number when i get to my destination. write, if you like. but don't try to find me.*
> *Laura*

I caught the bus to the train station, and bought a ticket for the train that would take me from Vancouver to Winnipeg. I said a small prayer of thanks for already having my bag packed, and ignored the aches all over my body. As I boarded, I tried not to think about the other train rides I had taken this month, tried not to think about how worried my parents would be, or whether I could really trust Nanveet to keep my secret. I made myself numb with not thinking about Paul.

It was good practice for what I was going to have to do.

Chapter 24
THEN

As I sat in the hospital waiting room, it occurred to me that this was the very same spot that I had sat next to Richard almost eighteen years before. The memory triggered a horrible sense of longing and apprehension that quickly transformed into anxiety and panic.

Tori was huddled beside me, still in pajamas, make up free and looking shell-shocked. She shivered, and I pulled her closer. Jordan sat across from us, while Tessa paced back and forth between the little room where we waited and the nurse's station in the hall. I hadn't bothered to comment on the fact that I had found her asleep in Jordan's bed at six-thirty. Some things could wait.

"Mrs. Lockhurst?" called a soft male voice.

I looked up and saw a man in scrubs standing in the doorway.

"Yes," I answered, barely above a whisper.

"I'm the surgeon who has been working on your husband," he told me. "I'll speak to you privately if you don't mind?"

I excused myself from my family, patting Tori's hand and squeezing Jordan's shoulder as I exited the room. I followed the doctor down a series of corridors until we reached an office.

"In these situations, I find it best to be honest from the outset," the doctor told me as I settled into a leather-backed chair.

"Is he dead?" I asked, unable to stop the question from coming out of my mouth.

"Not yet, Mrs. Lockhurst," the doctor said in a gentle tone. "There are some things that you should know now..."

This man would make an excellent funeral director, I thought absently, trying and failing to focus on his words rather than his soothing tone.

I caught every third sentence or so. "Damage to the blood brain barrier," I heard and then, "Glasgow coma scale."

I stared at the posters behind the doctor's head. An advertisement for breast self-examinations. A cat in a lab coat. The hypocratic oath, printed in swirling letters and forming the shape of a cross.

"Mrs. Lockhurst?" The doctor was asking me a question.

"Yes."

"Are you still with me?"

"Yes. No. I don't know, actually," I admitted. "Can you tell me again?"

The doctor looked puzzled for moment and then recovered his impassive face so quickly that I could've imagined his confusion.

"Break it down for me," I said, feeling like my brain and my words didn't want to work together. "Simply."

"You husband, Richard, was in a very serious car accident. The majority of the injury was to his head. We have put a catheter into his brain to release the pressure, but there is little more we can do." The doctor spoke slowly and apologetically.

"It's not your fault," I murmured.

"Pardon me?"

"Nothing." I shook my head, trying to find a place for my thoughts.

"Does your husband have a living will Mrs. Lockhurst?" the doctor asked.

"Yes," I said, blinking. "Richie has always been thorough about this kind of thing."

"Do you know what his wishes are, Mrs. Lockhurst? We have no record on file at the hospital."

"Richie doesn't get sick," I answered, wondering if maybe my detachment was a result of being in shock.

"I'll send the counsellor in to meet with your family as soon as we're done here," the doctor told me, perhaps sensing that I wasn't entirely present.

"An injunction," I answered.

"Mrs. Lockhurst?"

"I won't let him just go," I stated, sounding unreasonably angry and not being able to stop it.

The doctor put his hand on my arm. "That decision will be yours," he dropped his voice to the funeral director hum again. "But as I said, there are some things that you should be aware of. If brain death is determined, that will mean that Richie is no longer able to function on his own. Even the involuntary activity for the necessary sustainment of life will cease. He will need enteral nutrition, air through forced ventilation, and assistance in blood circulation."

"Best case a scenario?" I asked, pretending to absorb what I was being told.

"Even if brain death does not occur immediately, Richie will likely not recover. Gradual and progressive multiple organ failure is inevitable. If your husband's wishes do not include long term life support..." The doctor trailed off.

"I'd like a minute alone, please," I said.

As soon as the doctor left the little office, I buried my mouth into the sleeve of my coat and muffled a sob that threatened to become a scream.

Breath in. Breath out. I told myself. *Small steps first.*

I reached into my purse and dug around until I found the little card that listed all of our professional business contacts—our accountant, our doctor, and most importantly at this moment, our lawyer.

Chapter 25
THEN

I sat in the lawyer's office, watching Debbie Ling as she went through each page of the injunction methodically. She had been a friend of Paul's in his university days, and she was eager to make my wishes a reality. The file she held wasn't a large one for the enormity of its potential impact, but it did contain a lot of impressive medical jargon, legal precedents and our original will. She read each area out in a sincere and passionate voice while the team from the hospital listened impassively.

The surgeon who had operated on Richie—Dr. Daniel Friday—was there, along with Dr. Whitaker, a senior administrator, and two lawyers representing the legal side of the hospital. Dr. Whitaker kept reaching across the table to squeeze my hand reassuringly. None of rest of them had any strong reactions to my plea for the maintenance of my husband's life. Maybe it was just another day at the office for them.

When Debbie finished her presentation, the hospital's first lawyer spoke.

"We have no intention of contesting Mrs. Lockhurst's wishes," he began. "We understand that in situations like this, a sensitivity to the spouse's needs is an absolute necessity."

I released a breath that I hadn't realize I'd been holding.

Dr. Friday cleared his throat. "Without sounding coarse, and with respect for that sensitivity, we would like to make sure that we have clearly indicated the circumstances of this choice."

"On the record," added the second lawyer.

"On the record," Dr. Friday repeated, and shuffled through his own folder of notes. "Richard Lockhurst was admitted to this hospital eighteen days ago. He suffered a severe head injury as a result of impact in a collision related to inclement weather conditions. We performed surgery, diagnostic image testing, and have determined the presence of several intra-axial lesions, and damage to the blood-brain barrier. As well, the cranial nerve reflexes are largely non-responsive." The surgeon paused to look up at me with sympathy. "To be frank, it is a miracle that brain death has not occurred already. Mr. Lockhurst is currently in what is best defined a persistent vegetative state—and a fragile one at that. Typically with this kind of injury, death is likely in the first twelve to forty-eight hours. To have managed to carry on for three weeks—well, it is truly amazing."

Both of the lawyers cleared their throats.

Dr. Friday continued. "We can, via experience, anticipate that Mr. Lockhurst's state will continue to deteriorate. With his brain damaged the way that it is, seizures are likely, and could lead to instant death. If seizures do not occur, Mr. Lockhurst's organs will eventually begin to fail. He will be kept alive by ventilator, by enteral nutrition—which I understand is already in place—and assisted circulation. Heart failure is also a likely possibility."

"Enough," said Debbie.

"It's okay," I murmured, and then said in a louder voice, "I'm aware of all the circumstances. And I'm prepared for them."

"Laura," said Dr. Whitaker, "You may be prepared for them, but is your family?"

"The children are minors," Debbie stated for the benefit of the hospital team. "This is the decision of a wife on behalf of her husband."

I stared as coolly as I could at the man who had known my children since birth. "I have considered both Jordan's and Tori's opinions."

I tried to block out the remembered image of Tori's angry face.

"I'm on Dad's side," she had said.

"So am I," I had replied in a strained voice.

"Then let him go," she had said, pushing me away when I tried to hug her.

"I can't," I had said to myself as she stormed out of the room.

Dr. Whitaker pressed once more, sensing that this was the one area that might make me waver. "Their opinions, maybe. But what about their feelings? And their futures?"

"Enough," Debbie said again. "We're all in agreement. Let's sign the papers so that Mrs. Lockhurst can get on with her life."

I signed the papers leadenly, wondering if I would be able to get on with my life ever again.

❧ ❦

Tori stood in front of our artificial Christmas tree, placing decorations on it so violently that the tree shook with each shimmering ball and each plastic candy cane. Jordan sat on the couch, tossing a blown glass Santa from one hand to the other. I was sipping a rum and eggnog as I addressed the last of the Christmas cards at the coffee table. Bing Crosby played softly from the stereo. None of us looked toward the chair where Richie ususally sat on a family evening like this one.

Tori spun to me suddenly. "What did you put in your letter this year, Mom?"

I forced myself to swallow the sip I had just taken, and tried to ignore the sick feeling in my gut.

"The usual," I said cautiously.

"Like what?" she asked, with artificial sincerity.

I felt Jordan tense beside me, and put a hand on his knee. "I mentioned the scholarship that Jordan is up for," I told her, keeping my voice level. "I talked about my photography business."

Tori's tone slipped. "You didn't get around to my suspension from school?"

"This was a bad idea," Jordan muttered, trying to stand up. I kept my hand on his knee, forcing him to sit down.

"It's a Christmas update, Tori," I said through my teeth. "Teen drunkenness at a school function is not a usual topic."

"No?" My daughter went back to stringing tinsel in jerky motions.

I waited for the storm. Every conversation with Tori ended the same way.

"Did you mention my dad?" she asked without turning around.

"I explained the accident as best I could, yes." I waited some more.

"Mom," Jordan pleaded.

"In a minute," I murmured back.

I'm sorry if it's selfish, Jordan, but you are my only buffer against this torrent of anger, I thought.

"Was it easy for you? Did you say that you and Jordan are keeping him attached to a machine against his will? Did you say that he has a tube going into his stomach and that last week it got infected? Did you mention that the doctor said by this time next month he won't even be breathing on his own? Did you let our friends and family know that Dad is all but *dead*, and that you won't accept it?" Tori was shouting by the end. She grabbed a little glass angel and tossed it onto the floor where it shattered at my feet.

"I did not say those things," I answered.

"You didn't?" her voice was calm again as she stared me down.

I looked away first, and she stomped off triumphantly.

My son stood up, and I let him.

"I'll get the broom and clean that up before I go to Tessa's," he said.

"You don't have to," I told him.

"I want to, Mom."

I closed my eyes and lifted my feet wordlessly as Jordan pushed the bits of broken ornament into the dustpan.

"Mom," Jordan said when he finished sweeping.

I opened my eyes and looked up. His features mirrored Richie's so closely that it took my breath away. His eyes were the same piercing blue and his skin had the same pleasant year round tan. He was getting tall like his dad, too. He must've been at least six feet, and looked taller because of his still youthful leanness.

"Mom," he said again.

I downed the rest of my rum and eggnog before meeting his eyes. "Yes, Jordan?"

"You're doing the right thing," he said firmly.

"Am I?" Although I already knew that Jordan supported me one hundred percent, I did not know whether it was just for the sake of backing my decision, or because he agreed with my choice on principle. I wondered often how two children with the same parents could be so terribly different.

"Yes," he told me. "Tori forgets that you're a person, and not just her mom."

I looked at Jordan cautiously. I had been so careful to guard my emotions in front of the kids, trying to protect them and to be an example of strength. Maybe it wasn't the best thing for them, or for me, but it was all I could do.

"And what about you?" I wondered.

My son shrugged. "I would've made the same choice as you."

"Thank you, Jordan," I said gratefully.

He shrugged again. "I'm going to Tessa's now. Love you, Mom."

"Love you, too."

❧❦

I dropped the laundry and grabbed the phone as soon as I saw the hospital's office number come up on the call display.

"Hello, Dr. Friday," I answered.

"Mrs. Lockhurst," he responded with no preamble, "I have news, and it's not great."

In the four months since Richie's accident, I had truly come to appreciate the surgeon's straightforward attitude.

"Give it to me," I said.

Richie had been going downhill since New Year's. First he had started to drop a lot of weight, and they had needed to move his feeding tube from stomach to his small intestine. Then he had developed Septicemia. It had taken three different kinds of antibiotics and several days to clear the infection.

"Don't panic," Dr. Friday started, "But Richard stopped breathing twice last night. He was resuscitated quickly and easily both times."

I felt my body go cold. "Why didn't anyone notify me?"

"Tori convinced the physician on call that it wasn't necessary," the surgeon explained. "As I said, he was easily resuscitated each time and was in no more danger than usual."

"Tori? She was at the hospital last night?"

Dr. Friday was silent for a moment. "Mrs. Lockhurst, Tori is here almost every night. You weren't aware?"

"No," I answered flatly.

"Mrs. Lockhurst -

I cut him off. "It doesn't matter. You couldn't have known that I didn't know. I'll deal with Tori later. Please just tell me more about Richie."

"We've temporarily employed a simple laryngeal mask airway, but it's suitable for short term only. We'd like to insert an endotracheal tube with your permission," Dr. Friday stated.

"Okay," I said, sounding calmer than I felt. *This is how it starts*, I thought. *Or maybe how it finishes.* "Do you need me to come in and sign some more paperwork?"

I made some mental readjustments of my day. It was Friday, when the doctors did their weekly grand rounds, and the only day that I wasn't in the hospital by seven.

"You'll be in shortly after nine?" the surgeon asked, apparently aware of my usual schedule.

"I will," I confirmed. "Unless you need me earlier."

"Nine is fine. We'll schedule the surgery for eleven. You'll be able to spend some time with your husband after we fill in the paperwork."

"Thanks." I hung up the phone and stared blankly at the receiver. I felt a curious separation from my life, as if my identity was being ripped in two. I was coldly angry that Tori, the person, was visiting *my* husband in the hospital behind my back when at home she denied so vehemently that he be kept alive against his wishes.

But also I felt sad that I hadn't recognized that Tori, my daughter, still needed that time with her father.

When the phone rang again suddenly I was startled out of my reverie and I answered it mid-ring.

"Oh, hello," said my boss, sounding surprised.

"Hi, Karen."

"I thought you'd be, well, you know," she stumbled over her words the way people often did when talking to me now.

"At the hospital?" I filled in, trying to keep the impatience out of my voice.

"Yes," she said and paused awkwardly.

"On Friday mornings I go in a little later," I explained unnecessarily. "Just because the doctors are doing their grand rounds."

"Oh," she cleared her throat. "Can I help you with anything?"

"You called me," I reminded her.

"I was just going to leave you a message," Karen said.

"Now you don't have to," I stated.

She was hesitant. "You haven't been in for your shifts in a while."

I waited for her to realize the absolute absurdity of the statement. It only took a second.

"Laura, I'm so sorry. I didn't meant that at all like it sounded," Karen apologized. "I just wanted to know if you'd like a more permanent leave of absence?"

"Am I being fired?" I asked tonelessly. I knew that the measly eight hours or so that I put in a week could be filled by almost anybody, but somehow holding on to the job seemed important.

"Of course not!" She sounded embarrassed. "I just wanted to give you an option."

On the answering machine, I thought, but said nothing.

Karen babbled a bit, trying to fill the silence, and I tuned her out. When she started talking about changing the store hours, I cut in.

"Karen. Karen!" I said loudly, "I'll let you know as soon as I'm ready to start coming in again. If you need to replace me before then, fine."

"That won't be necessary," she said in a rush. "Thank you."

"Goodbye, Karen."

"Okay, Laura. Call me whenever you're ready."

I hung up the phone.

Chapter 26
WAY BACK WHEN

Forty-eight hours in a cramped sleeper car left my body feeling ragged and beat up. I had ignored the mechanized voice that had encouraged passengers to stretch their legs at each stop. The meals offered a-la-carte had been enough turn my stomach on sight alone, so I just sat in my bed nibbling on crackers and sipping on water. When the announcement came that we had reached our destination, I had to fight the urge to *run* out of the train. I forced my feet to move slowly, but as I stepped into the street, I couldn't resist gulping in the fresh air.

At eight thirty on an early fall evening, Winnipeg felt cooler and crisper than Vancouver did in the middle of December. I exhaled slowly, watching my breath hang in the air. I shivered a little against the cold.

"Need a ride, Miss?" asked a friendly voice.

I glanced in the direction of the question, and nodded at the young cabbie who had posed it. "Yes, please. I have an address."

I pulled out the little piece of crumpled paper, hastily torn from the hospital directory, where I had written down the contact information I needed. I handed it to the cabbie. If he recognized the house number or the name, he gave no indication.

We rode for twenty minutes in silence, and when we reached my destination, I paid him his fare. I also gave him a generous tip, grateful for the fact that he didn't ask me any polite but unwanted questions. I waited until he drove away before turning around to fully take in my new accommodations.

It was a large, white house with a wrap around veranda and a tidy picket fence. There was no sign to name it for what it was—from the outside it looked like it belonged to a wealthy family who cared enough to keep the old home in good order. But I knew that this was the place.

I knocked firmly on the door, and was greeted by a very young, very pregnant teenaged girl in overalls and pigtails. She took one look at me and shouted, "Vera! Late arrival!" She opened the door and moved aside. "What're you waiting for? C'mon in."

ॐ∾ॐ

I was ushered into a high ceilinged living room decorated with random furnishings—overstuffed couches, two reclining chairs, and a rocker—all inhabited by three other young women. They each pretended not to see me, and I pretended to ignore them back. The young girl in the overalls sat down heavily into the rocker, picked up a well-used novel and began to read. I stood awkwardly at the edge of the room, looking anywhere but at my new roommates.

"Greetings."

I turned toward the gravelly, female voice. "Hi," I said.

"I'm Vera." She was a middle aged woman with badly dyed black hair and a gap-toothed smile. "I believe we spoke on the phone."

I nodded. "I'm Olivia," I told her.

"Newton-John?" asked one of the girls at the same time another said, "Liar, liar, pants on fire."

Vera made an irritated noise, and the one who had called me a liar grinned and flipped us the bird.

"Excuse the girls," Vera apologized. "It's my experience that pregnancy makes *all* women crazy. Introduce yourselves, please."

Vera stepped out of the room, and no one said a word. I stared helplessly at a yellow spot on the wall.

The one who hadn't spoken at all yet finally tossed her long blonde hair over her shoulder and told me, "I'm Jane. From Montana. Due right around Easter." She patted her tummy and went back to watching TV.

The one with pigtails didn't look up from her book but said, "Ryder. Brandon, Manitoba. Due any week. Any day. Any second. Thank God."

"Don't blaspheme," chided the one who had made the 'Newton-John' joke. She was working on what looked like needlepoint. She pushed her glasses up on her nose and wound a piece of curly brown hair around her pinky finger. "I'm Kristen. And that's my real name," she gave the fourth girl a dirty look. "I'm from Prince George. This baby should be born in the New Year." She smiled at me. "The cranky one over there goes by Georgia."

"Like the peach that I am," Georgia said sarcastically. She stared at me unkindly. "No one gives their real name here," she informed me. "Or their real story."

"Speak for yourself," Kristen retorted.

Georgia rolled her eyes. "Is Olivia your real name?" she asked me. I said nothing.

"Didn't think so," Georgia told me. "But let me tell you a little bit about each of these girls. Kristen-Is-My-Real-Name over there is your average girl next door, smarty-pants, lawyer in the making. She started university with mighty expectations, got seduced by the first sexy professor she met, found out he was married and ran here."

Kristen kept her mouth shut, but stitched her little piece of fabric more furiously.

Georgia continued. "Jane was the homecoming queen. Pretty, but not too bright. Pep squad, jock boyfriend. Everything going for her. The kind of girl that Kristen wants to stab in the eye with the compass from her geometry set. Knocked up on grad night, jock boyfriend ditches her, forced here by her parents, covering it up with a story about an extended vacation."

Jane didn't look away from the TV.

"Now, little Ryder here, she's a seriously messed up case," Georgia's face lit up with the conspiracy of her story. "Backwoods Manitoba, not a lot going on there. Fifteen years old, not sure of her due date, lives alone in a cabin with her Daddy and her brother…You can make your own conclusions about the rest."

"You're disgusting," Ryder said without conviction, and then commanded, "Do Olivia."

I shuffled my feet uncomfortably as Georgia eyed me up and down. She stood up and walked around me in a circle. I was genuinely curious about what she thought she could see. I tried to keep my face impassive as she scrutinized me.

"Hmm. Bruised face. Broken heart," Georgia noted. "You fell in love with an older guy who you truly thought would be the one. He turned out to be an abuser—both of you and an illicit substance, or two. Or three. You had to leave as soon as you found out you were pregnant because no baby deserves to be in that kind of environment, and you have a real bad case of bleeding heart, right and wrong. You couldn't tell your parents, because that would be admitting that what they told you about the guy had turned out to be true. Which would actually be worse than having this baby. And here you are."

I shrugged. "It's as good a story as any," I said. "But what about you?"

Kristen laughed, ignoring the scathing look that Georgia sent her way. "Don't listen to her, Olivia. She also thinks that Vera is a retired drag queen turned midwife."

"Me? You want my story?" Georgia said innocently. "I'm just your average, run-of-the-mill whore who didn't have the sense to make my john wear a condom."

Just then, Vera came back into the room with a stack of paperwork in her hand. "Here you go." She handed me the forms. "Fill in as little or as much as you want. Just make sure that you read and sign the no-fault waiver. Don't need any lawsuits on my hand. The contact info for the adoption agency is included, but you can fill in the legal paperwork for that in their private office. I don't keep any of that around here. Too many nosy girls. There's also a list of typical house rules in there. No drinking, no smoking, no men, ten o'clock curfew, etcetera."

"There goes the weekend," Georgia muttered, and everyone laughed. Even me.

❧❧

I adjusted very quickly to life as Olivia Potter, my adopted persona. It was actually almost easier to be her than it was to be me. Although Vera ran a strict household and had high expectations for the daily chore schedule, she had no *personal* expectations. Nor did anyone else. We ate most meals together, sometimes pooling our meager funds to order in, sometimes indulging each other's weird cravings, happier to be eating with strangers than to eat alone. When we talked, it was usually to compare pregnancy notes. Certain subjects remained taboo—like the true identities of our 'sperm donors' as Georgia called them—but almost anything related to bodily functions was fair game.

I had been at the shelter for a little over a month when Ryder went into labour. One minute she said, "Pass the salt," and the next she made a face like she'd been kicked in the gut. Vera was at her side in a flash, and within what seemed like seconds, she had the little teen mom loaded into her old station wagon and bundled off to the hospital.

Georgia, Jane, Kristen and I ate the rest of our meal in uneasy silence.

"Another one bites the dust," Georgia finally said, shoving her plate away and stalking off angrily.

"I wonder who our next inmate will be?" Jane sounded more sad than bitter. She picked at her fish and chips idly, and then sighed. "I wasn't hungry anyways." She cleared both her and Georgia's plate. "Goodnight."

Kristen and I were left staring at each other.

"An un-hungry pregnant woman. Never thought I'd see the day," she joked half-heartedly.

"What happens now?" I asked.

Kristen shrugged. "Vera's strictly an antepartum deal. She's funded mostly by the private adoption agency she works for, so as soon as the baby's unloaded and all of the paperwork's taken care of, Ryder will be released into the hospital's care. Maybe then she'll go home. We'll get a new roomie."

"Are there so many of us?" I wondered.

Kristen looked as sad as I felt. "I hope not. But right before Ryder there was Lily, and just before you got here, a girl named Naomi left."

I looked down at my food, understanding why Jane had stopped eating. "What if I can't do it?"

Kristen understood immediately. "Give the baby up?"

"Yes," I whispered.

"They can't make you," my roommate told me.

"I wish that reassured me," I replied.

"Are you a Christian?" she asked me.

"If I say that I don't know, that probably means that I'm not, right?" I answered.

She smiled. "It doesn't mean that you don't have the potential to be one. I find that even in my situation, I can take comfort in the fact that God will help me make the decision that best reflects His will."

"Jesus Christ," Georgia swore, bursting into the kitchen suddenly.

"Yes," Kristen said, deliberately misunderstanding Georgia's words. "He is the topic of conversation."

"Can't a girl get some damned chocolate ice cream without getting a damned conversion thrown into the deal?" Georgia demanded.

Kristen finally lost her own appetite and threw her plate into the sink. "Screw you, Georgia."

"Who's turning the other cheek now?" Georgia asked mockingly as Kristen turned on her heel and stomped out.

I sighed and put my head down on the table.

Ѧѧ

After a few days, Vera came home without Ryder, and life returned to its normal state. Well, as normal as can be expected in a houseful of pregnant women under the age of twenty. Georgia received a GED package in the mail, and sought a delicate truce with Kristen in exchange for study help. A new roommate did arrive almost right away. The girl was from Montreal, spoke a refreshing blend of accented English smattered with French, and could cook unbelievable meals. She was pretty, blonde, and easy to get along with. Her name—or the one she gave us anyway—was Rachelle.

The same day she came, I received a postcard from home.

I had dragged Kristen and Jane out to get a chili cheese dog with extra pickles from my favourite restaurant in town. I also wanted to grab a little Christmas gift for each of the girls, and used that as an excuse to separate myself from my friends for a few minutes. I checked the post office on a weekly basis, and though I was getting used to coming back empty handed, I couldn't help but wonder how my parents were doing back home. Nothing like Christmas to make a bitter teen mom nostalgic.

The retiree who ran the parcel counter and assigned the safety deposit boxes waved at me when I came through the doors. "Look out there, Olivia, you're going to get trapped by the mistletoe!"

I looked up at the doorway and I laughed. "Mr. Humphries, I think that's ivy, not mistletoe. And aren't you married anyway? Anything come for me today?"

He smiled innocently. "That's your business," he told me.

"Uh huh," I replied, more excited than irritated. He usually just responded to my weekly inquiry with a sad head shake. I unlocked the PO box, reached in and pulled out a postcard with a cheerful Santa embossed on the front. I flipped it over. COME HOME, was all it said.

"Thanks, Mr. Humphries," I managed in a tightly cheerful voice.

"Merry Christmas!" he called back.

My hands were shaking by the time I hit the sidewalk, and my whole body was shivering as I dropped the postcard into the first garbage can I saw. I stood there, watching crystalized snowflakes obscure Saint Nick's face. Sighing, I grabbed the postcard and fished around in my purse for a pen. I crossed out the words written on it, and instead wrote 'NO' is dark, capital letters. Then I added, 'Return to sender'. Without checking to see if Mr. Humphries was watching, I shoved the postcard in the big red mailbox outside the office.

Chapter 27
THEN

I was covered from head to toe in garage dust. I had been digging through our storage boxes for several hours, dodging calls from Amanda Lockhurst, from Tori, and even from Jordan. The side of my face ached from where a badly balanced box had landed on it. I was also ignoring the biting pain radiating from two of the fingers on my left hand. I had ripped the nails back while peeling the packing tape off of a cardboard box labelled "Wedding Stuff."

When I came back into the house to use the bathroom, I glanced at myself in the mirror and was forced to confront my frightening state. I resisted the urge to dry heave into the sink. I looked more than a bit crazy. I had the beginnings of a black eye and a blood soaked cloth wrapped around my hand. I hoped vaguely that I hadn't bled into the wedding tape—the object that had caused me to tear through our garage in desperation. I clung to the little black cartridge as I stared a my scary reflection.

Who was this dirty, haggard woman staring back at me? I didn't recognize her as any of the selves I knew. I closed my eyes and sagged hopelessly against the sink.

"Laura," said a soft voice beside me, and I immediately felt Cindy's familiar presence at my side.

"Hi," I replied, not being able to think of anything else to say.

"I've been calling you all day," my friend told me.

"You have? I was out in the garage," I said. I opened my eyes and our gazes met in the mirror.

Cindy put her hands on my shoulders and tried to pull me away, but I held tightly to the sink.

"Do you know what the hardest thing about being a wife and mother is, Cindy?" I asked softly.

"Besides everything?" she quipped half-heartedly.

My reflection smiled a macabre smile. "The hardest thing is losing yourself. One second you're looking in the mirror, and you're you. And the very next moment you're looking back at a stranger."

I touched my hand to my face, leaving a bloody fingerprint on my cheek.

"Oh, my God," my friend exclaimed, "You're hurt. What exactly were you *doing* in your garage?"

I showed her the old VHS tape. "Richie's been saying for years that we needed to convert this into a DVD, but he never found the time to do it. Now it's up to me to preserve our memories."

Cindy wet a cloth and wiped my face.

"Laura, you're not alone." she said softly.

"Not yet," I replied.

☊❧

I left Richard's hospital room to get a cup of coffee, and while I was a gone, an eternity had passed.

A half dozen medical professionals surrounded his bed, and the room looked like a scene from one of those evening TV dramas. They were all moving very quickly and seemed to be shouting at each other. I caught words like "cardiac arrest" and "arrhythmia". I stood dumbly in the doorway watching, until a very young looking intern pushed by me roughly, causing me to drop my coffee cup. Dr. Friday was at my side in an instant.

"Laura," he said softly, "You shouldn't be in here."

"Is he dying?" I asked.

"His heart stopped, but we were able to restart it," the surgeon told me. "Your husband had a seizure. He knocked out both his respirator and his feeding tube. The team has already placed a new valve into the airway, but the intestinal tube will have to be put in again surgically."

I sagged down into a chair in the corner of the room. "I was gone for less than ten minutes."

"This isn't a scenario we haven't prepared you for," Dr. Friday reminded me.

"But what if I wasn't here?" I asked in a desperate voice.

"I can't promise that won't happen. But I expect that he will continue as he has. A slow progression. And I can promise you that I will call you the second I hear that anything has gone wrong," he assured me.

"How long?" I wondered.

"As long as he's stable, a month. Six weeks, maybe," the doctor said. "It's hard to be definite because his brain is already so inactive in all the traditional senses, but my best guess is that he's already been having mini seizures for at least a few weeks. His heart can't take much more, Laura. There are bypass options…But that's not a permanent solution."

"No," I answered. "It's almost done, Dr. Friday. If I'm not here and you can keep him alive, then do it. But I'm not sure my own heart can take anymore either."

❧

It was after midnight when I got home from the hospital, and my body was aching with exhaustion. I dragged myself from the car to my bedroom, feeling each muscle groan in protest. I wished that I could make my body go to sleep, but no matter how tired I felt when I finished my vigil at Richard's side, I was always restless again by the time I put my pajamas on. I had given up months ago trying to sleep in the bed that my husband and I shared. I could lay on my side of the bed, but it was always cold and left me feeling hollow. I no longer expected to turn over and find him beside me, but it didn't stop me from rolling onto my side every few minutes to confirm it. My only consolation was that I never slept long enough to have nightmares. And I knew that both Jordan and Tori suffered from them on an almost nightly basis.

Thinking of my kids reminded me that I hadn't checked in on either of them when I came in. I sat up, knowing that it was just an excuse my fitful brain was using to get me back out of bed, but I caved in anyways.

I looked into Jordan's room first. I stood at his door for a second before opening it. It was dark and silent outside his room, but the door was ajar so I pushed it open. He was on his bed with ear phones tucked in and the covers pulled up snugly around his chin. It was dark inside the room too, but when I opened the door a little further Jordan opened his eyes and sat up.

"Dad alright?" he asked, and I nodded. He smiled and closed his eyes again.

"Can't sleep either?" I wondered, and he shook his head.

"Nothing helps," he told me without opening his eyes.

"I know," I said. I waited for him to say something else, but he remained silent. Sighing, I left his room, closing the door behind me.

Tori's light was on, so I knocked. She didn't answer. There was a likelihood that she hadn't heard me, but there was just as much of a chance that she was ignoring me. I hadn't seen my daughter in over a week. I left for the hospital before she went to school—when she went at all. She was never home when I came in to make dinner, though she did seem to eat whatever I left in the fridge for her. When I came home late from my second stint in Richie's room, Tori was usually in bed. If I got home earlier, she was either out with friends or at the hospital herself. The nurses now reported her comings and goings to me. I knocked again, a little more insistently.

"What?" called a gruff male voice.

I swung the door open quickly and stared at the occupant of Tori's room. He was sprawled on an angle across my daughter's double bed. He was huge, maybe six foot five, and well over two hundred pounds. His forearms were covered with dark tattoos. I could only assume that they continued on up under his shirt sleeves to his shoulders. He was wearing thick, army-print shorts and heavy boots. A ring protruded from his lip, and his head was covered in dark stubble.

"Goodness," was all I could say. *At least he's not under the covers, or worse, naked,* I thought and then felt guilty immediately.

The big man—he really was more of man than a boy—sat up and looked at me with interest.

"Hey," he said. "I'm Buzz."

"Of course you are," I replied.

"Are you Tori's…sister?" he asked with a raised eyebrow.

"Funny," I said. "Have you seen my daughter?"

"Yeah," Buzz laughed. "She's totally hot. But she's a girl. *You.* You're a woman."

My jaw actually dropped. "You're aware that I'm her mother?"

"Yeah, but she's gone out for some smokes," he told me and then rubbed his crotch in an appalling gesture.

It was like watching a train wreck. I couldn't tear my eyes away from Buzz, even though looking at him was making me feel sick to my stomach.

"Do you have an..err…erection?" The words were out of my mouth before I could stop them. I tried to recover. "You know that I'm probably twice your age, right?"

Just then my daughter walked into her bedroom. "What the hell is going on?" she demanded.

"You took the words right out of my mouth," I said back, before realizing that Tori had directed her angry question at Buzz, not at me.

Her guest somehow managed to smirk at her while still leering at me. "What's the matter? Can't handle a little competition?"

Tori's face went red and I thought that she was going to cry. I reached over to calm her, but she waved me off and then burst into laughter.

"Jesus," she said. "So you actually *were* hitting on my mom?"

Buzz shrugged and stood. He towered over Tori and me.

"God," I stated. "You've got to be over six and a half feet tall!"

He grinned at me. "You bet I am. Wanna come for a ride?"

My daughter was still giggling helplessly. "I really. Think it's time. For you to go," she said to him in between breaths.

Buzz appeared unembarrassed. "My smokes?"

Tori grabbed them from her purse and tossed them in his direction. Buzz caught them in one meaty fist, winked at me and then helped himself to handful of my rear end on his way out the door. I watched him leave with an incredulous look on my face.

My daughter sat down on her bed, winded and red-faced from laughing. "That was the funniest thing I've seen."

"Tori, next time you want my attention, just get a tattoo or something," I suggested, but I felt a smile tugging on my lips.

"I'll keep that in mind," she said, and as I made to leave the room she asked, "Could you do me favor?"

"I think that I just did," I reminded her.

Tori ignored my comment. "Could you lie with me until I fall asleep?"

I stopped in my tracks, completely surprised. "Of course."

We both climbed fully clothed into Tori's bed. It was a tight fit.

"How did it come to this?" she asked me, as if she were the adult and I was the child.

"I honestly don't know, sweetheart," I replied. "I just don't know."

I waited for her to say something else, but the only thing I heard was the occasional giggle. And then that subsided into even, steady breathing.

"Goodnight, Tori," I whispered in the dark, knowing that she was already asleep.

Chapter 28
WAY BACK WHEN

A soft knock on my bedroom door dragged me out of that state right in between wakefulness and sleep. Wrapping my blanket around my body, I stood up and stumbled to the door.

"Hi," said Kristen. She was holding two steaming mugs. "I have tea. Can I come in?"

I opened the door wider. "Do you have food, too?"

My friend smiled and patted the pocket of her robe. "Raspberry filled cookies."

"Then absolutely you can come in," I said.

"I couldn't sleep," she told me as we settled on my bed.

I nibbled on a cookie. "What's on your mind?"

"The same thing that's always on my mind. Food," she told me. "But I'm thinking mostly about what my life's going to be, you know, after."

"What was your life like before?" I wondered, knowing that I was unlikely to get an honest answer anyway.

Kristen smiled. "Pretty straight forward. I'm a legal assistant for a tiny law firm. I live with my dad, my older brother and my mom. What about you?"

"I'm a photographer," I told her. It was partly true.

"Is that your one thing?" she asked.

"My one thing?"

"All of the girls seem to bring one thing from home. Something that connects them to their past," Kristen explained. "I brought my Bible. Georgia brought a sewing machine and a suitcase full of patterns, if you can believe it. Did you bring a camera?"

"Oh," I said. "Sort of."

I yanked my backpack out from under my bed and dug through it for a minute before finding one little black film canister.

"This is all that's left," I stated sadly. "I forgot my camera—well, somewhere that's not important anymore. I didn't even get to use this roll."

Kristen turned the canister thoughtfully in her hand and then pocketed it. "Just a second," she said, and stepped lightly out of the room.

Moments later, she returned carrying a shiny black box. "I think that this is for you." She handed it to me and I opened it right away.

"It's a camera," I stated, feeling the pleasant weight of it in my hands. "A Canon Rebel."

"It was a gift," Kristen told me. "But I won't ever use it. And… well, let's just say that I don't talk to the person who gave it to me anymore. I probably never will."

I got the impression that I shouldn't ask her who it came from.

"I don't know what to say," I whispered with catch in my voice.

"Say thank you," Kristen laughed.

"Thank you!" I repeated back obediently and gave my friend a grateful hug.

∂∾ঔ

I stood in the knee-high snow, marveling at how powdery and light it was compared to the wet, sloppy stuff we got in the Vancouver area. My new camera felt solid and comfortable around my neck as I snapped photos of my friends in the subzero Winnipeg weather.

That morning, the girls had been chatting loudly as I joined them at the breakfast table. Rachelle nudged Georgia when she saw me, and suddenly they all went silent.

"What?" I had wondered suspiciously.

"Eat fast," Kristen said to me. "We've got a surprise for you."

Jane had quickly piled toast, eggs, and sausages onto my plate. I shoveled the food into my mouth as fast as I could, and had then let my friends herd me out to the minivan that Vera let us use for trips into the city. We drove for a little over an hour, passing farms and fields, until finally Georgia had shouted, "Stop! This is the place."

Everyone had unloaded into the wintery field, and now they were posing for me in snow, noses red with the cold and faces glowing with the fun of it.

I felt alive and whole for the first time in months.

రొుం

I woke three days after Christmas to find a heavy, whimpering form beside me.

"Hello?" I whispered in a frightened voice.

The weight on my bed shifted, and Georgia propped herself up beside me.

"Olivia," she said. "I'm scared."

Her face was pale and shiny in the dim light coming through my window.

"Georgia?" I asked disbelievingly.

"I think I'm in labour," she told me.

I sat up quickly. "Let's get Vera."

"Please. No," Georgia begged. "I want to keep her. The baby."

"Vera can't make you give your baby away if you don't want to," I replied.

She gripped my hand, and I could feel the terror in her hot palm. "She will. I know she will."

I shook my head. "She can't."

Georgia's eyes met mine in the dark. "She's done it before. Listen. I saw from the bruises on your face when you got here that you'd been beaten."

I nodded my head, keeping guiltily to my cover story.

"So was I," she confided without her usual bitterness. "And my older sister. Our stepdad beat the crap out us of every time he drank."

"I'm sorry," I whispered back.

"My sister, she got pregnant last year, and her fiancé started hitting her, too. She came here to have the baby and give it away.

Didn't want her kid to grow up the way we did. But at the last second her fiancé found her and came to take her away, said he was getting help. But Vera *made* them leave the baby behind."

"That's against the law," I argued.

Georgia shook her head. "Unless it's the law they're threatening you with. Vera said that she was going to turn them into child services, and then the baby would wind up in foster care."

I felt a fearful sympathy grip my heart. I got out of bed and found my purse. I counted my money slowly, and placed it all in Georgia's hand.

"This almost three hundred dollars," I told her. "The people who live three doors down are the Browns. They're big time pro-lifers and they think that Vera's running some kind of brothel. Ask them to call you a cab. Go anywhere but St. Boniface."

"Are you serious?"

"As I've ever been," I answered.

Georgia kissed my cheek and padded silently out of the room. I closed my eyes, but was awake long past the time that morning light crept through my window.

∢‪

New Year's came and went without much celebration, and no one commented to me on Georgia's disappearance. In passing, Vera mentioned that every now and then she got a runner, but if I hadn't known better, I would've assumed that she was speaking in general terms rather than referencing our cranky old roommate. No one came to take Georgia's room, and then when Kristen went into labour suddenly late one mid-January night, she was ushered out quietly. The large house suddenly began to seem very empty.

One particularly dreary evening, Rachelle and I were sitting at the living room table playing a few hands of Crazy Eights when Jane decided to join us. The pretty cheerleader usually preferred fashion magazines to card games, so I was surprised when she asked to be dealt in. But we had all been feeling a little alone lately.

"Looks like I'm up for execution next," she said morosely as she organized her hand.

"*Pardon?*" Rachelle asked. "I think maybe I misunderstand."

Jane laughed.

"She means that her baby is coming next," I explained.

"And then I disappear," Jane added. "Do you really think that Georgia got out?"

"If that's what she wanted, then me, I 'ope so," Rachelle answered.

"Me, too," I stated a little too quickly.

I felt a twinge in my chest. I truly hoped that Georgia had made the right decision. I wondered where she had gone, knowing that she wouldn't have—couldn't have—gone home to her abusive stepfather.

"It's like a revolving door of pregnant girls." Jane said, and then sighed. "But right now I have to pee. Don't start the next hand without me."

"Vera should be back today," I commented.

With nobody on the brink of delivery, the mistress of the house had gone for a weekend visit with her sister's family. She had promised to bring us a batch of homemade fudge. Thinking of it made my stomach grumble almost painfully.

"*Oui,*" Rachelle agreed. "Is all okay, Olivia? You have a look *étrange* on your face."

"Fine," I grimaced, but stood up to stretch a suddenly cramped leg.

Rachelle was out of her seat in a second. "I don't think you're fine, Olivia. You're bleeding."

I looked down, and saw that blood was indeed soaking my pants.

"Crap," I said, leaning weakly against the table. "Crap."

I heard a ringing in my ears, and then I was surrounded by gentle hands and concerned voices.

లు ఌ

I watched Vera's face through a cloud of pain. The girls at the house had called her immediately after calling the paramedics, and she had beaten the ambulance to the hospital. Although she had been barking orders at the nursing staff since I arrived, her eyes remained on my face, and they were sympathetic. Each time she spoke to me, her voice went from commanding to soothing, and I was grateful for her presence.

"There is a story I tell all my girls who lose a baby," she said softly as a painful cramp subsided. "Do you want to hear it?"

"Yes, please," I answered in a strained voice. "Why won't it stop hurting?"

"Give it time," she said. "Your body still has a lot of stuff to clear out, and it will be a while before you normalize."

"The story? Distract me," I begged.

"I grew up in the prairies," Vera started, and I drifted with the sound of her voice. "My dad was a doctor, and in a little town like that one, well, you get to see and hear an awful lot of stuff in a physician's home. It's hard on a little girl, knowing about cancer and broken ribs and everyone's private business."

She paused as I breathed my way through some more pain.

"One day, my dad went off on a house call, and was gone overnight," Vera continued. "When he came back, it was the wee hours of the morning, and he looked worse that I'd ever seen him. I listened to him talking to my mom about his case. A little girl, only thirteen—that was just a year older than me at the time—had died trying to give birth to a baby in her bathtub. Everything that could go wrong, did."

I moaned a little as another bad cramp overwhelmed me. "*This* is the story you tell miscarrying mothers?" I asked as it subsided.

"Do you want me to stop?" Vera asked.

"No," I said.

"The baby was breach and five weeks premature. The girl had been concealing her pregnancy from her parents—they never did find out who the father was—and she hadn't received any prenatal care. The chord was wrapped around the little one's neck, and when he came out his face was blue and my dad knew that he wasn't going to make it. The mom started to hemorrhage pretty bad, and Dad couldn't get the bleeding stopped. By the time the ambulance got there, they were both gone already." Vera watched me, gauging my reaction.

I stared at her in alarm.

"This is the reason I started my shelter," Vera told me. "And the reason that I became a midwife."

"That's awful. Why? Why would you tell someone who just lost a baby that story?" I asked, unable to keep the revulsion out of my voice.

"To remind her that unlike the girl in my story, she still has a life. And a future."

And then Vera gave me an injection that melted away the last of the pain, and put me to sleep.

൭�ൟ൭

I watched listlessly as the nurse checked my pulse and pushed on my sagging stomach. Twenty-four hours had eased some of my physical pain, but none of the emotional. The nurse misread my expression.

"Don't worry, sweetie. In a month or two, you'll be back in a bikini," she told me.

I tried to smile back at her. But I felt empty. Guilty. Angry. She made a note on my chart and exited the room.

"Does it get easier?" I asked the nurse's receding back.

"For some," Vera answered.

I hadn't realized that she was sitting in the corner of the room.

"Do you want to to know the sex of the baby?" Vera wondered.

At the word 'baby', my heart lurched. "No. I don't think that's a great idea."

"Some do, some don't," Vera told me impassively.

"I don't," I stated emphatically.

"Rachelle gave me this to give to you. Said it was from Kristen, for after you had the baby." Vera handed me a plastic bag.

"Thank you," I said, taking the proffered item. I opened it and examined the contents. A business card was stapled to a blank sheet of lined paper. The card read, *Kristen Myres, Legal Assistant.* It had a phone number and a Prince George address on it.

So she was telling he truth, I thought, relieved.

"Thank you," I repeated as I set the paper on the hospital nightstand.

I closed my eyes and slept again for a bit. I dreamed of a tiny baby boy with Paul's blue eyes and my pointed chin.

Chapter 29
THEN

"What will happen?" I asked Dr. Friday softly.

I couldn't take my eyes off of my husband's frail body. The forced air pumped through the ventilator in slow, steady movements. I could barely recognize him as the man I had shared my bed with for so many years. Richie's hair had become waxy grey in colour, and his skin was stretched tautly across his face, bordering on translucent in some spots. His once naturally muscular frame was near to gaunt and he was almost the same shade of white as the hospital sheets.

But against all odds, my husband's body was still alive.

Dr. Friday watched me watching Richie.

"When we turn off the machines, his body will likely shut down. He will probably breathe on his own. For a short time anyway. His heart may give out from the effort of trying to maintain a body that can no longer be maintained," the surgeon told me.

"Will it hurt?" I asked.

Dr. Friday put his hand overtop of mine in an uncharacteristic gesture of sympathy. "From a clinical perspective, it is unlikely that Richie has the ability to feel pain. He has no reflexes, virtually no responses. Not even the automatic kind. So from a personal perspective, and years of experience, I can tell you this: don't worry about your husband's suffering. The only person who will feel any pain is you."

"I'll have to make my decision soon, I guess," I said.

"There's still no rush," he replied.

"Can we be alone?" I asked softly.

The surgeon left the room quietly, and I stared down at my husband helplessly. I pulled a chair up beside him and laid my head on his thin chest.

"It's not supposed to be like this," I said to him. "I love you, you know? I swear it. I've never been very good at showing it. And you didn't deserve that, just like you don't deserve this."

For months, the specialists had been telling me that it might help me to talk to Richie, but I hadn't been able to make myself do it. If they felt that he couldn't hear me, what was the point in chattering at him like an idiot? But suddenly, the words couldn't get out fast enough.

"I'm so sorry for being afraid to share myself with you. I don't know why I held it in all this time. Sometimes, I don't think I even knew I was doing it. Almost two decades ago, my life was changed by someone else, and I've never been..." I trailed off as a seething anger gripped me.

"Damn you, Paul!" I shouted, and a nurse passing in the hall jumped a little.

"How am I supposed to get closure, here, with him, if I could never get it from you?" I wondered out loud.

Someone behind me cleared his throat, and I turned in surprise. A teenaged boy was standing beside the bathroom door. He was wearing a baggy grey t-shirt and khaki pants. A shock of red hair hung down in front of his eyes and his face was deeply freckled in a pleasant way.

"Hello there," I greeted him uncertainly.

"Hi, Mrs. Lockhurst," he answered. "I'm Kieran. Sorry to intrude."

"It's okay," I assured him, embarrassed by my emotional outburst. "Are you a friend of Jordan's? He's not here."

Kieran looked a little younger than my son, but I couldn't think of another logical reason for his presence.

He smiled at me, exposing a mouthful of braces. "Actually, I'm Tori's boyfriend," he told me.

"Oh," I said, trying to cover my surprise.

Kieran's smile got bigger. "I know. I don't have any weird body parts pierced and I have an IQ above ninety. In the interest of disclosure, I'm a year younger than your daughter."

"Oh," I repeated.

"She's embarrassed to introduce us," he informed me.

I couldn't help it. I laughed. It sounded unnatural in the solemnity of the room.

"Sorry," I apologized. "But if you had *seen* some of the boys she's brought home…" I thought of Buzz.

Kieran grinned at me. "I've heard."

"Maybe she's embarrassed because you're so, well, normal," I suggested.

"I am a bit of a smart ass, though," he stated with a straight face.

"I see," I replied with a little smile. "I have to admit, I didn't know she'd, um, branched out."

Kieran grabbed a chair from the other side of the room and slid it over to sit right beside me. He put his hand overtop of mine in a familiar way. It was a warm and oddly soothing gesture. I left my hand under his, accepting the unexpected sympathy from this stranger.

"Tori and I met online a couple of months ago," he told me. "In a forum for teens grieving the loss of a parent. My dad died two years ago. He had cancer."

"I'm sorry."

Sadness passed across of his face, quickly replaced by a soft smile. "Don't be. He suffered quite a bit."

"Oh." I seemed to be saying that a lot.

"I want to tell you something." Kieran looked at me hesitantly, meeting my eyes and holding my gaze. "Tori believes that you made the wrong choice."

"I know," I said, unable to keep the bitterness out of my voice.

"But she's spent a lot of time here with Mr. Lockhurst, and she's thankful for having the opportunity. She's mad, but not at you," Kieran stated. "You seem kind of angry yourself."

It was a disarmingly and inappropriate personal observation, but I just sagged sadly in response. "I am. And I have nowhere to direct it. I can't blame the kids or Richie. I don't want to take it out on my friends."

"You and Tori are so much alike," my daughter's boyfriend told me.

"That's what I hear," I replied.

"Who *are* you mad at?" he asked, looking me straight in the eye.

I shrugged. "Circumstance? God? I don't know."

Kieran leaned closer, bending so that his open face was level with mine. "I don't think that's the truth," he said.

I hung my head. "Paul," I whispered. "I'm mad at someone named Paul."

"Then go tell him."

"I can't," I started to explain, but then wondered, *Why not? What's stopping me from confronting him?*

"Nothing's stopping you," Kieran said, answering the question I hadn't voiced. "I bet once you've done that, everything else will fall into place."

I stared at my daughter's boyfriend, a crazy idea forming in my mind. "How old did you say you were?"

"I'm fourteen," he told me.

"I think, Kieran, that I'm very glad to meet you."

સ્જ

I stared at the phone, willing it to spring to life.

Ring! I commanded mentally.

Since my impromptu meeting with Kieran in the hospital, I had only stopped running around to call my lawyer. My mind had been moving as fast as my body, working in overdrive to plan how I would do what I suddenly *needed* to do, consequences be damned.

After I had her assistant page her a third, and then a fourth time, Debbie Ling finally returned my calls. She listened in silence as I rapidly explained my wishes to her. When I finished speaking, Debbie still said nothing.

I cleared my throat. "Are you still there?"

"I'm here," she said finally. "Laura, you realize that in doing this, you run the risk of not being here when—if—Richard passes."

"I do," I replied, amazed to find that my voice wasn't shaking.

"Tori's still only sixteen," she reminded me. "This is a big burden."

"That's why I've included Amanda and Cole Lockhurst in the decision," I said.

"And Jordan?"

I swallowed uncomfortably. "My son doesn't have a thick enough shell."

"And does your family fully understand what you're asking them to do?" Debbie asked.

"I haven't told them," I admitted quietly.

My lawyer was silent again.

"Please," I said. "I just need five or six days, and they you can have them sign the paperwork."

"Laura, what you're asking me to do..." she trailed off.

"Please," I said again.

Debbie sighed loudly. "I'll fax over the paperwork that you need to sign. When you're done that, just leave it at my office and I'll take care of the rest."

"Thank you. I'll talk to you very soon." I started to hang up, and then realized that she was still speaking.

"Laura, I have to ask you. Are you planning on coming back?"

I pressed the headset into the receiver. Maybe she wouldn't realize that I had heard her question. But then again, maybe she would.

෴

I stood at the foot of my bed, staring into my partially packed suitcase. I couldn't remember the last time I had done anything truly spontaneous. I had grabbed random items from my closet and tossed them into the bag with my toothbrush, hairbrush, and makeup bag. I also hadn't put on makeup since before Richie's accident, and I wondered just how clumpy mascara could become if it sat unused for almost a year. Probably very.

I zipped the suitcase up and gave it a critical look. It had been a wedding gift—something to take on the honeymoon that never happened. We had used it once, to take the kids to Disneyland many years before.

It was not a suitcase that fit at all with what I was about to do. I stared at it disparagingly. It was the kind of suitcase that alluded to careful planning and controlled decisions. It was the kind of suitcase that a thirty-eight year old, married woman with two kids would use.

I unzipped it and defiantly dumped the contents onto the floor. I stomped to my walk-in closet and began pulling out clothes from the very back. I tossed aside old blankets and long forgotten baskets of mismatched socks, digging for what I knew was there.

"Aha!" I said out loud, yanking my prize from its hiding place and setting it lovingly on the bed.

Aside from dust, the twenty year old backpack still looked like new. The enormous Canadian flag, stitched on by hand, still lay flat against the main pocket. The zippers all ran smoothly and the clasps seemed to be functioning normally.

I smiled. This would suit my needs much better.

কৈ

I made my second attempt at packing a little more deliberate. Spontaneous did not have to equate to carelessness. And rummaging through my closet would give me time to rummage through my mind as well.

The vague call I had placed to my mother-in-law had left me in a more pensive mood. It had been almost too easy. Amanda Lockhurt hadn't asked a single question. If anything, she had been enthusiastic about keeping Jordan and Tori for a week or two, stating that having the teens around would keep her mind off of things. I had considered asking to speak to either one of the children but I too was afraid that the contact would be enough to break into the small bubble of anticipatory euphoria that I had created for myself. I felt relief when Amanda told me that Tori was plugged into both her iPod and her laptop, while Jordan had decided to see a matinee with some friends. I pictured my daughter's dark head of dyed "not-quite" black hair bobbing in time with a ska tune that probably predated her birth by twenty years. If Tori was online, she was probably chatting with her friends. Maybe with Kieran. If she was offline she was probably writing song lyrics or poetry. Either task would keep Tori absorbed for hours at a time, and she had a strict do-not-disturb policy when she was engrossed in her fusion of electronics, social life, and creative outlet. I hoped that my son and his friends would choose a comedy at the theatre. I couldn't really remember the last time I had heard my son's laugh. I tried to remember its distinct sound but it blended with my memory of Richie's own deep chuckle, so I pushed it away.

I steered my thoughts away from my children, relieved that I had not had to have a forced conversation with either of them. And the relief instantly made me feel guilty. Richie had been Amanda and Cole's only son in houseful of daughters. I couldn't imagine the depth of loss the older woman must be feeling.

So why do I not want my own children here now? I wondered. *Why won't I tell them what I'm about to do?*

It was a time when I ought to be drawing my family close, to be tightening the bonds on my loved ones, sharing things that I had never before shared. I tried not to think too hard about why I didn't feel the need to do those things, and instead concentrated on my haphazardly planned trip.

I had booked my flight on the internet before even calling Amanda. It was a non-refundable trip with a flexible return date. I hadn't considered whether I might be unable to make the flight work, or whether my children or extended family might ask me to stay home. This was not a trip that I wanted to be talked out of. It was a trip that I *would* not be talked out of.

I examined the pile of my clothes spread across my bed and floor. There were two pantsuits, bought with the hope that they would motivate me to choose a career where I might need them. There were several sweatshirts and t-shirts that I considered to be standard mom gear. There were multi-function blouses and pants, designed to be dressed up or dressed down as the occasion called for it. The one actual dress that I owned—worn to every formal event for the last five years—was crumpled in a ball at my feet.

I moved a little hopelessly back to my closet. None of it was appropriate, and none of it fit properly anyway. In the last ten months I had lost about fifteen pounds—ironic in that for all of my work out and fad diet attempts in the past twelve or thirteen years I had never been able to lose an inch. My comfy jeans, always a fail safe choice in the past, now hung loosely on my hips, and my t-shirts bunched in areas that they ought to hug. I had paid so little attention to my appearance over the last year that my ill-fitting clothes hadn't mattered until this very moment. I considered whether or not I ought to just purchase a new wardrobe when I arrived at Heathrow. I tried to imagine myself explaining to the border guard that I hadn't been able to bring any personal belongings because they reminded me too much of my dying husband and my distant teenaged children. They would probably think me a crazy woman on the run.

And they might be right, I admitted to myself.

I reached into Richie's side of the closet, grabbing one of his old plaid shirts, inhaling to see if I could catch the scent of him. I allowed myself a moment of overwhelming sadness. I closed my eyes and pictured my husband's face as it had looked before the crash, warm and alive. I pushed aside the memory of his body hooked up to the devices that fed him and breathed for him. I folded my husband's shirt and placed it decisively into my old backpack.

I can do this, I thought resolutely, trying to climb back into a hopeful mental state.

Thinking of Richie had reminded me suddenly of my "skinny bin". It had actually started out as several boxes—clothes I had put aside after first having Jordan, and then more after I had Tori. I had pared down the boxes over the years, but there were a few items that I hadn't been able to part with. I had considered throwing away the entire bin on more than one occasion. I had once left it out with a few boxes for donation, only to find that Richie had brought the bin back into the the house. I found him standing defensively in front of the bin, armed with a sharpie and a roll of masking tape. I had watched incredulously as my husband labelled the bin with the words: Skinny Bin, Keep the skinny dream alive!

Richard had slung his arms around my shoulders and whispered into my ear, "One day, Laura, you will fit into every item in here."

I smiled bittersweetly at the memory. I was sure that every one would fit me now.

Chapter 30
WAY BACK WHEN

I woke with a start, and glanced anxiously around the room. Vera was gone from her seat. I thought about what to do next, and then remembered Kristen's business card in my purse. I fumbled through my bag, found it, and then dialed quickly before I could change my mind.

"Hello?"

"May I please speak with Kristen?" I asked nervously.

"Who's this?" The voice on the other end was male and suspicious.

"This is Laura," I said, and then remembered. "But tell her it's Olivia."

"Pardon?"

"Olivia," I said with false surety. "It's Olivia."

I heard the phone be set down somewhere, the sound of footsteps and muffled voices, and then Kristen picked up an extension.

"I've got it," she stated, and then waited for other phone to be hung up. "Olivia? Are you okay?" she asked, concern filling her voice.

"It's done," I whispered. "I lost it."

"Lost what?" Kristen sounded confused, and I met her question with silence.

"Oh," she said finally, in a small sad voice.

"Yes," I replied.

"Are you okay?" she repeated.

I tested out my emotions. They felt raw and overextended. The shame and the sadness were the worst. "I think so," I lied.

"Liar," my friend said automatically.

"Thanks," I replied.

Kristen was silent for a minute. "Can you come to Prince George? At least for a few days before you go on and do whatever it is you're going to do?"

I felt an immediate sense of relief. "Really?"

"Yes," she said with no hesitation.

"Two days," I told her. "I'll be on my way in two days."

⁖⁗

Kristen stood grinning and waving at me from the Prince George bus depot. The ride had been a long and dreary one, and it had been hard to be trapped inside my own head for so many hours. But I felt myself smile now, in response to my friend's enthusiasm. It was the first time I had been able to feel anything positive in days.

"Hi!" I said happily.

My friend greeted me with an enthusiastic hug and guided me to her car, chatting about the weather and her brother's new kitten.

"You seem so, I don't know, *balanced*," I remarked enviously as we pulled out into the street.

She let her smile falter only a little. "I've had more time than you to adjust," she told me. "And I remind myself everyday that someone who really wanted a baby, who really deserved one, got one. And without me, they couldn't have."

I sighed, wishing that I could be that practical. "I don't know if I will ever be balanced again."

"You will," Kristen assured me.

We drove in silence, and after about ten minutes Kristen pulled into a gravel driveway in front of a pretty little rancher. She turned off the car, but made no move to get out.

"Do you want my advice?" she asked, and I nodded.

"Find the next big thing," she advised me. "I have a lot on my side. I've got a strong faith in God, a good job as a legal assistant and a very supportive family." She avoided looking at me, knowing that my relationship with my own parents was tenuous at best. "I'm not trying to make you feel bad. I know that I should be thankful for those things. I *am* thankful. But I promise you that it's not being so blessed that's helping me stay sane—it's having a plan that keeps me going."

"A plan?" I wondered how long it would take before I would feel normal enough to think about the future.

Kristen put her hand overtop of mine. It was a warm, soothing, and most importantly, *genuine* gesture. "I know that it seems hard right now. But I also know that it works, making plans. I can't honestly say that I never think about my baby," she confessed with a sad smile. "And for you, I don't know…This might be even harder. But by this time next year, I'll have finished the second half of my BA and with any luck I'll be starting my LLB in Nova Scotia. And knowing that I still *have* a future—well it's really something. You have a future, too."

"Kristen," I asked in a strained voice. "Did you love him?"

My friend stiffened beside me.

"I'm sorry," I apologized quickly.

"It's okay," she assured me softly. "Sometimes. Maybe. The truth is, Georgia was right. He *is* married. Older. And already has two kids of his own."

"Oh," I said.

"Did *you* love *him?*" she wondered.

"Yes, I think that I did," I admitted.

We both stared out the windshield.

"That's that, then," Kristen finally said lightly.

"That's that," I agreed more somberly.

❦❧

Kristen and I sat on the same side of the booth in the little coffee shop where we had been eating breakfast every morning for the last week. She had picked up a day old, Vancouver newspaper at the grocery store, and had already circled several potential apartments that fit my needs. The whole of the classifieds was spread out on our table, and Kristen was as excited as if we had been searching for the various compartments of her new life versus mine.

My friend was making a two sided list in her little notebook. One side was filled with job ads and their wages, the other with apartments and their rents. She had colour coded the list so that I could tell which jobs made which homes affordable.

"See here," she said enthusiastically pointing at the newspaper. "This one is walking distance to the sky train. And this one allows cats. You could get a kitten!"

I laughed. "Right now I'd settle for a job that pays more than six dollars an hour and an apartment that's bigger than a cardboard box."

Kristen made a face. "You're too much of a pessimist," she told me, and then brightened. "But at least you've got your sense of humour back."

"You were right," I admitted. "It's easier to act normal if I'm making plans. Thank you."

"Hey," she said lightly. "You'd do it for me. Right?"

"Maybe not as efficiently," I joked.

She blushed a little and then reached suddenly for her purse. "I have something for you."

"It's not a kitten is it?" I asked suspiciously.

Kristen laughed. "Much better than a kitten, if there is such a thing. But you have to not be mad."

In an almost shy way, she handed a long white envelope to me.

"What is it?" I wondered out loud. It had my name, but Kristen's address on it. I opened it and read quickly. "An acceptance letter?"

"It's just an interview," Kristen assured me.

I read the letter again, more slowly. "It's for a photography program," I said.

"A really good one. I know it was totally wrong, but I sent them some of your photos—the ones you took at Vera's of all of us when we were pregnant. I mailed them away as soon as you said you could come for a visit. I wasn't even sure if I'd hear anything, but...I got this letter yesterday." Kristen watched my face.

"You sent my pictures away?" I asked stupidly. "That's...I don't know. You opened it?"

"I'm so sorry," she apologized. "It was a long shot at best. I'm really so sorry."

"But I got accepted," I stated.

"Yes," my friend agreed.

"Kristen," I said slowly, a wave of love and gratitude overwhelming me. "Don't be sorry. This is fantastic."

"It is?" she asked.

I jumped up from the table, knocking my coffee mug over onto the newspaper. I hugged my friend as hard as I could, tears forming in my eyes. For a moment—just one moment—I forgot what had brought us together in the first place and I allowed myself to consider that Vera might've been right. I might really have a future after all.

Chapter 31
THEN

As soon as the plane landed, I pulled out my cell phone and dialed Cindy.

My friend answered on the fifth ring, sounding a little breathless. "Hello?"

"Cindy."

"You sound funny. Like you're in a tin can," my friend stated.

I had to laugh. Since the accident, most people has been so *careful* about what they said to me.

"*You* sound normal," I said, my voice full of relief.

I heard the sound of something crashing followed by rambunctious laughter.

"Just a sec," said Cindy and then called out in her mom voice, "Boys! If you want to play soccer *at all* for the next *month*, you will cease and desist this very moment!"

There was a moment of silence and then Cindy spoke into the phone again. "Sorry 'bout that. Typical Mike and Lee."

I needed no further explanation.

"No worries," I told her her, and meant it. It was just good to hear the sound of life carrying on.

"Now you sound even funnier."

"I'm in London."

There was a silent pause, and I could picture my friend shrugging.

"Not funny like far away funny. Funny like you just ate piece pie at the world's best restaurant and you want to keep it a secret."

I grinned into the phone and asked guiltily. "Is that bad?"

"No. It's *good* to hear you sounding like that."

"Thanks."

"Okay. Do you want to share this metaphorical restaurant with *me*?"

I hesitated. "Not just yet, but -

Cindy jumped in. "If anyone asks, you're taking some personal time, you're coping okay, and don't want to be bothered. Oh, and you have enough food."

I exhaled. "Yes. Perfect." I hesitated again. "Cindy?"

"Hmm?"

"I promise that I *will* take you to the world's best restaurant with me someday."

I flipped my cell phone shut and stared down at it for a moment before opening it again and pressing the red power button—off. For one wild moment, I pictured myself tossing the little black device, with all its connections to my other life—my real life—into one of the large metal garbage bins in the airport terminal. I could disappear into the city of London, get a job as a waitress at a gloomy pub, serving pints and shots of whiskey to travelers and locals alike, and pretend that I belonged.

I closed my eyes, feeling the throng of strangers around me, sucking me into a lulling anonymity before I took the next step.

කංග

I watched the scenery pass by as I rode the train from Heathrow to Brighton, marveling at how easy it had actually been. A quick train change at Victoria Station, and I was on my way. The countryside was dotted with trees and hills. It had been too dark last time to notice much of anything, and I had been asleep most the time anyway. The ride was almost too fast—less than an hour—and I laughed at myself for expecting delays like the one I had experienced with Paul years before.

No dead bodies or mechanical problems this time around, I thought.

When the train pulled into the station, my heart jumped a little in my chest and I tried to ignore the heavy feeling in my stomach. I grabbed my bag, slung it onto my shoulder and headed out into the street. I could remember exactly how the smell had hit me last time I was here, and I was equally affected now. The closeness of the ocean was evident in the salty air and the sound of birds nearby. I closed my eyes and breathed it in.

I visualized Paul's parents' house with its salmon coloured paint and chipping white trim. I imagined them sitting on their raised deck with it's view of the ocean. I smiled and opened my eyes.

I weighed the idea of catching a cab versus walking, and quickly opted for walking. The exercise would let me stretch my legs after almost twenty hours of sitting. It would also give me the chance to fine tune the speech I was preparing in my head. I headed down toward the beach with the smile still on my face.

ঙ়ক়

The street-front house looked only a little different than it had twenty years earlier. The numbers on the door frame were still brassy, and the '3' was still hanging loosely from a single screw. The deck on the top floor with its pretty French doors had been extended to span the width of the house, and the trim looked freshly painted, but otherwise it was the same.

I took a breath and headed up the little walk, figuring there wasn't much sense in delaying. I had flown over seven thousand kilometres, and another ten steps seemed a very small distance indeed. My feet felt leaden as I walked hesitantly up to the door. I made myself ring the doorbell and waited, picturing Aggie's stout figure lumbering toward the door.

"Hul-lo?" called a young male voice from the other side of the door.

"Uh, hi?" I answered.

"If you're selling something, I'm not buying," came the reply.

"I'm not selling anything!" I called back. "I'm just looking for Aggie and Will!"

"Why didn't you say so?"

The door swung open and I stepped back. A man in his late twenties, dressed in a black v-neck t-shirt and pink plaid flannel pants eyed me up and down.

"Sorry that I'm still in my PJ's," he said. "We don't get much company during the day. I'm Kendall. Come on in. Any friend of Aggie's is a friend of mine."

He couldn't have looked less dangerous, so I shrugged and stepped into the house. I followed Kendall, assessing the furniture as I went. The floral print sofa that I remembered being in the sitting room had been replaced by a black leather couch and matching love seat. The heavy oak coffee table was gone and a glass-topped one had taken its place. At the far end of the room, two tall bar stools and a cocktail table stood beneath a framed set of inkblot paintings. Kendall perched himself on one of the stools, and took a sip from a martini glass. I stood awkwardly on the zig-zagged black and white rug until Kendall pointed to the couch and said, "Sit."

I balanced on the edge, trying to remember the speech I had prepared for Aggie, complete with a demand to know Paul's whereabouts. I wondered if I should present it to this stranger instead since he seemed to know the family.

"Drink?" Kendall asked after a moment.

"No. Well. Maybe?" I fumbled.

"I'll take that as a yes." He downed the rest of his own beverage and then hopped up and left the room.

I sighed in frustration. I hadn't prepared myself for this contingency. I should've considered that Paul's parents might have moved on. I was lucky that the new resident had even *heard* of them.

"Here you go," said Kendall, handing me a martini glass as he breezed into the room. He joined me on the couch. "So. You knew Aggie and Will?"

"Sort of," I responded. "Their son, Paul, is—was—a friend of mine."

I sipped my drink. It was very strong and quite delicious.

"Oh, I *love* Paul," Kendall said to me enthusiastically. "He rented me and Mario the whole house when his mom passed. I had the room upstairs before that."

"Aggie died?" I asked, feeling a slight head rush coming on.

"Oh, you didn't know. I'm sorry. Eight—no, nine years ago," Kendall said, shaking his head sadly. "She was a grand old gal, but she essentially went downhill when her husband got ill. She let me the room—Paul's old one, you know—to help pay the bills. And then when Will died, the place just became too much for her. She moved into the spare room when I met Mario, and it just made sense that we take the master. It worked out splendidly, too, since Paul moved back in to take care of poor Aggie in her last year. He stayed for a while after, but...I'm talking too much, aren't I?" He laughed. "Mario says that I do."

I was a little light-headed, and I shook my head as I tried to process everything Kendall had just said. Will and Aggie were both dead. Paul had lived here, but now he didn't. He still owned the house. I took another big sip, knowing that it wouldn't help un-muddle me at all.

"Where is he?" I asked.

"Mario? At work. I'm the housewife in this relationship," Kendall laughed.

"No, Paul."

"Oh. Back at his apartment in Scotland, I would think." Kendall shrugged. "He used to come by every month to get the rent. And then he started having a mate come by instead. And then about five years ago, he asked us to send it to a London post office box. We've been doing that ever since, and it's been near to seven years since we've seen Paul himself. Too bad, too. He was a great addition to our little club scene. Mario and I loved taking him out with us back in the day. Danced and drank like a man in his twenties, Paul did, and I think he was nearer to forty. Attracted guys like you wouldn't believe. I should be so lucky at his age!"

I pictured Paul and his rock star good looks, trying to make adjustments for the years, maybe a little grayer and a little heavier, gyrating at a gay bar. A man who was partying like that a few years ago couldn't have much to tie him down.

"He's not—" I cut myself off, surprised at my strong reaction to the information I was receiving.

"Queer? No, though there are plenty of men around here who would try to change that if they could!" Kendall laughed again.

I swallowed the rest of my drink. "I was going to say married," I said. "I already kind of know that he's not gay."

"Oh!" exclaimed Kendall, and then got a funny look on his face. "You're not Laura Morgan, are you?" he asked.

The pleasant affect of the alcohol in my system let me smile without blushing, even though I felt a school girlish excitement building in my stomach. I knew that I must be a little tipsy. "He mentioned me?"

"Only a gazillion times!"

I nodded. "I *am* Laura Morgan. Or I was."

"That's cause for a celebration. Would you like a refill?"

"Why not?"

Kendall made a quick exit and returned with a full martini shaker. He poured us each a fresh drink.

"Let's chat," he said.

∾∾

Midway through our third round, Mario had appeared in the living room. He was much more reserved in appearance and mannerisms than Kendall. He was clean cut, dressed in a stylish business suit, and spoke English with a soft Italian accent. He greeted Kendall with a quick kiss and me with quizzical smile.

"Laura," my host had said as way of explanation.

Mario's eyes had widened in instant recognition and an animated discussion between the two men began immediately.

Before I had time to digest what was going on, Mario was on the phone, booking me a red eye flight from Heathrow to Edinburgh.

"I don't understand," I said, my words sounding a little slurred, even to me.

"Mario's a travel agent," Kendall explained. "This is the least we can do for the famed Laura Morgan."

Mario hung up the phone with a satisfied smile and turned to me. "*Gratis*," he said.

"Free?" I translated, feeling stunned.

"His boss is a romantic," Kendall told me, and then whispered, "And so is Mario."

"I've got a meeting with a very rich, very irritating client in London in the morning," Mario said, pretending that he hadn't heard Kendall. "I'll drive you up myself."

I swayed a little bit in my seat, and he put a cool hand against my forehead.

"You need a rest," Mario told me.

I didn't argue.

"Would you like a blanket for here? Or would you like to nap in Paul's old room?" Kendall asked.

I pictured the heavy blue curtains and the rickety stairs leading up to them. The memory was a painful one. I swallowed. "I'm fine here," I said, and was nodding off before the two men brought me the promised blanket.

Chapter 32
THEN

I attempted to think of a more logical way to begin my search for this man whom I haven't seen in twenty years. Every angle I tried led me back to the entire illogic of my situation and added to my growing anxiety. Paul wasn't listed in the phonebook, and Kendall and Mario hadn't been able to find him in the online directory either.

I reached into my purse and fingered the computer print out that detailed the terms of my open ended return. I wondered how much suspicion it would arouse if I just turned back around to the airline counter and cashed it in. Maybe other people were doing stuff like this all the time—making spontaneous vacation decisions and then canceling them when reality set in. I doubted it.

I walked quickly to the nearest women's bathroom, trying not to look like I was panicking.

I splashed cool water on my face, and examined myself in the mirror. I felt equally comforted and confused by my appearance. I had selected my outfit—with Kendall and Mario's assistance—to be carefully casual. The jeans were from the notorious "skinny bin" and were so old that they could probably quite literally be labelled as retro. The hip-length, fitted tank top had actually been purchased as a Christmas gift for Tori. But with my daughter's recent predisposition toward clothes that ranged from grey to black only, I had no qualms about reclaiming the forest green shirt. And it did go very well my favourite, button front, cable knit sweater. I knew that I looked as good as I ever had, and considering the last year of events, I should probably have been at my worst.

I forced a guilty smile onto my face and pretended to adjust my hair as I tried again to sort out a plan.

I made myself sift through all the sensible pieces of my current situation. I had options. I had credit cards and cash enough to book myself into a hotel if I wanted to. I had the return ticket as well, so in case of an absolute failure, I could head home with an hour's notice. Conversely, I did not feel a pressing need to be home—or anywhere else—at a specific time, and I could approach my search with little to no urgency. These were reassuring facts, and once I had mentally listed them, I felt better.

Tentatively, I allowed myself to think about the more variable aspects of finding Paul. I had flown into London, and headed straight to Brighton because that was the where I had seen him last. When that hadn't panned out, I had taken Kendall and Mario's advice and headed straight for Edinburgh. It made some sense because that *was* where he had lived years before, and reportedly where he had lived again most recently. But truthfully, Paul could be anywhere in Britain. He wasn't even Scottish, after all. Or he could've left the continent altogether. Even if by some miracle I did find him, there was a big possibility that I wouldn't be able to say what I had come to say. He might not even be willing to listen, or care enough to bother. As much as I couldn't picture it, I had to acknowledge that he could be married himself, maybe have his own children.

I decided that I would deal with those things if necessary, but for the moment, I needed a starting point.

The Happy Traveller Hostel, I thought. *And The Bonnie Lass Pub.* Those were the two places that I knew were walking distance from Paul's old flat, so that's where I would start.

"Good!" I said loudly, and smiled apologetically at the woman at the next sink over who jumped back, startled.

"Sorry." But my smile widened.

It was always good to have a plan.

❧☙

I got into the cab hesitantly, hoping that the driver was going to be patient with me.

"Awrite! Welcome to Edinburgh, Auld Reekie! Scootland at it's finest!" greeted the cabbie as he opened the door for me.

"Hi," I said, smiling and feeling glad that I had a native Scotsman to guide to me.

"First time in Scootland, ma'am? Ah can recommend th' best places tae eat!" He rubbed his ample belly for emphasis.

I laughed in spite of the nerves roiling around in my stomach. "Second time actually—but the first time was a really long time ago."

"Welcome back then!" he said heartily.

"Thanks. I take it you're a local?"

"Born an' bred."

"Perfect. I have two places I need to go, both *very* local," I told him.

"Nae problem. Auld Gregory can gie ye thaur th' fastest, Ah tryst." The cabbie closed the door behind me and settled himself into the driver's seat. "Whaur tae?"

"There used to be a hostel not far from here. It was called *The Happy Traveler*. Do you know if it's still there? It was in a big brick front building?" I asked.

"They aw hae brick front dornt they?" Gregory laughed. "But Ah ken th' place. Th' nam got changed tae th' *Jolly Hunter Inn* at a point, but Ah hink it's closed. Did ye want me tae drife by? It's ye cash, not mine!"

"Yes, please," I said. I wanted to see it anyway.

The ride was quick—quicker than I remembered, and after only a few minutes I found myself staring up in amazement at the old building. Time had not been kind, and it was clearly in poor repair. The bricks were dirtier and mossier than I remembered, and the old wooden door had been replaced by a cheap looking metal one. One of the front windows was cracked, and there was no sign to indicate what function—if any—the old hostel served now. It made me feel a little sad, even though I had never been inside.

"Naw whit ye min'?" Gregory asked as I stared out the taxi window.

"No," I answered, and the cabbie didn't press it further.

"Whaer tae next then?"

"A pub. Close to here. It was called *The Bonnie Lass*," I told him.

"Och, och aye. Ah ken th' pub. Sham abit 'at place." The cabbie swiveled his neck around to look at me more closely. "Wa diz a bonnie quine loch ye want tae gang tae these rin doon places?" He shook his head and answered himself as he pulled back out into the street. "Nane ay mah business, ah suppose."

"What happened to *The Bonnie Lass*?" I asked, not offended. "Did it get shut down, too?"

"Nae. Ah heard 'at th' owner got killed. Th' son took ower, but he's nae a true highlander loch Nathaniel was." Gregory shrugged, clearly think that this was enough of an explanation.

He made two more quick turns and we were suddenly there. I looked out my window. It was exactly as I remembered it. The heavy door frame was the same grainy wood, the windows had the same red velvet curtains hanging inside. I could see a few late lunch stragglers through the double paned windows.

I handed the cabbie his fare and a generous tip, and climbed out slowly.

"Dae ye want me tae bide haur? Sae ye can see if thes is th' reit place?" Gregory called.

I shook my head. "This is it," I answered softly. "This is definitely it."

෨ං ෬

As I got a little closer, I realized that the pub wasn't *exactly* as I remembered it. The stain on the wooden door looked fresh and shiny, and I was sure that it had been peeling a bit twenty years before. Two barrels that had been turned into planters framed the wide stairway, and though they were meant to have an antique look, the craftsmanship was definitely recent. Pretty yellow and purple flowers were planted in the barrels and they gave off a fresh scent that didn't quite mask the smell of beer and smoke that wafted from within. A little handwritten sign announced that the pub was closing at five for a private function. I checked my watch. Plenty of time.

Pausing on the doorstep, I leaned in to inhale the flowers' sweet aroma.

"Dae ye hae a broken heart, hen?"

"Oh!" I exclaimed and jumped back, almost landing on the tiny Scottish lady who had asked the question.

The woman was under five feet tall, at least eighty, and grinning impishly at me from underneath a plaid tam. "Ah saw ye smellin' th' Heartsease, an Ah coodnae help but wonder if someone broke ye poor bonnie heart?"

I smiled back. "In a way, I guess that's what happened," I said.

The little woman reached into one of the planters and plucked out one of the flowers.

"Bend doon, hen," she instructed, and I obeyed.

She tucked the flower behind my ear. "Folklore says 'at ye can brew it intae a tea tae heal ye broken heart. But Ah think 'at wearin it in yer hair is much prettier an' mair effectife than onie loove potion anyway."

"Thank you," I said, genuinely touched.

The lady nodded her head toward the pub. "A pint micht nae dae ye tay bad either, hen!"

"It might be just what I need," I agreed as the old lady walked away.

❦❧

As I walked into the pub, I half expected to find three drunken Scotsmen dancing on a makeshift stage. But the inside of *The Bonnie Lass* had changed significantly from what my hazy memory could recall. The old stage, made of wood planks balanced on top of wine crates, had been replaced by a more formal structure. An electric-acoustic band kit sat on the new stage like it belonged there, and I wondered how often the musicians played. Judging by the caliber of the equipment I could see, I thought that they must be professionals. It was a far cry from the karaoke kings I had seen here twenty years earlier.

In fact, as I inspected the pub from the doorway, I found that the atmosphere was different, too. The tables were tidily organized, and polished to a hardwood shine. Each one had a tiny floral arrangement in the centre, and each little vase was topped by a Scottish flag. The dim sconces which had lined the walls and evoked such a feeling of continuity in me all those years before had been replaced by white shade covers that gave off a modern and soothing light. A couple of fans had been installed in the ceiling and twirled slowly, attempting to keep the air fresh.

I laughed out loud to myself. *Of course* the old cabbie had described *The Bonnie Lass* as going downhill. It had completely lost its hole-in-the-wall charm. I seated myself at one of the empty tables.

"Oi, miss," said a bored and vaguely familiar voice. "You want a menu, or just a pint?"

I looked up and had to laugh again. The serving woman was older, of course, but her bleach blonde hair, exaggerated earrings, and loud mouth we the same.

"Oi," she again, sounding irritated and not bothering to mask it. "I don't like the uniform either, but the boss wants us to wear 'em, so wear 'em we do. No reason to stare." The server indicated her ridiculously short kilt and frilly white blouse.

I grinned, too pleased at finally seeing a face from my past to be offended by the waitress's tone. "I'll take a menu, please and a pint as well. And just so you know, I'm a generous tipper."

కరుడు

The overly made up server sauntered up to me as I sipped my second pint.

"My shift's about done," she informed me. "Anything I can grab you before I clock out?" Her tone said that she hoped not.

I felt the affects of the beer clouding my judgment. "Join me for a drink?" I asked spontaneously.

"You buyin'?"

"Sure."

The waitress eyed me a little skeptically. "Not a queer, are you? 'Cause they can do what they like on their own watch, but I'm not the type."

I laughed, tapped my wedding ring pointedly and said, "My intentions are honourable, I promise."

"Alright then. Clocking out. I'm all yours for the next hour and then I've gotta get ready for the do that we're puttin' on a little later." She yanked off her apron and called loudly in the direction of the kitchen, "Hank! I'm done! Bring us two pints!"

"Get 'em yerself, Jackie!" a man—presumably Hank—shouted back.

"Oi! I said that I'm done!"

A few seconds later, a lanky young fellow with a resentful face carried two beers to the table.

Jackie took a long pull of her pint before she turned back to me. "Well, then, you're here. And I'm going to assume that it's not your husband you're meeting."

I shook her head. "No."

"Mind if I smoke?"

I shook my head again, and Jackie lit one, staring thoughtfully across the table.

"But it *is* a man?" she asked.

I nodded, feeling a familiar lump grow in my throat. "My husband was in a terrible accident." It was the first time I had allowed myself to think about it in two days, and the words felt hollow and unreal.

Jackie lit another cigarette and handed it wordlessly to me. I took it, and inhaled deeply. I began to cry, my carefully held in emotions finally rushing to the surface. I sobbed until my throat was dry and sore and the cigarette was a soggy mess.

"I'm sorry," I finally apologized to Jackie. "I never told him."

"About the other man?" the waitress asked.

"No," I said. "That I smoked."

Jackie pulled a thick bar cloth from her discarded apron and used it to blot my eyes like I was a small child.

"Was he the kind of man who would've cared, you reckon?" she asked me sympathetically.

"No, probably not," I admitted softly.

"Then you've not got to be sorry," she told me, and signaled to Hank that we needed a refill.

I sipped my fresh pint thankfully, and let the waitress light me another cigarette. I looked around the bar again, trying focus my thoughts away from Richie and the hospital. I wondered if Paul had also sat here, and what he thought of the changes that had been made.

I stared up at the bagpipes on the wall above the bar, and suddenly noticed a collage of framed photographs.

⤙⤚

The photographs were of people—the kind of shots that I appreciated. Diverse, not retouched, beautiful. And they were familiar.

I stood up and walked toward them, feeling entranced. I could hear Jackie calling me, but her voice faded into the background as I got close enough to see the tiny details of the pictures.

An old taxi driver with a raised eyebrow and a sheepish grin. A petite redhead with a sweet smile. The distant profile of a bearded man, clearly the subject of the photograph though he barely in focus, and almost obscured by the crowd surrounding him.

I gasped a little, and put one hand on the counter to steady myself. The bartender said something in a concerned voice, but I waived him off and continued to stare at the framed collection.

A statuesque blonde woman in a navy blue uniform, looking embarrassed and proud at the same time. A short man with black hair and an awkward thumbs up. An African man, sizable even on film, with a straight face but a twinkle in his eyes.

And in the centre of the six photographs was a small drawing of two love knots. I put my hand self-consciously on my hip, feeling as though my corresponding tattoo was going to burn through my jeans. I tried to read the tiny inscription plate on the bottom of the frame, but my eyes were suddenly bleary. I made myself sit down heavily on one of the bar stools.

Jackie was at my side with a cool hand on my arm. "You alright?"

"These are mine," I tried to say, but the words were a breathy squeak.

"You like the pictures?"

I nodded.

"Belong to the boss, they do. Or did, I guess I should say," she told me.

My heart quickened.

"That little nameplate up there? It reads, *Snapshots by Laura*," she went on.

I felt the blood drain from my face. "It says what?"

Jackie repeated herself and then added, "Long lost love. Unrequited, maybe. She was a foreigner, like you."

"Laura Morgan," I managed to get out, and Jackie looked at me with renewed interest.

"What did you say *your* name was?" she asked me.

"They're mine," I said again. "I took them."

"Oh, God." The waitress had a look on her face that I couldn't place. "You couldn't have...Ms. Morgan."

"Yes?" I replied softly. "Does Paul run the pub now? I'd like to speak to him."

My waitress and the bartender exchanged a worried glance, and Jackie's face went pale.

"Glad you're sittin' down, Ms. Morgan. I'm so sorry to tell you. Paulie died this last week."

Chapter 33
WAY BACK WHEN MEETS THEN

I stood in front of my parent's door unsurely. I couldn't decide whether to knock or let myself in. If I opened the door, there was a strong possibility that my mom or dad would think that I was a thief and call the police. Or even attack me personally with whatever makeshift weapon was handy. But knocking on the door seemed odd, too. This was the house where I had spent the first eighteen years of my life, and where I would likely spend the next few weeks or months as well. So I stood there, dumbly, willing myself to make a decisions.

My choice was abruptly taken away as the door opened a crack and my father peered through suspiciously.

"What?" he asked.

"Hi," I answered uncertainly, and then he recognized me.

He swung the door open and a smaller, paler version of the man who raised me stood staring at me with a mix of concern and unconcealed happiness. He was leaning on a cane and one side of his face drooped a little as he grinned at me.

"Hi," I said again, this time with a little more warmth.

"Look what the cat dragged in," my dad teased, setting his cane against the doorframe and reaching out his arms.

I hugged him shyly, surprised and relieved at the warmth I felt from him. I pulled away reluctantly.

"You look..." I trailed off.

"Older?" he suggested.

"Like home," I amended.

I heard my mom call out from the living room. "Was someone there, Gerry?"

"You bet!" my dad yelled back.

"I told you I wasn't imagining things! Tell whoever it is that we're not buying and close the door!"

"It's me, Mom," I answered her with muted apprehension.

She didn't respond. I pictured my mother sitting in her easy chair, reading one of the Clive Cussler novels that she loved as she sipped on her herbal tea. In my mind, I could see her rolling her eyes and taking another slow and purposeful swallow.

"You had better come in here," she called at last. "Because I'm sure as heck not coming out there."

"Of course not," I muttered to myself and followed my dad down the hall.

My mom didn't look up as we came in. She did indeed have cup of hot liquid in her hand and a book in her lap. "Told you I heard something," she said to my dad.

"You're rarely wrong, Melissa," he conceded as he sat down on the couch.

I stood on the periphery of the scene, watching my parents. It seemed that something had changed. Always before my father had bowed to my mother's stubborn will.

No one said a word. Finally I sighed and reluctantly crossed the room to seat myself beside my dad.

"You can see that your father's gotten worse," my mom told me.

"Has he?" I replied with as little emotion as I could.

"Right. I guess you didn't see him after his first stroke. Well this is what he looks like after one more," she persisted.

My body stiffened involuntarily, but I refused to be goaded.

"I'm fine, Laura," my dad assured me. "I missed you."

So that was it. The change. My mom had driven me away, and my dad disapproved.

"I didn't know, Dad," I said.

"How could you know?" my mom asked. "I followed your instructions. Though I did send you a postcard when he had his other stroke."

"I answered it." I still kept the feeling out of my voice. I gave my dad an apologetic look and he smiled back.

My dad crossed and uncrossed his legs, clearing his throat. "Will you be moving back home?"

My mother finally looked at me, and I couldn't stop an uncomfortable heat from creeping into my face as she stared my down. But I didn't pull my eyes away.

"Your room is the way you left it," she said in a resigned tone. Then she picked up her novel and lifted it pointedly between us.

I sighed, and turned my attention to my father. I kept my voice pleasantly even in spite of the fact that I really wanted to run back to Prince George. Or even up to my old bedroom.

"I'll only be here for a few days. Maybe a week," I announced. "I've got a job interview lined up at a bookstore downtown. Well, almost downtown. I have interviews for a couple of studio apartments tomorrow as well."

"Good for you," my dad said sincerely. "Stay here as long as you like."

My mother just strummed her fingers against the cover of her book.

I could feel my defensive hackles rising. "And I'm going back to school," I added. *If I get in*, I thought. "A paid photography internship."

My dad patted my knee and my mom stopped her tapping. We sat in silence for a few moments, and then I excused myself, stopping just short of running up the stairs to my familiar old room.

Tomorrow, I told myself. *Tomorrow is the first day of the rest of my life.*

Chapter 34
THEN

I felt the world give way abruptly, and when I awoke, I was surrounded by strangers with Scottish accents. My head was in Jackie's lap, and she was holding a cool compress in place.

"Where am I?" I asked.

"Paul's apartment," she told me, and I felt myself grow faint again. "Hold on, there, Ms. Morgan."

"Why are all these people here?" I asked.

"Dropping off food and the like," Jackie told me.

"Oh."

I closed my eyes and counted to ten. Then to twenty. When I opened them again, the room was empty except for Jackie, me, and two middle-aged men in a traditional kilts. I looked around cautiously. I recognized my surroundings then. I stared up at the high, slightly smoke stained ceiling, and glanced at the handcrafted coffee table. The old fashioned turn table and stack of vinyl records was in the same spot as it had been twenty years earlier, and the house still smelled vaguely of lemon.

"How did we get here?" I wondered.

"Not to worry," Jackie said quietly. "Ewen and Ely carried you up the from the pub."

She indicated the two older gentlemen, who nodded at me politely. I flushed in embarrassment.

They carried me three blocks? I cringed.

"We've seen waur plenty ay times. Ewen, mah brither thaur, he's bin a medic in th' Scottish Regiment gonnae oan thirty years. An' ye didne bump yer heed at aw," the taller of the two—Ely—reassured me.

"Broocht up yer backpack, tay," Ewen told me gruffly. "Ye shood feel better efter some rest an' mebbe some water."

"Ur a wee bit ay Scotch," Ely added.

"Thank you," I said faintly.

Both Scotsmen stood staring at me. I finally cleared my throat self-conciously.

"When was the last time you talked to Paulie?" Jackie asked me softly.

"I haven't spoken with him since we…Since I was here twenty years ago," I explained with a catch in my throat.

Ewen frowned a little. "Twintie years, ye say?"

"*He* asked *me* not to contact *him*," I said, feeling defensive at the way they were all looking at me.

"Ah dorne kin…" Ely trailed off. "But it doesnae matter, Ah suppose. Paul wanted whit he wanted. And Ah dinnae hae a min' tae argue wi' a deid man."

"Ely's a lawyer," Jackie told me, watching me for a reaction.

I just felt confused. "Oh."

"It would seem 'at Paul still had verra strong feelings fur ye, Ms. Morgan," Ewen said.

"Laura," I replied. "Call me Laura. I don't understand. Please tell me what's going on."

"We waur supposed tae dae thes efter thes evening's wake," Ely sighed. "But Ah wasnae expectin' 'at yoo'd be haur at all."

He reached down, picked up a briefcase, and set it on the table. He kneeled awkwardly on the floor and opened the briefcase.

"Thes is Paul's will." Ely pulled out a folder full of papers. "Ah was gonnae draft ye a letter. Paul's left everythin' tae ye."

"Left everything? To me? Why?" I struggled to process what was happening.

"Everythin'—th' pub, his flat. Th' place in Brighton. E'en his motur," Ely listed off.

"Paul owned *The Bonnie Lass*?" I asked. Nothing was making any sense. *Why would Paul leave all of this to me?*

Jackie smiled. "Sure. When his Dad passed a few years back, it went straight to Paul."

I remembered that Gregory, the cabbie, had told me that Nathaniel's son—a non-native Scotsman—had taken over *The Bonnie Lass*.

"Nathaniel was Paul's father?" I asked, finally making the connection. "He never said."

"It was a touchy subject. For both of them," Jackie explained. "Stubborn men. Nate left Paul's mum high and dry when Paul was just a boy. It wasn't 'til he was about twenty that Paul finally came up here to confront his dad. I remember it—my first week in the pub. Near came to blows. But when things settled down, Nate agreed to apprentice Paul as a chef, teach him the trade and the like. Paul stayed for a good four years, and after that he was in and out whenever it suited him. Drove Nate crazy. But as soon as Paul inherited, he made a real effort to keep the place up."

I listened in silence. *Four years. Until he was about twenty-four. When he met me.*

"He told me that he didn't love me," I said to the room.

"It appears 'at wasnae exactly true," Ewen replied in a gentle voice.

"Didn't Paul have any family?" I wondered.

Ely met my eyes. "His da's third wife is mah ain wife's sister. And that's as close as it gits. Sae, nae. Nae real fowk."

"What happened?" I asked. "How did Paul die?"

"Och, loove, ye dornt want tae hear abit it," Ewen said to me.

"I think that I need to know," I insisted.

"Near to a year ago, Paulie was diagnosed with leukemia," Jackie told me. "It was already too late."

"Wasted awa' tae naething," Ewen added.

I wondered how near to Richie's accident Paul had received his diagnosis.

Ely snapped his briefcase shut. "There's quite a bit ay paperwork tae be dain still. Will ye be in toon long?"

"I need to think," I whispered.

"We should get down to pub, anyway," Jackie said. "Get ready for the mourners. Put out the food and the like."

"Will ye be able tai fin' yer way back tae *The Bonnie Lass* oan ye ain?" Ewen asked.

I nodded. "I just need a bit of time."

Chapter 35
THEN MEETS NOW

Almost immediately after I closed the door behind Jackie, Ely, and Ewen, I heard a soft knock. I opened the door a crack, and peered out. Jackie was standing there, slightly out of breath. She was holding a lumpy grocery bag.

"I might as well give these to you," she said, and handed over the bag.

"What are they?" I asked.

She shrugged. "Paul's mail—some of it's been collecting since he first got sick. Some of it came after he passed. I think people didn't know where to send their cards, so they just mailed 'em here."

"Thanks," I replied, and clutched the mail to my chest.

I closed the door behind her again, and wandered aimlessly from the bedroom to the living room and back. Finally I went into the kitchen. It was dusty and grimy, with stacks of paper and dishes strewn about. I dumped the mail out onto the table, and the room looked even worse.

Paul would hate his kitchen this way, I thought, remembering how pristine it had been twenty years ago.

And so to distract my mind and to ease the heartsick feeling I had, I decided to make it my personal goal to clean up the mess. For Paul's sake.

And I started with his mail.

Chapter 36
NOW

I sat on Paul's couch with the black envelope in my hands, the paper cut forgotten. *Laura Morgan*, I thought again as I slowly read the silver lettering. My heart was beating fast and hard in my chest.

My Dearest Laura,
I have hopes that this will find you. I want you to understand. I'm sick, luv. Really sick. I need to tell you some things. There never was another girl. It was silly now, it seems, to try to make things easier in the long run by breaking your heart in the short. No matter, now. I'm going to try to do right by you soon, as I should've twenty years ago. I hope that you can forgive me, luv. I really do. Look for a man called Ely McCrae. He'll sort you out, I promise. There's a small white box in my closet. It will answer some questions, though perhaps not all. All my love,
Paul
PS Richard, if you've managed to intercept this one, please. Take heart and pass along my message, whether you think it's fit or not.
P.

I put the letter down slowly, trying to digest its meaning. It was true then, that Paul had never stopped loving me. Ewen had been right.

I flipped over the envelope and examined it carefully. It was addressed to mine and Richie's house, and stamped. But obviously it had never gone through the postal system. I wondered if Paul had waited too long to mail it, or if he had just changed his mind.

I felt a little chill. Perhaps he had just known that eventually I would have to come to Scotland in search of him, or to claim my new property. I wondered also, what kinds of question he thought could possibly be answered only after his death.

৵ৎ

I dug through Paul's closet with shaking hands. I found the white box easily enough. It was larger than a shoe box, heavy, and well worn. I sat on Paul's bed with it in my lap, dreading the thought of opening it. I felt very alone, and wished for a moment that I had asked Jackie to stay with me.

Sighing, I pulled the lid from the box, and then stared down at its contents in puzzled curiosity. It was full to almost overflowing with envelopes. Some were identical to the one addressed to me that I had found in Paul's stack of mail. The others were varied in colour—white, grey, or even floral. They were jammed in so tightly that when I tried I pull one out gingerly, ten more came bursting with it. They landed in a haphazard way on the bed, and as I read the addresses, my palms started to sweat and my heart skipped a beat.

Laura Morgan, two of the black ones said. They were still sealed.

Richard Lockhurst, read four more, also unopened.

An off-white one and a light blue were each addressed to *Mr. Paul Macdonald* in handwriting that I recognized instantly. They were from Richie, there was no doubt in my mind. On these, the seal was open, and the edges looked frayed, as though they had been read again and again.

How long had they been writing to each other? And why? With my heart and my thoughts racing, I grabbed four envelopes at random from the box. Two were dated from over fifteen years ago. One was only a little over a year old. I tore open one of the letters that had my name on it an scanned it. The words rambled, like a diary entry, confusing me and making my heart ache.

Laura,
Today I came by the shelter in Winnipeg, where your mom said you'd gone. (She seemed unhappy to see me by the

way.) The lady at the shelter told me you'd already left and wouldn't tell me where you'd gone.
What about the baby?

He's been in Canada. He'd known about the baby. Our baby. And my mom. He'd met her. She'd known, too. My body felt numb, and I when I touched my face, it felt foreign.
I opened another.

Paul,
I've intercepted three letters from you to my wife. I think that it would break her heart to read them. I'm not an unkind man, but I will send back everything that comes to us from you.
R.P. Lockhurst

Richie's words shocked me. I had never thought of him as a secretive, and I had never suspected that he had even an inkling of Paul's existence. But then I remembered. We had been dating for months before he told me about his estranged sister, Cara. We had been married for several years before he told about Trina's suicide, and over a decade before letting me know that Cole was not his biological father.

I flipped madly though several more letters. Richie, letting Paul know that we had moved from our apartment into our split level home. Paul, telling Richie that he'd been right—watching me in the park with Jordan and Tori proved that I seemed happy. I quickly pulled out all of the letters, and began to arrange them in chronological order. Paul and Richie had each meticulously dated their letters, and I was able to hastily reconstruct a timeline of correspondence. There were more than two hundred letters in total. Doing a mental calculation, I realized that they must've been writing each other on an almost monthly basis. I knew that I would eventually want to read each one slowly and carefully, but I was eager to get a taste of Paul and Richie's letters now.

So I skimmed bits and pieces to satiate that need. At first, all of the letters were about me. Paul's writing was passionate and intense—especially the letters that he had written directly to me but never sent. Richie was matter-of-fact, practical, and possessive of our life together. They conceded that each loved me as much the other. Richie told Paul that he had been able to locate my hospital records, and that I had lost the baby. Paul mourned the loss, and my husband was sympathetic. Eventually, the letters grew more personal, and I felt intrusive reading them. Richard detailed concerns at work, and shared stories about our children. Paul reported the death of his stepdad and then his mom, and in response, Richard talked about how his own father had abandoned him as a child. I felt tears form in my eyes as I relived the gradual growing respect and care forming between these two men who had meant so much to me. It was almost unreal.

Paul's phone rang abruptly from his nightstand, startling me. I picked up the handset uneasily.

"Hello?"

"Oh, good. You answered. Wasn't sure that you would." It was Jackie on the other end.

"I'm surprised that I did," I agreed.

"Paulie's wake is about to get started," she told me, and I assured her that I would be down immediately.

I hung up, reluctantly placed all of the letters back into the box, and prepared myself mentally for the hard hours that were to come.

છ⊷ૐ

I stood outside *The Bonnie Lass*, feeling like an intruder. I could see a small crowd of people through the thick glass, and I couldn't make myself go in. The stage was occupied now by a wide table topped with an ornamental urn and a framed photograph of Paul. A woman with bagpipes stood nearby, poised to play.

A family—mother, father, and two teenaged children—stepped up to pay their respects, and I felt a longing for my own family. I wondered how Tori and Jordan were doing at their grandmother's house.

I dug through my purse until I found my cell phone. I turned it on a waited for the signal bars to load.

99 Missed Calls. The words flashed across the screen. *48 New Text Messages. Voice Mail Full.*

My stomach dropped. It must've happened.

Oh, God. Richie, I thought.

I selected Delete All under my text message options, and watched the screen clear. But the little phone vibrated in my hand as soon as I flipped it shut. I opened it slowly.

Missed Call From Tori, the display announced.

I held down the '1' to access my voicemail. The first message was indecipherable—my daughter crying into the phone. I erased it. The second message was from Debbie Ling, the lawyer. She cut in and out, and I surmised that she must've been calling from the hospital with its notoriously bad reception. Then there was a message from Dr. Friday, and then a second, third, and fourth, all urging me to call the hospital as soon as possible. Finally, Jordan's warm voice came through.

"Mom," he said, and his voice was full of something other than despair. "Mom. Come home. Dad opened his eyes."

EPILOGUE
AFTER

She sat on the side of his hospital bed, watching his chest rise and fall with deep, even breaths. She resisted the urge to shake him awake, to make sure that he *could* still be woken. Her hands trembled as she restrained them tightly against the white box in her lap. After a moment, she realized that she was crushing the cardboard, and the box's precious contents. She forced herself to let go, drawing in a shaky breath.

At last, he opened his eyes and smiled at her. It was little lop-sided, and would remain so always. She reached over and softly stroked the paralyzed side of his face. His eyes brightened at her touch. She maneuvered the mechanical bed into a sitting position.

"Good morning, my love," she said tenderly.

He made a humming noise in the back of his throat and his mouth moved as he tried to form a word. The doctors had assured her that his dysarthria was temporary. All of his muscles—including the ones in his mouth—were weak from disuse. They assured her that with time and therapy he would soon begin to regain his ability to speak, to move, and even to walk. But she was in no rush.

"I'll get you a popsicle from the freezer," she told him, and her husband made a sound that might've passed for a laugh.

As she started to stand, he brought his hand up and clutched at her shirt. His grip was as weak a baby's, but she instantly sat down again. He inclined his head ever so slightly toward the white box.

"You want me to read some more?" she asked, and he nodded slowly.

She lifted the lid, and pulled out one black envelope and one yellow. She held them out to her husband. "Were we reading from you, or one from Paul?"

He tapped the yellow envelope.

"Ah, yes. This one is dated February 11th, 2000," she said, and then began to read. "Greetings from Canada...Life here carries on..."

Made in the USA
Charleston, SC
30 June 2011